Praise for Erle Stanley Gardner and his Perry Mason mysteries

"Gardner [is] humorous, astute, curious, inventive—who can top him? No one has yet."
—*Los Angeles Times*

"Erle Stanley Gardner is probably the most widely read of all . . . authors. . . . His success . . . undoubtedly lies in the real-life quality of his characters and their problems, for which he can draw on his own dazzling accomplishments as a trial lawyer."
—*The Atlantic*

"A clean, economical writer of peerless ingenuity."
—*The New York Times*

By Erle Stanley Gardner
Published by The Ballantine Publishing Group:

The Case of the
Glamorous
Ghost

Erle Stanley Gardner

FAWCETT BOOKS • NEW YORK

A Fawcett Book
Published by The Ballantine Publishing Group
Copyright © 1955 by Erle Stanley Gardner

www.randomhouse.com/BB/

ISBN 0-345-43786-1

This edition published by arrangement with William Morrow & Company, Inc.

Manufactured in the United States of America

First Ballantine Books Edition: December 1982

10 9 8 7 6 5 4 3 2

FOREWORD

GEORGE BURGESS MAGRATH HAS EXERTED A TREMEN-
dous influence in the field of legal medicine and in the
detection of crime.

Dr. Magrath's life is a splendid example of the manner
in which a man's dynamic personality can spread out over
the years, affecting the lives of others long after he is
gone.

Many of my readers will remember what I have written
about Frances G. Lee, the fabulous character who is
mainly responsible for founding the Department of Legal
Medicine at Harvard Medical School; a woman in her
seventies who is respected by police officers everywhere,
who is an authority in the field of homicide investigation
and who has been appointed a captain in the New Hamp-
shire State Police.

The fact that Captain Frances G. Lee became interested
in legal medicine was due to the influence of Dr. Magrath.
The fact that Captain Frances G. Lee invented her famous nutshell studies in unexplained death has been responsible for training hundreds of competent officers so
that they can detect murders which otherwise might go
not only undetected but unsuspected.

One of Dr. Magrath's greatest contributions to investigative science was his devotion to truth.

In every one of his field notebooks he wrote just inside
the front cover a quotation from the writings of Dr. Paul
Brouardel, the noted French doctor who was one of the
first pioneers in legal medicine.

The quotation is as follows:

"IF THE LAW HAS MADE YOU A WITNESS, RE-
MAIN A MAN OF SCIENCE: YOU HAVE NO VICTIM

TO AVENGE, NO GUILTY OR INNOCENT PERSON TO RUIN OR SAVE. YOU MUST BEAR TESTIMONY WITHIN THE LIMITS OF SCIENCE."

Dr. Magrath was a colorful personality. There was about him a flair for the dramatic. He was tall and heavy-set with superb shoulders and one of his greatest pleasures was rowing, or, more properly, sculling on the Charles River. He wore his hair long like Paderewski, his dress was informal, usually of soft tweeds, and his tie was invariably a dark Windsor.

There was about his personality something compelling that enabled him to dominate situations without apparently making the slightest effort to do so. He was in spirit a pioneer, blazing a trail in the investigative field, and he had all of the personality of the true pioneer. He was born on October 2nd, 1870. He died December 11th, 1938. During his lifetime he examined over twenty thousand cases of unexplained deaths, and the present highly efficient science of homicide investigation is in large measure due to the trail blazed by Dr. Magrath. The blaze marks on that trail are Truth, Accuracy, Efficiency and Scientific Integrity. Today many feet follow along that trail, and the wayfarers either follow those same blaze marks or become hopelessly lost in the forest of prejudice.

The truly scientific investigator of homicide remains on the one trail that follows those same blazes which Dr. Magrath used for his own guidance.

And so I dedicate this book to the memory of:

GEORGE BURGESS MAGRATH, M.D.

—Erle Stanley Gardner

CAST OF CHARACTERS

◼ 1 ◼

IT WAS DELLA STREET, PERRY MASON'S CONFIDENTIAL secretary, who first called the lawyer's attention to the glamorous ghost.

"Why the grin?" Mason asked, as Della Street folded a newspaper and handed it to him.

"This should interest you."

"What is it?"

"A ghost that people saw last night out at Sierra Vista Park, a very glamorous ghost. A seductive ghost. It should make a case you'd be interested in."

Mason said, "You've already interested me."

He took the newspaper Della Street had handed him and read in headlines:

SEXY SPOOK STARTLES SPOONERS
GIRL GIVES CHASE WITH JACK HANDLE

The story had been written up in a light vein, a combination of news and humor. It read:

Last night was a night of witchery. The moon was full and fragrant wisps of breeze gently rustled the trees and greenery.

George Belmont, 28, of 1532 West Woodwane Street and Diane Foley were sitting in their parked car, looking at the moon. Suddenly a beautiful wraith, apparently in the nude save for a fluttering diaphanous covering, drifted out of the shadows toward the car.

According to George, the wraith was making the motions of a classical dance. Diane, outraged, described the same occurrence to police with far less imagery—a difference in viewpoint, no doubt.

1

"We were sitting there talking," Diane told Officer Stanley of the park patrol, "when a girl appeared in little or nothing and deliberately started vamping my boy friend. She wasn't dancing, she was giving the old come-on, and don't think I didn't know it."

"A seductive come-on?" Officer Stanley inquired.

"Call it seductive if you want to," Diane snorted. "It was just a wiggle as far as I'm concerned."

"And what did George do?"

"He said, 'Look at that,' and started to get out of the car. That was when I went into action."

"What did you do?"

"I grabbed up the first thing that was available and took after her, saying that I'd teach her better than to come prancing around without any clothes on, making passes at my boy friend."

According to police the "first thing that was available" was a jack handle which would certainly have inflicted what the law refers to as "grievous bodily injury," and, beyond any question, was within the classification of a deadly weapon.

The ghost, however, did not seem to realize its desperate plight. It was too busy getting out of there— but fast. Diane Foley, hampered by her more conventional garb, took after the ghost in a headlong pursuit which was punctuated from time to time with infuriated screams, arousing the attention of residents who bordered on the park and resulting in more than half a dozen calls to the police.

According to Diane the ghost did the screaming. According to neighbors Diane certainly was doing some screaming herself. As one man who telephoned the police said in a later report, "It sounded like a couple of coyotes out in the desert—and you know what that sounds like. One sounds like half a dozen. Two sound like . . . well, that was the way it sounded out there in the park. I certainly thought someone was getting murdered, or that at least it was a hand-to-hand hair-pulling match."

Be that as it may the "ghost," which George

described as having a figure "simply out of this world," won the race and a breathless, indignant Diane, still carrying the jack handle, returned to the car.

Police, however, alerted by a dozen calls, converged on the neighborhood and soon were rewarded by picking up a young woman walking demurely along clad in an opaque raincoat. In view of the cloudless night the raincoat seemed incongruous.

Interrogated by police, the young woman professed complete ignorance as to her name or address. Her mind, she said, was a blank.

Once at headquarters, it was soon discovered that her mind wasn't all that was blank. Under the raincoat, her only apparel was the remains of an expensive, gossamer slip, torn into the equivalent of Salome's seven veils.

Police felt they had apprehended the ghost, but the evidence was circumstantial. Diane was vague as to any identification and she refused to permit George to be called as a witness.

In view of the seeming amnesia the "ghost" is at present being held in the emergency hospital while police seek to learn her identity.

"Well," Mason said, "it would make a most interesting problem in identification. She should have committed some crime. It's too bad."

"Don't bewail your luck so soon," Della Street said. "I didn't call your attention to the article in the paper simply to send your thoughts woolgathering, but in my official capacity as your secretary.

"The half sister of this glamorous ghost is impatiently waiting in the outer office."

"The deuce!" Mason exclaimed. "What does she want?"

"Apparently the family wants you to represent the ghost. There seems to be a consensus of opinion that the ghost is up to her neck in a scrape of some kind and that you must get her out."

"What's the half sister's name, Della?"

"Mrs. William Kensington Jordan, and she seems to have the trappings of wealth and respectability."

Mason grinned. "Your build-up, Della, is excellent. By all means, let's see Mrs. William Jordan—but first tell me what she looks like."

"Neat, refined, well-groomed, nice clothes, neat ankles, expensive shoes . . ."

"How old?"

"Twenty-eight to thirty."

"Good-looking?"

Della Street hesitated a moment. "The lips are just a bit too thin. She tries to build them up with lipstick and . . . well, somehow it throws her face out of balance. A full mouth just doesn't go with that type of face. But she has nice, intelligent eyes."

"Well, let's take a look at her," Mason said. "I'm interested in the ghost."

"You would be," Della said dryly, heading for the outer office.

Mrs. Jordan, on being ushered into Mason's private office, stood for a moment in the doorway, regarding the lawyer with searching scrutiny. Della Street said, "This is Mr. Mason, Mrs. Jordan."

"Thank you," Mrs. Jordan snapped without moving her eyes in the slightest.

Mason smiled affably. "How do you do, Mrs. Jordan?"

She came forward and gave him her hand. "How do you do, Mr. Mason? It's a pleasure to meet you—and see that your looks measure up to your extraordinary reputation."

"Thank you," the lawyer said gravely, avoiding his secretary's amused eyes.

Mrs. Jordan's speech had that sharp, precise articulation which should go with thin lips, and her manner was incisive.

"Do sit down," Mason said, indicating the client's comfortable chair, "and tell me what you wanted to see me about."

"Have you read the paper?" Mrs. Jordan asked, seating

herself, crossing her knees and carefully smoothing the skirt down over her legs.

Mason glanced at Della Street, nodded to Mrs. Jordan.

"Well," she said, "then you've read about this ghost, this exhibitionist in Sierra Vista Park who made a naked spectacle of herself in the moonlight."

Mason nodded. "I take it," he said, "from your description that you are not a believer in the supernatural."

"Not when Eleanor is concerned."

"And who is Eleanor?"

"The ghost. She's my half sister," she said.

"You have communicated that information to the authorities?" Mason asked.

"No."

"Why not?"

"I . . . I want to know where I stand first."

"Perhaps," Mason told her, "you'd better explain."

Mrs. Jordan made no attempt to disguise the bitterness in her voice.

"Eleanor," she said, "is an exhibitionist and an opportunist. She's also a liar."

"Evidently you have very little affection for your half sister."

"Don't misunderstand me, Mr. Mason. I hate the ground she walks on."

"I take it," Mason said, "that you have recognized the picture that was published in the newspaper, the picture of the young woman who has amne—"

"Amnesia my foot!" she interrupted. "She doesn't have any more amnesia than I do. She got in a jam once before and pulled that amnesia business to get herself out. She's done something that's a lulu this time and this is just her way of arousing sympathy and easing herself back into the family fold."

"I think," Mason said, "you'd better give me *all* the circumstances."

"About two weeks ago," Mrs. Jordan said, "Eleanor ran away with Douglas Hepner."

"And who's Douglas Hepner?"

5

"A drifter, a traveler, a fortune-hunter and an opportunist. He's as phony as a three-dollar bill."

"And you say your half sister ran away with him?"

"That's right."

"Marriage?" Mason asked.

"That's what *she* says."

"You were not at the ceremony?"

"Of course not. They simply took off. My husband, my father and I were away for the week end. When we returned we found a wire stating that they were happily married."

"Where was the wire from?"

"Yuma, Arizona."

"Lots of marriages are solemnized in Yuma," Mason said dryly. "People go there simply to get married."

"That's probably why they went there."

"To get married?"

"No, because Yuma has that reputation."

"You don't think they're actually married?"

"I don't know *what* to think, Mr. Mason. As far as Eleanor is concerned I've given up trying to think a long time ago."

"Well, suppose you tell me about her."

"My maiden name was Corbin. I'm Olga Corbin Jordan."

"Is your husband living?"

She nodded.

"You're living together?"

"Of course. Bill and I are very happy. I came here alone because he couldn't get away."

"But he knows you're coming?"

"Certainly. I don't have any secrets from Bill. Dad doesn't know all the details. I simply told him I was going to see a lawyer and that he wasn't to say a word to the police or to the newspapers until after he heard from me."

"You recognized your half sister's picture in the paper?"

"Yes. It's a good likeness. Other people will recognize it too. That's why I was so impatient trying to get in to see you. We don't have much time."

6

"All right, just what do you want me to do?"

"Eleanor has been in four or five scrapes. Someone has always come to the rescue and got her out. Dad has always been most indulgent with her and . . . well, I think she's the apple of his eye. She's spoiled and thinks she can wrap any man around her little finger. She's loaded with sex appeal, and does she use it!"

"Is she oversexed?" Mason asked.

"No, but the men whom she comes in contact with think *they're* oversexed. You've been around, Mr. Mason. You know that type of woman."

"How does she get along with women?"

"She doesn't deal with women. She makes her play for men and, believe me, she's clever at it. Of course, it's flattering—she makes them think they're wonderful—but when you have to live with that sort of thing day in and day out, week in and week out, when you know each new victim will be a sucker, you become disgusted with the whole thing."

"Particularly if you don't like her in the first place," Mason said dryly.

"Well, I don't like her," Olga Jordan blazed. "She's been a devastating influence on Dad ever since she was five years old."

"Is your mother living?"

She shook her head.

"You say Eleanor is your half sister?"

"I'll give you the highlights, Mr. Mason. I was born when Father was thirty years old. I'm twenty . . . I'm thirty now. Dad is sixty. Mother died when I was five years old. Then when I was eight this Sally Levan came into Dad's life."

"She was Eleanor's mother?"

"That's right. And she had one definite, fixed idea in mind from the time she first met Dad. That was to throw her hooks into him and take him for all she could get. She raved about Dad and about how she loved every hair of his head. She wanted to raise a family and Eleanor was the result—not because she gave a hang about a family but she knew that as long as Dad had me she

7

couldn't compete with that bond unless she had a child of her own who would be Dad's daughter and . . . Oh, I was only eight years old at the time, and I know an eight-year-old child isn't supposed to notice those things, but, believe me, I saw it just as plain as day."

"She died?"

"Rather suddenly. Yes, she died. And I'll tell you, Mr. Mason, I've never made a point of being a hypocrite. I was eleven years old then, but I could see things just as clearly as I can see them now, and I was glad she died. I was glad then and I've been ever since."

"And thereafter you and Eleanor grew up together?"

"Thereafter I had the job of trying to be an older sister and a mother. Dad called me in and explained my responsibilities. I determined to do the best I could. I liked Eleanor at that time. I hated her mother, but I didn't have any feeling against Eleanor."

"That came later?" Mason asked.

"That came later."

"How much later?" Mason asked, glancing at Della Street.

"Not a lot later," Mrs. Jordan confessed. "By the time Eleanor was five years old you could see that she was her mother's child all over. She has beautiful large blue eyes, blond hair that gives her an innocent sweet look—it's so fine and has such a sheen to it that it's almost like a halo, and she started cultivating that angelic look. She was just such a sweet, poor little motherless morsel that people fell all over themselves to help her.

"She used that technique until she learned about men —and then there was no stopping her."

"Go on," Mason said.

"Well, she would have caused Dad a lot of heartbreak if Dad had known about it. Dad never did know all the details. Bill and I helped cover things up. On occasion we lied our heads off. One time when we were on a vacation and Eleanor was supposed to have been with us, we backed up her alibi and lied like troopers."

"She wasn't with you?"

"No. Heavens knows where she was. But she told Dad

she was going up to join us. We probably never would have learned anything about it if it hadn't been for the fact that we called up Dad to see how he was getting along and Dad asked how Eleanor was enjoying the trip. It took me just half a second to get the picture and for his sake I told him she was having the time of her life."

"Your father is fond of her?"

"Dad has been hypnotized by her, just as he was hypnotized by her mother. But I think Dad is beginning to get his eyes open just a little bit."

"And now you believe that she's this ghost who . . . ?"

"I know it," she interrupted. "I could almost tell it even if it weren't for the picture in the paper. That technique is Eleanor's. It's just like her. She ran away with Douglas Hepner. Heaven knows what happened. Whatever it is you can expect the worst. All right, she had to come back to the family fold, but she's afraid of something. Something's happened so she has to make a plea for sympathy and sneak up on Dad's blind side.

"So she goes out in the moonlight, doing the dance of the seven veils and manages to get herself caught by the police—which, of course, she'd planned all along—and looks at them with those wide blue eyes of hers and says she doesn't know who she is, that she hasn't the faintest idea of the past. It's all a blank to her. So the police take her to the hospital, her picture is published in the paper and then the family is supposed to come running to her. There'll be a reunion. We'll get psychiatrists to get her memory back and in the midst of all that sympathy and sweet helplessness the thing that she'd done that she's afraid of will come to light and she'll be forgiven."

Mason's eyes narrowed as he studied Mrs. Jordan. "Then why not go to the hospital and identify her," he asked, "and get it over with? If that's the game she's playing there's not much you can do about it. Why consult a lawyer?"

"I'm consulting you, Mr. Mason, partially because I'm tired of this whole business, and partially because I want to spare Dad as much as I can. I'm afraid—afraid of what Eleanor's done this time."

"Why?"

"This is . . . well, this is carrying things plenty far, even for Eleanor."

"And what do you want *me* to do?"

"I want you to go to the hospital with me. I want you to be there when I make the identification. I want you to take charge of things. You'll know how to handle the resulting publicity. You'll know how to handle reporters, and then I want you to sit down with Eleanor and I want you to *force* her to tell you *what* it is she's running away from, what it is that's happened, what has caused her to adopt this weird method of trying to arouse public sympathy and get herself reinstated with the family."

"And then?" Mason asked.

"And then," she said, "I want you to use every bit of resourcefulness at your command to try and square things, to try and clean the mess up so that . . . so that the newspapers don't get hold of things and so that Dad doesn't have too much of a shock."

"Is your father in good health?"

"Physically," she said, "he's straight as a ramrod, but he's in a peculiar position. Dad's in the wholesale jewelry business. He specializes in diamonds. People trust him. His word is as good as a written guarantee. If something should happen that would humiliate him, if there should be a big family scandal—well, it would crush him."

"And you think Eleanor may have . . . ?"

"I think that whatever Eleanor's done this time," she interrupted, "it's *really* something. This isn't just an ordinary scrape. This is a dilly."

Mason hesitated. "I'm afraid, Mrs. Jordan," he said at length, "that you're letting your suspicions and your prejudices build up a set of circumstances in your mind that are purely imaginary. Why don't you wait until . . . ?"

She shook her head impatiently. "There isn't time, Mr. Mason. Quite a few people know Eleanor. In all probability the hospital is receiving calls by this time, telling them who she is. We're going to have to work fast."

Mrs. Jordan opened her purse, took out a folded oblong of paper. "I know you're a busy and a high-priced lawyer. I have made out a check payable to you for twenty-five hundred dollars. Mr. Mason. That is in the nature of a retainer."

Mason raised his eyebrows. "Usually," he said, "people go to an attorney and ask him how much . . ."

"I know," she said, "but this is different. This is an emergency."

Mason asked, "You want me to go to the hospital with you and then what?"

"I'll identify Eleanor, and then I want you to talk with her privately and alone after you've got rid of the reporters."

Mason said, "You will, of course, identify her as your half sister?"

"Naturally. And as far as the public is concerned the scene will be one of great affection and sympathy. Outwardly I'll do everything that the situation requires."

"Do you expect to have your father see her?"

"Not until after you've found out what has really happened."

"Do you think she'll tell me?"

"Probably not. You're going to have to talk with her and get clues. You'll need detectives. We will, of course, pay all expenses."

"What do you think Eleanor will do?" Mason asked.

"I can tell you *exactly* what she'll do. She'll look at us and turn her head away in bored indifference, a poor child who doesn't know who she is or anything about her past. And then I'll say, 'Eleanor, don't you know me?'

"She'll turn those big blue eyes on me as though I'm a total stranger and then suddenly the eyes will begin to widen. She'll blink. She'll do a double take. There'll be a ghost of a smile and then suddenly memory will come back with a rush and she'll exclaim, 'Olga! Olga, my *dar*ling' and throw her arms around me and cling to me like a drowning man clinging to a piece of driftwood."

"And then?" Mason asked.

"And then there'll be the terrific shock of readjustment. Memory will come pouring back to her in a flood. She'll pull out all the stops—and finally she'll wind up by re-

11

membering everything about her past life up until the moment she disappeared with Douglas Hepner, and from that time on her memory will be a complete blank. She simply won't know where she's been or what she's been doing during the past two weeks.

"She'll ask about Dad. She'll ask questions that show that in her poor little deranged mind she thinks it is still two weeks ago. It will come as a shock to her when I explain that there's a missing gap of two weeks."

"And she won't remember anything that happened? Even the show she put on in the park?"

"She'll look at newspaper reporters with shocked incredulity when they tell her about it."

"To carry through a situation of that sort is going to take a good deal of histrionic ability," Mason said. "Do you think she can do it and do it convincingly?"

"She'll fool everybody on earth," Mrs. Jordan said, "except one person."

"Who's that?"

"Me. I'm telling you that in advance, Mr. Mason, because she's going to fool *you!*"

Mason smiled. "Lawyers become somewhat cynical."

"She'll fool you," Olga Jordan asserted positively. "She'll fool you and when she finds out what you're there for, she'll hypnotize you. You'll be just like all the other men. You'll want to protect her. Don't misunderstand me. I *want* you to protect her and help her out of the scrape she's in because that's the only way you can help Dad and do a job protecting the family."

"When do we go to the hospital?" Mason asked.

"Now," she said, looking at her watch. "We haven't much time."

Mason nodded to Della Street. "I'll be out for an hour or an hour and a half, Della. Come on," he said to Mrs. Jordan, "Let's get going."

■ 2 ■

THE HEAD NURSE IN THE FRONT OFFICE SAID, "OH YES, Mrs. Jordan. The police have been trying to reach you for the last hour. They're anxious to see if you can make an identification."

"There's a very great resemblance to my sister," Mrs. Jordan said. "I feel certain it is she."

"Yes. We've had several telephone calls since the picture was published in the paper from people who have told us they were sure it was Eleanor Corbin."

"Eleanor Hepner," Mrs. Jordan corrected firmly. "She was married about two weeks ago."

"Oh, I see. Well, would you mind going up, Mrs. Jordan? The doctor left word that you were to be admitted as soon as we could get in touch with you. He feels that the emotional shock of seeing you may do a good deal to restore the patient's memory. Of course, you understand in these cases we never know just what's going to happen. The nurse in charge will be with you. She has instructions from the doctor. You will have to follow her guidance.

"In case it should appear that your presence disturbs the patient then you'll have to withdraw. You will, of course, have to be very careful not to do anything that would tend to annoy or excite the patient unduly. But in case the emotional shock of seeing you *does* bring about recognition and breaks through the amnesia—well, then, of course, we'll have to be governed by circumstances."

"I understand," Mrs. Jordan said.

"And you'll co-operate with the nurse?"

"Certainly, but Mr. Mason is to be with me," Olga Jordan said.

The nurse hesitated. "There were no instructions about Mr. Mason, but . . ."

"Very definitely he must be with me," Olga Jordan said firmly, "in case she should recognize me and break through this amnesia. I noticed several reporters waiting around outside, and—well, Mr. Mason has certain things to do in order to see that the publicity doesn't get out of hand and . . . there are certain things that he understands."

"Very well, we *have* been having a bad time with the reporters," the nurse said. "You will, of course, understand that you're to do the talking, Mrs. Jordan—that is, until we get a reaction. The nurse will advise you. Here she is now—Myrna, this is Mrs. Jordan, the sister of the patient in 981, that is, we *think* she's the sister. And this is Mr. Mason, the lawyer. Will you take them up, please, and see if Mrs. Jordan's presence brings about a recognition?"

The nurse nodded, turned with rubber-heeled efficiency and said, "This way, please."

She led the way, moving on silent feet, the starched skirt giving a faint rustle as she guided them to the elevator, up to the ninth floor, then down to room 981.

The nurse opened the door. "Go right in," she whispered. "Walk up to the bed. Stand beside her. Watch the expression on her face. If she shows any sign of recognition call out her name."

"I understand," Olga Jordan said, and she and Perry Mason moved on into the room.

The young woman who lay on the bed, attired in a hospital nightgown, was staring at the ceiling with vacant eyes. There was a helpless expression on her face that was pathetically appealing.

Olga Jordan moved over toward the bed.

The blue eyes detected motion within the room. They turned casually, making an appraisal of the newcomer, then as casually turned away.

Abruptly the eyes turned back again, studied Olga for a moment, started to turn away again, then with a start

14

the eyes widened, the neck stiffened. The woman on the bed raised her head slightly.

"Eleanor," Olga Jordan said softly.

For a moment the eyes lighted with utter incredulity, then the girl blinked her lids a couple of times as though just waking up and snapped upright in bed.

"Olga!" she cried.

"Olga! My darling! Oh *dear, dear* Olga! I'm *so* glad to see you!"

She held out her arms.

Olga enclosed Eleanor in an embrace. "You poor darling," she said. "You poor, poor dear." Her voice was vibrant with sympathy.

Mason stood by the head of the bed. His eyes sought those of the nurse. The nurse smiled reassuringly, nodded at Mason, and moved quietly into the corner of the room where she could listen but wouldn't be readily visible to the patient.

"Oh Olga, it seems like it's ages since I've seen you and yet it couldn't have been . . . couldn't have been over an hour or two. Where am I, Olga? This room . . . ?"

The blond head turned from side to side. Abruptly she noticed Perry Mason.

"Who's he?" she asked.

"That's Perry Mason, an attorney who's come to help you."

"An attorney? What do I want with an attorney to help *me?*"

"We thought you'd better have one."

"What for, I don't need a lawyer," Eleanor said, but she flashed a quick smile at Perry Mason. "But if I did need one," she said, "I'd want one just like you."

"Thank you," Mason said.

"Well, wherever I am and whatever it's all about," Eleanor said, "I'm going to get some clothes on right now and get out of here."

She flung back the covers on the bed, exposing shapely legs with creamy skin, then, realizing the position of the nightgown, hastily grabbed at the hem and pulled it down.

Olga pushed gently on the girl's shoulders.

15

"You'll have to stay here for a little while, Eleanor."

"Where's here and why do I have to stay?"

"It's a hospital, darling."

"A hospital!" Eleanor exclaimed.

Olga nodded.

"But what am *I* doing in a hospital? Why, Olga, it's absurd! I just left home. I . . . now wait a minute. Oh yes, there was that auto accident. What day is it?"

"Tuesday."

"Well, that's right," Eleanor said. "Yesterday was Monday. We left Monday night, the second."

"Where's Douglas?" Olga asked.

"Douglas? Good heavens, where *is* Doug? He was driving the car. What's happened? Is he hurt? Tell me, Olga. Don't try to break it to me gently! Where is he? Tell me."

"We don't know, darling," Olga said. "This is Tuesday, dear, but it's Tuesday the seventeenth, not Tuesday the third. We received a wire from Yuma, Arizona, and several post cards saying you had been married."

"Then they must have been sent *after* the accident, so Doug must have been all right."

"What accident, darling?"

"The one Monday night. The big white headlights came boring out of the darkness like two great big eyes trying to tear me apart, and then this awful . . ."

She broke off and hid face with her hands.

Olga patted her shoulder. "There, there, dear, you mustn't worry. Don't try to remember anything."

"I'm all right," Eleanor said, "only I've got to find out what happened. If I've got a perfectly good husband running around loose somewhere, this doesn't fit in with my idea of a honeymoon. I guess I must have had a bump on the head in the auto accident."

She raised her hands to her head, moving the tips of her fingers through her blond hair. She turned to Mason, regarded him with frank appraisal, said, "You're either going to have to get out of here or turn your back because I'm going to dress."

"Now wait just a moment," Mason said. "You must stay quiet. You've had a little trouble with your memory."

"I guess I got knocked out," Eleanor admitted, and then laughed. "But that's nothing. Lots of people get knocked out. Prize fighters get knocked out so often that they just bounce up and down like a rubber ball every time they hit the canvas. I guess I took a delayed bounce. What was the report on the accident? Who hit us?"

"We don't know about any accident, darling," Olga said.

"Well, of all things. It certainly should have been reported. How did you happen to come here if you didn't know about the accident, Olga?"

"I saw your picture in the paper."

"My picture . . ."

"We were hoping perhaps you could tell us what had happened," Mason interposed.

"Well, all I know is that Doug and I were on our way to Yuma to get married. . . . Then I saw those headlights right in front of me and felt that terrible impact and . . . well, here I am in the hospital—at least you tell me it's a hospital."

Olga said, "Listen, Eleanor darling, no one knows what's happened. You've been out doing things on your own. No one knows what. You were picked up by the police last night, wandering around in a park with nothing on but a raincoat and a diaphanous slip . . ."

"I, in a park, without clothes! Well, I'll be damned!" Eleanor exclaimed, and then suddenly began to laugh.

Olga raised inquiring eyebrows.

"Well," Eleanor said, "I've heard the expression 'being knocked into the middle of next week,' but I guess that automobile accident knocked me into the middle of the week *after* next. So you're to be my mentor and guardian, Mr. Mason."

"I wouldn't go as far as that, but maybe I can help. Can you remember anything about the last two weeks?" Mason asked.

"I can't remember one single thing after we had the accident."

"The accident," Mason said, "was probably two weeks ago."

17

"Well, all I can remember is that I was lying here with my mind a blank and people gliding in and out and then I looked up and saw Olga and I felt a dizzy spinning sensation in my head and, all of a sudden, I woke up—and here I was—I mean here I am.

"I'm perfectly normal. I can remember everything that happened up until the moment that car came rushing toward us."

"Where was that?" Mason asked.

"Some place on the road to Yuma."

"You can't remember just where?"

"No. Now that you speak of it, things get fuzzy when I try to focus my mind on things that happened that night. . . . I get all dizzy. . . . I feel I'm slipping. . . ."

"Don't try to recall anything, then," Mason said. "Just lie there and relax."

"Thank you, I feel a little tired all at once."

The door to the room swung open silently. A crisp-mannered, professional man entered the room.

Mason stepped quickly between the bed and the new arrival.

"Who are you?" Mason demanded.

The man stared at Mason with surprise and some indignation. "Who are *you?* I am the doctor in charge of this case."

Mason turned to the nurse for confirmation. She nodded.

Mason grinned. "I'm the attorney in charge of this case. My name is Mason. I thought you might be a reporter."

"They've had a field day already with the police." The doctor turned to Eleanor. "You look as though you were feeling better."

"Better? I'm well! And I'm on my way."

"Doctor, Mrs. Hepner has regained her memory. She seems to be all right physically. We appreciate all you have done for her, but we want to get her out of here quickly and quietly."

"Now wait just a minute, Mr. Mason! This patient—"

"You undoubtedly know Dr. Ariel."

The doctor nodded.

18

"I'm going to call him immediately. We want Mrs. Hepner under his care—elsewhere."

"The police—"

"No charges have been filed against Mrs. Hepner, so the police have nothing to say about it. Mrs. Hepner will expect a bill for your services, Doctor, an *adequate* bill."

"And the reporters?" the doctor asked grimly.

Mason thought for a moment. "Tell them your patient has been identified and that she has been discharged from the hospital. That and nothing more. I can assure you that your co-operation will be appreciated."

The doctor studied Eleanor Hepner frowningly. Then he shrugged. "All right, if that's the way you want it."

He turned and opened the door into the corridor. "Nurse, I'd like to speak to you a moment."

The nurse followed him into the corridor and closed the door behind her.

"Olga, I *like* Mr. Mason," Eleanor sighed. "I'll take him any time."

Olga Jordan ignored her sister. "Mr. Mason, are you sure you know what you're doing?"

"I've got a pretty good idea," Mason said coolly. "Now if you will hand me that telephone, please. . . . Thank you."

He called Dr. Claude Ariel, a client of his, and explained the circumstances. He emphasized that in his opinion Eleanor should be kept quiet and that above all she should have no visitors.

"That's fine," Dr. Ariel said. "I'll call the hospital. I'm on the staff there. I'll also make arrangements to have the patient moved to a private sanitarium. I'll have that done by ambulance. Now the sanitarium I would suggest is the Pine Haven Sanitarium up above Glendale. Do you have any preference?"

"No, the Pine Haven's fine with me," Mason said.

"All right, I'll get on the job. I'll put on a special nurse I can trust right away, and I'll be there myself within half an hour. At that time I'll arrange for an ambulance to move the patient. I'll make all necessary arrangements at the sanitarium. There aren't any police charges against this patient, are there?"

"Not as yet," Mason said, "and I don't think there will be, but if there are, I'll put up bail and get her out, so you can go right ahead with your plans. Now it's very important that for the moment she receive no visitors."

"I understand," Dr. Ariel said. "You can trust me on that."

Mason thanked him and hung up.

Some ten minutes later there was a gentle tap on the door.

"Who is it?" Mason asked.

"I'm a special nurse. Dr. Ariel wanted me to take charge of the case and to see that the patient wasn't disturbed."

Mason opened the door. The nurse entered the room, promptly proceeded to close the door firmly. She smiled at Mason and said, "You believe in direct action, don't you?"

"It gets results," Mason said.

The nurse smiled at the blonde on the bed. "How are you feeling?" she asked.

"Better," Eleanor said cautiously. "I feel fine except when I try to recall certain events that took place."

"Then don't try to recall them," the nurse said.

Eleanor looked helplessly at Perry Mason and said, "I'd like to help you, Mr. Mason, I really would."

"That's all right," Mason said. "It may come back to you later."

"I remember," she said, "we were going to get married. We were driving to Yuma and . . . and there was Douglas' mother. He telephoned her and told her and . . . and I talked with her. She had a sweet voice and . . ."

"Where did you place the call from, do you know?" Mason asked.

"It was a service station somewhere where we stopped for gas."

"Where does his mother live?" Mason asked.

"Salt Lake City, but heavens, I don't know the address. And then we drove on and there were these head-

20

lights coming right toward me . . ." She put her hands over her face again and said through her fingers. "Mr. Mason, I have to hold on to myself. I get all dizzy when I start thinking of that. You don't mind, do you?"

The nurse looked at Mason and placed a finger across her lips.

Mason said, "No. Don't try to think about it at all."

"I can't help it. I just keep thinking up to that point and then my mind starts going round and round."

"The doctor will be here in a few minutes," Mason said. "He'll give you something to quiet you and then you'll go to a sanitarium where you can rest for a while."

Mason turned to Olga. "I think it'll be a good plan for us to leave now, Mrs. Jordan."

"I think so too," the nurse said. "The doctor has given orders that the patient is to have a sedative if she becomes at all restless."

"I don't want a sedative," Eleanor said. "I want to get out of here. I want to get my clothes on and find out what happened to Douglas."

Mason smiled understandingly. "You'd better rest and wait until after Dr. Ariel has had a good talk with you. Then he'll fix things so you can be discharged and . . ."

"But you said I'd have to go to a sanitarium. I don't want to go to a sanitarium. What do I want to go to a rest home for? A rest home is for people who are beginning to break up. I'm . . ."

Once more she threw the covers off the bed, kicked out a pair of smooth, well-shaped legs.

The nurse hurriedly interposed herself between the bed and Mason, pulled the covers up, and said, "You mustn't do that. You must keep quiet. Just a few minutes longer and Dr. Ariel will be here."

"I don't want Dr. Ariel. I want Doug." Eleanor looked as though she would cry.

The nurse picked up a package she had carried with her into the room. There was the brief smell of alcohol, then Eleanor said, "Ouch, that hurts."

"Just hold still for a minute," the nurse said. "This is what the doctor ordered."

21

The nurse withdrew the hypodermic, turned to Mason and Olga, and nodded toward the door.

"She'll be all right now," the nurse said. "Dr. Ariel wants me to go along to the sanitarium as a special. I understand there are to be no visitors. You don't need to worry."

Mason took Olga Jordan's arm. "Let's go," he said.

Out in the corridor, Olga turned to Perry Mason. "Pretty good act, wasn't it?"

"Act or no act," Mason said, "let's get down to brass tacks and see what we have to do."

"Well," Olga said, "she's given you the information that she wants us to have. There's been an accident. She doesn't know where Douglas is. It's up to us to try and find him. We're also going to have to try and find out where the marriage took place. We're going to have to find out about Douglas Hepner's mother in Salt Lake City. And something seems to tell me we're going to have to move pretty fast because whatever it is that Eleanor has pulled this time it's really a lulu and when it catches up with her there's going to be quite a commotion. You're going to have to work fast, Mr. Mason."

"Fast work is going to mean a lot of expense," Mason said. "Are you prepared to pay for the necessary detective work . . . ?"

"We're prepared to pay for anything within reason, Mr. Mason, but for heaven sakes get started and get to work on it fast."

"All right," Mason said. "What can you tell me about this man Hepner?"

"Not very much."

"When did you first meet him?"

"On that last trip to Europe, that is, on our way home from Europe. He was on the boat."

"Do you have any pictures?"

"Yes, I think I can find you some pictures. They're just snaps but . . ."

"That's all right," Mason said. "Get the snaps. Get them up to my office just as fast as you can. Now can you describe him?"

"Yes. He's tall—around six feet, I guess. He has dark hair and a snub nose, a ready smile and a magnetic personality."

"How old?"

"Twenty-seven or twenty-eight."

"He must have cut quite a swathe on the ship coming over from Europe," Mason said.

"You can say that again. You know how travel is these days. Men have to stay home and work. The women travel. Good-looking men are scarce as hen's teeth. Most of the men are the ones who have retired twenty years too late."

"You sound rather bitter," Mason said.

"I've done lots of traveling. Dad is in the wholesale jewelry business. We go to Europe quite often and . . ."

"Wait a minute," Mason said. "You're married. Does your father take you and your husband and . . . ?"

"Oh, whenever Bill wants to go Dad takes him. But for the most part Bill likes to stay home and hang around the country club. He's quite a tennis and golf enthusiast and he likes horses. He doesn't care too much for Europe."

"You leave him and go with your father?"

"Yes. Dad needs us to act as traveling secretaries, to make appointments and keep track of his purchases and things of that sort."

"So Eleanor goes along?"

"I'll tell the world Eleanor goes along. She hasn't missed a trip to Europe in the last ten years. Don't be silly. Whenever there's any traveling little Eleanor is right along."

"Where did she meet Douglas Hepner?"

"On the ship."

"What does Hepner do?"

"Apparently nothing. He seems to be a gentleman of leisure. He's one of the most enigmatic individuals I ever knew. He simply won't talk about himself or his background. I think that's why Dad dislikes him. The man is as elusive as a Halloween apple in a barrel of water."

Mason said, "But he seems to be able to attract people and . . ."

"There's something strange about him. His personality seems to . . . well, it sort of holds its breath on you. Now that isn't what I'm trying to say. But . . . well, you get the idea he's playing poker with you. He's affable and polite and friendly, and all of a sudden you catch him looking at you as though he were sizing you up. Eleanor was crazy about him. We thought it was just a shipboard romance, and Lord knows she's had plenty of those."

"But it turned out to be serious?"

"Well, there again it's hard to tell just what *did* happen. No one could be certain whether they were serious or not right up until the minute they left for Yuma."

"How long ago was this cruise?"

"About three months ago."

"Eleanor and Douglas had a crush on shipboard?"

"Yes, but Douglas was in circulation. He was talking with everybody. That's one thing about the man. He's a great mixer when he wants to be, and he certainly got all over that ship."

"Then after you landed he kept up with Eleanor?"

"Well, for a while he didn't—I guess a month or so. And then all of a sudden he began to cultivate Eleanor and she was going out with him—nobody paid too much attention to it until it began to look as though she were serious about it."

"And what did your father say?"

"Dad never did like the man. He took an instinctive, intuitive dislike to him. And Dad's pretty hard to fool."

"But Hepner got Eleanor to go to Yuma and get married?"

"Apparently. Now there again, Mr. Mason, when it comes to telling you anything that Eleanor did or didn't do, all we know is that she left two weeks ago Monday night, that was the second. We got a wire from Yuma, Arizona, that was delivered early on the morning of the third, stating that she and Doug had been married, to please forgive her, that she was crazy about him and they were very happy. We got a couple of post cards, one sent

24

from Yuma and one from Las Vegas, Nevada, and after that there was an interval of complete silence."

"So apparently from Yuma they went to Las Vegas."

"That's what her post card would indicate."

"And the postmarks on the cards?"

"They were from Yuma and from Las Vegas."

"Did you save those?"

"I'm sorry, we didn't. We saved the wire."

"All right," Mason said, "send up whatever snapshots you can find of Douglas Hepner, send up that wire and anything else you may have that you think will help. I'm going to get detectives on the job. We can trace that wire."

"You have confidence in this doctor you retained?" she asked.

"Absolutely," Mason said.

"He'll keep her out of circulation?"

Mason nodded. "Of course," he said, "newspapers will get part of the story. We don't know how much the first nurse overheard, and they may get at her."

"Oh, of course," Olga said, "that's the way Eleanor planned it. She was talking for publication. But the minute you started to pin her down she became afraid of you. She was afraid you'd cross-examine her and bring out the truth, so things began to get all fuzzy and she started getting dizzy, and she threw back the covers so you could see her nice legs."

"And you think all that was put on?" Mason asked.

She looked at him appraisingly. "My God, Mr. Mason, don't be naïve!"

■ 3 ■

From a pay station Mason called Paul Drake's office.

"Drake in?" he asked.

"Is this Mr. Mason?"

"That's right."

"Yes, he's here. I'll put him on the line."

A moment later Mason heard Drake's voice on the line. "Hello, Paul," Mason said. "I have a job for you. It's an emergency."

"All your jobs are emergencies," Drake protested. "What is it this time?"

"Been reading the newspapers?"

"I always read the newspapers. It's part of my job."

"Have you read about the glamorous ghost of Sierra Vista Park?" Mason asked.

"You mean the nearly nude ghost that was traipsing around the park?"

"That's the one."

"Now there's the kind of an assignment a detective would like to have. If I'd had a pair of night binoculars and had been commissioned to sit out there in the moonlight and . . ."

"All right, Paul, here is where you go to work. The ghost is really Eleanor Hepner who was Eleanor Corbin. She left her home on the second of the month. Apparently she and Hepner went to Yuma, Arizona, and were married.

"Find out when and where. Get certified copies of the records.

"They were in an auto accident on the road. Get the facts on that. I want to know the name of the other party involved in the accident.

"After they were married, they went to Las Vegas. Cover the hotels and motels. Also I want you to find Hepner. He has a passport. Get what you can from the passport office. I'll have pictures up at your office within an hour.

"Get some men lined up. Trace Hepner and get a line on what he does, how much dough he has and where he got it.

"On the night of the second he placed a call to his mother in Salt Lake City. That call was put in from a phone booth at a service station on the road to Yuma where they stopped for gas. We don't know the place; however, figuring they started out with a full tank the place will probably be Indio or near Indio. Cover all calls from there to Salt Lake City on the night of the second.

"Find Hepner's mother. See if she knows where he is now. Find Hepner. See why he and Eleanor have split up. Get a pipeline into police headquarters, find out all they are finding out about Eleanor and see if they are intending to do anything.

"Don't waste time on Eleanor. She can't give us much help at the present time. For your information she's buried. I have her out of circulation."

"Okay," Drake said. "When do you want all this stuff, Perry?"

"Just as soon as you can possibly get it," the lawyer said and hung up.

■ 4 ■

OLGA JORDAN WAS ACCOMPANIED BY HER FATHER WHEN she brought the photographs and the telegram to Mason's office. She was more than twenty minutes late and started apologizing to Mason almost as soon as she had entered the office and introduced her father to him and Della Street.

"I'm terribly sorry, Mr. Mason. Usually I'm very prompt, but Father pointed out it would be ever so much better to get the negatives rather than merely bring you the photographic prints."

"That will help a lot," Mason said, his eyes on Olga's father.

Homer Corbin could have posed for pictures of a typical Southern colonel. He was a spare, erect man, with a white Vandyke beard carefully trimmed, bushy eyebrows and steel-gray, cold eyes in which the pupils seemed to be mere pinpoints.

"My daughter," he said, speaking with some dignity, "is a very estimable companion, a competent secretary and a rather poor photographer. However, these pictures give you a good idea of the man. I'm glad you're working on that angle, Mr. Mason. I think Douglas Hepner holds the key to whatever has happened."

"Sit down," Mason invited, and then to Corbin said, "You think something has happened, Mr. Corbin?"

Corbin said, "I believe it takes a great emotional shock to bring on amnesia."

"There has, of course, been a physical shock," Mason said. "As I understand it there was an automobile accident."

"Yes, yes, I know. Of course that could have happened, but Olga is rather shrewd, very observant and she is quite familiar with Eleanor's temperament. In fact Olga had to be something of a mother as well as an older sister to Eleanor."

"So she told me," Mason said.

"She very definitely feels that there is some emotional shock in the background, something that has brought on this attack of amnesia. If, of course, that is true, when we discover the event we are going to be faced with another problem, that is how to spare Eleanor from further suffering.

"Eleanor is very dear to me, Mr. Mason. I certainly trust that she hasn't married that bounder Hepner. If she

28

has I feel that this amnesia can be turned to very great legal advantage. I feel that the ceremony can be annulled. Evidently, Mr. Mason, she remembers nothing after that automobile accident, therefore any marriage ceremony must have been performed while her mind was a blank."

"Except," Mason pointed out, "that she knew who she was after that accident and after the wedding ceremony. She sent you this telegram."

"That's true," the older man admitted, reluctantly.

"And some postal cards," Mason went on.

"Two postal cards—one from Yuma, one from Las Vegas."

"They were in her handwriting?"

Homer Corbin stroked his Vandyke, bringing his fingers down to the very point of the beard with a caressing motion. "Well there, Mr. Mason, we're confronted with a peculiar situation. I simply didn't notice the handwriting on the post cards, that is, I took it for granted it was Eleanor's handwriting. I may say that it bore a resemblance to her handwriting, but that, of course, is a far cry from being able to say definitely and positively, 'Yes, that is Eleanor's handwriting.'

"Now as far as the telegram is concerned that could have been sent by anyone. Personally I wouldn't put it a bit past this bounder Hepner to have taken advantage of Eleanor's befuddled mental condition, to have talked her into a marriage and then, in order to keep her family from finding out her real mental condition, sent a telegram in Eleanor's name and forged those postal cards. After all, the postal cards were rather brief and . . . they hardly seemed like Eleanor. There was a certain element of restraint in them and one doesn't usually associate Eleanor with restraint."

Olga started to say something, then changed her mind.

"Just what would have been his object in marrying your daughter?" Mason asked.

"I think the man is a bounder, a cad, a fortune-hunter."

"I take it that Eleanor has good financial prospects?"

Corbin fastened his cold eyes on Mason and then shifted them slightly toward Olga and then back to Mason. "On my death Eleanor will inherit a very substantial sum of money. Both of my children will be very well fixed as far as this world's goods are concerned."

"All right," Mason said, "let's take a look at the photographs."

"I have here some prints that I tore rather hastily from my photograph book," Olga said. "I've circled Doug Hepner. Here he is standing with Eleanor and another girl. Here he is in a group. Here he is talking with Eleanor at the ship's rail. This probably is the best one of all. Eleanor took this with my camera. It shows him alone, standing by the rail, about the only time I ever saw him on the ship when he didn't have some woman making a pass at him.

"Now here are the negatives. You can find the negatives that go with these pictures. . . . You will get to work at once, Mr. Mason?"

"*Get* to work?" Mason exclaimed. "Good Lord, I've *been* working for an hour and a half. The Drake Detective Agency has men out. We're trying to trace the automobile accident. We're trying to trace that telephone call that Eleanor says Douglas Hepner put through to his mother in Salt Lake City . . ."

"But you don't know where the call was placed," Olga said.

"I'm assuming that they started out with a full tank," Mason said. "Probably they stopped for gas either at Banning or at Indio, possibly Brawley. We're checking all three places. We're also checking all reports of accidents on the night of the second. We're checking car registrations and . . . perhaps you know what kind of a car he was driving."

"He had an air-conditioned Oldsmobile," she said, "one of the big ones. He was very proud of it."

The unlisted telephone on Mason's desk rang sharply.

Since only Della Street and Paul Drake had the number of that telephone Mason motioned to Della Street to hand him the phone and said, "Here's Paul Drake on the line now. He may have something to report."

Mason picked up the telephone, said, "Hello, Paul,"

and heard Drake's voice saying, "We struck pay dirt on the phone call, Perry."

"Go ahead," Mason said. "My clients are in the office now. I'd like to get the information."

"Well," Drake said, "your hunch was right. It came through from Indio. It was put in at nine-thirty-five on the evening of August second. It was a person-to-person call put in by Douglas Hepner to Sadie Hepner at Salt Lake City. The number is Wabash 983226."

"Have you made any investigation at the other end?" Mason asked.

"No time yet," Drake said. "I thought I'd pass it on to you and see what you wanted to do."

"I'll call you back," Mason said.

He hung up the telephone, turned to Homer Corbin, and said, "We've traced Hepner's mother in Salt Lake City. Now if you want to work fast on this I suggest that I call her and tell her I'm interested in locating her son. If time isn't so essential I can get detectives at Salt Lake to find out something about the woman and we can make a more indirect approach."

Olga and her father exchanged significant glances. It was Olga who answered Mason's question. "I think you'd better put through the call," she said.

Mason said, "Della, put through a call, a person-to-person call. We want to talk with Mrs. Sadie Hepner at Wabash 983226, and you'd better monitor the conversation when the call comes through."

Della Street picked up the telephone. "Give me an outside line, Gertie."

She put through the call, asking the operator to rush it as it was quite important, while the little group sat in tense silence.

Abruptly Della Street nodded to Perry Mason.

Mason picked up the phone.

"Here's your party," the operator said.

"Hello," Mason said.

A richly mellow, feminine voice at the other end of the line said, "Yes, hello."

"Mrs. Hepner?" Mason said.

31

"Yes. This is Mrs. Hepner."

"Mrs. Hepner, this is Perry Mason. I am very anxious to get in touch with your son, Douglas Hepner. I wonder if you can tell me where he could be reached?"

"Have you tried Las Vegas?" the voice asked.

"Is he there?" Mason asked.

"He telephoned from Barstow when he was on his way to Las Vegas two or three nights ago—now wait a minute, it was . . . I can give you the exact date . . . it was the thirteenth, the evening of the thirteenth."

"And he was on his way to Las Vegas?"

"Yes, he said that he thought he might get up to see me but he evidently couldn't make it."

"You don't know where he was staying in Las Vegas or what he was doing or . . . or whom he was with?"

"No, I'm sure I can't help you on that, Mr. Mason. May I ask what your interest is?"

"Could you," Mason asked, avoiding the question, "tell me if your son is married or single?"

"Why, he's unmarried."

"I believe there was an Eleanor Corbin who . . ."

"Oh yes, Eleanor Corbin," the voice said. "Yes, he called me up . . . oh, it must have been two weeks ago. He was with Eleanor Corbin at the time and he said something that led me to believe his intentions might be serious, but when he called up from Barstow he was with another girl whom he introduced to me over the phone as Suzanne. May I ask why you're interested in locating him, Mr. Mason, and how it happens that you're calling me?"

"I'm trying to find him," Mason said, "and I don't have any other way of reaching him."

"How did you get my address?"

"I happened to know that you were his mother and that he kept in close touch with you."

"And how did you know that, Mr. Mason?"

"Through friends."

"What is your occupation, Mr. Mason? Are you a reporter?"

"No, definitely not."

"What *is* your occupation?"

"I'm an attorney."

"Are you representing my son?"

"No. However, I'm interested in . . ."

"I think perhaps, Mr. Mason, I will have to refer you to my son for any further answers to questions. I'm sorry, perhaps I've been a bit indiscreet. I thought you were a friend of Doug's. Good-by."

The telephone clicked at the other end of the line.

Mason said to Della Street, "Jump down the hall to Drake's office, get him to put Salt Lake detectives on Mrs. Hepner. Find out everything they can about her. Get some elderly woman operative who has a sympathetic approach to get in touch with her and win her confidence, start her talking."

Della Street grabbed her shorthand book. "Shall I repeat the conversation to Paul Drake?"

Mason nodded. "Give him all of it."

"We'd like to know what it was," Olga Jordan said as the door closed behind Della Street.

Mason repeated his conversation with Mrs. Hepner. When he reached the references to Suzanne, Olga and her father exchanged glances.

"Now then," Mason said, "do you know anyone whose first name is Suzanne? Think back over the passenger list. Think carefully. See if you can remember anyone on the ship with that first name. She would probably be some young, attractive woman who showed an interest in Hepner, a rather . . ."

Abruptly Olga Jordan snapped her fingers.

"You have it?" Mason asked.

She turned to her father. "Suzanne Granger!" she exclaimed.

Her father's bushy eyebrows drew together, his eyelids lowered as he considered the problem, then he said slowly, "Yes, it *could* well have been Miss Granger."

"Who is Suzanne Granger?" Mason asked.

"As far as we know she's just a name—that is, we met her, of course. Eleanor knew her better than we did. She was in that crowd that played around together—they usually put the ship's bar to bed every night after the dancing and . . . I think she lives here in the city."

"Any chance you can get her address?" Mason asked.

"I . . . now wait a minute. Eleanor has an address book that she jots down names in and keeps track of people she meets. . . . I'm wondering if she took that book with her or whether it's in her desk. I can see if Bill's home. He could . . ."

Olga reached toward the telephone.

Mason handed it to her, said, "Just tell the girl at the switchboard to give you an outside line."

"An outside line, please," Olga said into the telephone, then her fingers flew rapidly over the dial.

After a moment she said, "Hello. Hello, Bill. Bill, this is Olga. Bill, this is important. Don't stop to ask questions. Run up to Eleanor's room. Look in her desk. See if you can find her address book. See if you can find Suzanne Granger's address. If you don't find it there, see if she didn't save the passenger list on the ship home—there were some autographs and addresses on it."

Mason said to the father, "We can find it from passport information if we have to, or we may locate it from a directory, but this may be faster."

He picked up the other phone, said to the girl at the switchboard, "Gertie, look through the telephone directory. See if a Suzanne Granger has a listed telephone."

Mason held on to the phone while Gertie was looking up the information and Olga held on to the other phone while she was waiting for her husband to look through Eleanor's address book.

A few moments later Gertie relayed the information to Perry Mason. "I don't find any Suzanne Granger listed, Mr. Mason. There's an S. Granger and an S. A. Granger and an S. D. Granger and . . ."

"I have it," Olga interrupted triumphantly from the other telephone.

"Never mind," Mason said. "Skip it, Gertie."

He hung up.

Olga said, "It was on the passenger list. Suzanne Granger autographed it and her address is on there—the Belinda Apartments."

Into the telephone she said, "Thanks, Bill. We're at Mr. Mason's office. We'll be home shortly. Better wait."

She hung up.

"Well," Olga said, "this gives us a definite lead. Of course it's rather a delicate matter, Mr. Mason. You can't come right out and ask a young woman if she spent a week end with the husband of your client who is suffering from amnesia."

"Mr. Mason will know how to handle it, Olga," Homer Corbin said. "As a lawyer he will understand that we can't any of us afford to lay ourselves open to an action for defamation of character."

"That, of course, is the danger in a matter of this kind," Mason said. "I think I'll handle this personally."

"I wish you would," Corbin said. He got to his feet. "Come, Olga," he said, "I think we've done everything we can here. You have the negatives, Mr. Mason, you have the telegram and you have the information about Suzanne. You'll know what to do with all of that.

"There is only one other matter that I thought I might call to your attention. When she left the house on the second, Eleanor had some rather expensive and very distinctive luggage.

"We do quite a bit of traveling and as you are probably aware, on these large steamers the problem of getting luggage through Customs is rather complicated. There is usually a considerable delay finding and collecting all one's luggage in one place because luggage usually looks very much alike. So I had some distinctive luggage made for the two girls and myself. Olga's luggage has a pattern of orange and white checkers. Eleanor's is red and white. Eleanor has two suitcases and an overnight bag. I feel certain that anyone who saw those cases would remember them because of their unique color design. When you start trying to trace Eleanor's movements in Yuma and in Las Vegas you might remember that point about the luggage."

"Thanks," Mason said. "That could be very valuable.

35

Her luggage was simply in alternate squares of red and white?"

"Completely checkerboarded," Corbin said. "It is very conspicuous. It was purposely designed to be conspicuous."

"Thanks," Mason said. "Now I think I'll see what I can do with Miss Granger."

"You will, of course, be circumspect," Corbin cautioned. In the doorway he turned. "Spare no expense, Mr. Mason. Employ all the assistance that you need. Do anything that you think is required under the circumstances."

Mason nodded.

Corbin walked two steps through the door, then turned, retraced his steps and said, "That is, spare no *reasonable* expense, Mr. Mason." With that he turned and marched from the office.

■ 5 ■

THE BELINDA APARTMENTS HAD AN AIR OF SUBSTANCE and dignity. It made no outward attempt to compete with the more ornate apartments in the neighborhood.

The clerk on duty regarded Mason and Della Street superciliously.

"Suzanne Granger," Mason said.

"Your name, please."

"Mason."

"The initials?"

"The first name is Perry."

If the name meant anything to him, the clerk gave no sign.

"Miss Granger is not in at present."

"When will she be in?"

"I'm sorry. I can't give you that information."

"Do you know if she's in the city?"

"I'm sorry, sir. I can't help you."

"I suppose," Mason said, "you would place a message in her mailbox?"

"Of course."

Mason extended his hand. The clerk, with punctilious formality, took a sheet of paper and an envelope from under the desk and handed them to Mason.

Mason took a fountain pen from his pocket, hesitated a moment, then wrote:

Della:
    There's something a little fishy about this. It's a little *too* cold, a little *too* formal. His face froze when I mentioned my name. I'm going to write a note. You stand where you can watch the girl at the switchboard. See if you can pick up anything.

Mason pushed the note over toward Della Street, then suddenly said, "Wait a minute, I think I'll set forth my business in detail. May I have another sheet of paper, please?"

The clerk silently handed him another sheet of paper.

Mason went over to a writing desk and seated himself. Della Street remained for a moment by the reception counter, then sliding her elbow along the edge of the counter, she moved slowly and apparently aimlessly toward the switchboard.

The clerk retired behind a glassed-in partition to a private office.

Mason waited for some three minutes, moving his pen as though writing on the paper. In the end he wrote simply:

Miss Granger:
    I think it will be to your advantage to get in touch with me as soon as possible after you return to your apartment.

Mason signed his name, folded the note, sealed it in the envelope, and taking it to the desk, wrote on the outside, "Miss Suzanne Granger."

Della Street said in a low voice, "He stepped into the office and called apartment 360. He's still talking on that call. You can see the line is still plugged in."

The clerk looked out through the glass-enclosed office, almost immediately hung up the telephone, came out and extended his hand for the note.

Mason, with his pen poised over the envelope, said, "What's the apartment number?"

For a moment the clerk hesitated but Mason's poised pen had about it an air of compelling urgency. The clerk's cold, slightly protruding eyes looked down at the point of the pen for a moment, then he said, "Apartment 358—although that's not at all necessary. Miss Granger will get the message."

Mason wrote down the apartment under her name, handed the envelope to the clerk. "Will you see that she gets this as soon as she comes in?"

Mason took Della Street's arm, escorted her across the lobby to the street.

"Now what?" she asked. "Suzanne Granger in 358, and he telephones to 360! What goes on?"

"That," Mason told her, "is something we'll have to find out. We don't *know* that Suzanne lives in 358."

"If you could find some way to drop a firecracker down the collar of that stuffed shirt at the desk it would suit me fine."

Mason nodded. "I have a feeling, Della, that several people are conspiring to give us a run-around. Let's just walk around the block."

"Walk?"

"That's right," he said, holding her elbow and starting out briskly. "We'll leave the car parked where it is and see what we can find. After all, there must be some way of getting service to these apartments, taking things in and out and . . . Here's an alley. Let's turn down here."

They walked down the alley, came to the back of the apartment house and saw a wide door paneled by thick glass backed by steel mesh. Mason and Della Street entered and saw a sign, *"Service Elevators."*

Mason pressed the button and a slow, lumbering elevator came up from the basement.

An assistant janitor looked at them inquiringly.

Mason said indignantly to Della Street, "The idea of treating us like garbage and telling us to go back to the service elevator."

Della Street said angrily, "Well, some day we'll get even with him."

They entered the service elevator. Mason snapped, "Third floor. . . . I take it *you've* no objection to garbage."

"What's the matter?" the janitor asked.

"Nothing," Mason said irritably, as though spoiling for a fight. "I'm a vulgar tradesman, that's all. The front elevators it seems are reserved for guests."

"Well, don't take it out on me. I have my troubles too," the janitor said, pulling the control and sending the elevator slowly upward to the third floor. "Lots of people don't like the guy you're thinking about."

Mason and Della Street got out, oriented themselves by studying the sequence of several apartment numbers and walked down to apartment 360.

Mason pressed the buzzer to the right of the door.

A woman in her early thirties, dressed to go out, opened the door, started to say something, then stepped back in open-mouthed surprise.

"You!" she exclaimed.

"Exactly," Mason said and volunteered no other information, but simply stood there.

"Why, I . . . I . . . what are you doing here?"

"Maybe the clerk at the desk got his signals mixed."

She had a look of such apparent consternation on her face that after a moment Mason said, "Or perhaps you did."

"What do you want?"

Mason did not reply to her question. "You seem to know who I am," he observed.

"I recognized you from your pictures. You're Perry Mason, the lawyer, and this is your secretary, Miss Street."

Mason remained perfectly silent.

"Well, you are, aren't you?" she asked.

"Yes. I want to talk to you."

She looked at him frowningly. Then Mason and Della Street entered the apartment.

Mason noticed that there were morning newspapers on the floor, that someone had neatly snipped the account of the park ghost from the paper. There was no sign of what had been done with the clipping, but the newspaper lying on the floor bore mute testimony to someone's interest in the case.

"Are you sure *you* are not the one who is confused, Mr. Mason, that you haven't got me mixed up with someone else? I'm certain you have never even heard of me. My name is Ethel Belan."

Mason caught Della Street's eye and gave her a warning glance. "Sit down, Della," he said, and settled himself comfortably in one of the overstuffed chairs.

"No, I'm not confused, Miss Belan. It is you I want to talk to. I'm representing the young woman you've been reading about," Mason said, indicating the mutilated newspaper on the floor.

Ethel Belan started to say something, then apparently changed her mind and was silent.

"Nice apartment you have here," Mason said.

"Thank you."

"You get a view out over Sierra Vista Park from those front windows?"

"Yes, it's nice having a park right across the street."

"Double apartment?" Mason asked, looking around.

"Yes."

"Someone share it with you?"

Ethel Belan looked around the apartment as though looking for something that would give her an inspiration as to how to handle the situation. Her eyes rested momentarily on the telephone, then moved toward the window. "I took a lease on it some time ago. I had a very congenial young woman living with me but she was transferred to a position back East and I . . . well, I haven't as yet found anyone to share the apartment. I think it pays to go easy in matters of that sort."

Mason nodded. "Do you smoke?" he asked Ethel Belan, taking his cigarette case from his pocket.

"No, thank you. I don't smoke."

"May I?"

"Of course."

Mason lit a cigarette, settled back in the chair.

Ethel Belan said pointedly, "I was just going out."

Again Mason nodded, smoking in silence.

"Mr. Mason, may I ask just *what* it is you want?"

Mason seemed somewhat surprised. "Don't you know?"

"I . . . I'd prefer to have you tell me. I . . ."

Mason studied the smoke eddying upward from his cigarette. "In representing a client one has to exercise a certain amount of caution. It is very easy to make a statement which can perhaps be misconstrued and then the situation becomes complicated. It's much better to let the other party make the statements and then either agree or disagree."

"Well, Mr. Mason, I've got nothing in the world to talk to you about. I realize, of course, that you're a highly successful and reputable lawyer, but . . ."

Mason's eyes bored steadily into hers. "Was that your raincoat Eleanor was wearing?"

The question took her completely by surprise.

"Why," she said, "I . . . oh, so *that's* what brought you here! You traced the raincoat!"

Mason gave himself over to contemplation of the smoke spiraling upward from his cigarette.

"Mr. Mason, did Eleanor *send* you here or did you come here because of the raincoat?"

Mason abruptly turned to Ethel Belan. "We want to get her things," he said.

"Why . . . I . . ."

"I brought my secretary along," Mason said, "in case there should be any packing to be done."

"Well, I . . . what gave you the idea that I had any of Eleanor's things here, Mr. Mason?"

Mason shook his head.

"I understand her mind was a complete blank as to

41

where she had been and what had happened for the last two weeks," Ethel Belan said.

Mason's smile was as enigmatic as that of the sphinx.

"Very well," Ethel Belan said abruptly, "I guess it's all right. You're a reputable attorney and you wouldn't be here asking for her things unless she'd sent you for them. This way, please."

She led the way into one of the two bedrooms, opened a closet door and said, "All of those things on the hangers are hers. That's her suitcase in the closet, that's her two-suiter there, and . . ."

"And her overnight bag, I take it," Mason said, indicating the red and white overnight bag.

"Exactly."

Mason said quite casually to Della Street, "You'll try packing them as well as you can, Della?"

Della Street nodded.

"We may as well go out and sit down," Mason said. "Della Street will pack the things."

"I . . . I have an appointment, Mr. Mason. I . . . I'll wait here and close up as soon as Miss Street has them packed. Perhaps I can help."

Mason nodded.

The two women took clothes from the hangers, put them in the suitcases. Ethel Belan opened a drawer and took out handkerchiefs, lingerie and nylon stockings which she handed to Della. Della Street packed them silently.

"Well, I guess that's all," Ethel Belan said.

"We will, of course, trust your discretion in the matter," Mason said significantly.

Ethel Belan hesitated a moment, then said, "Actually, Mr. Mason, there was another week's rent due."

"Oh yes," Mason said, taking his wallet from his pocket. "How much was it?"

"Eighty-five dollars."

Mason hesitated perceptibly.

"Of course," Ethel Belan said rapidly, "that's not exactly half of what I'm paying for the apartment but that was the price that was agreed upon."

"I understand," Mason said, counting out a fifty, three tens and a five.

He handed the currency to Ethel Belan.

"I'm wondering," he said, "since I'm acting in a representative capacity and will necessarily have to submit an expense account, if you'd mind . . . ?"

"Not at all," she said.

She took a piece of paper and wrote:

> Received of Perry Mason, attorney for Eleanor Corbin, eighty-five dollars. Rent from August 16th to August 23rd.

She signed it, and Mason gravely pocketed the receipt, said, "If you can carry the overnight bag, Della. I'll carry the other two."

Ethel Belan's curiosity suddenly got the better of her. "I don't understand how you . . . how you got up here," she said.

"After the clerk phoned you," Mason said, "we felt that we could hardly count on his co-operation."

"But didn't . . . you didn't ask for *me!*"

Mason smiled. "An attorney has to be discreet. He has to be *very* discreet, Miss Belan."

"I see," she said gravely. "I hope you can be as discreet about my connection with this as you are about other things, Mr. Mason. I have a rather responsible position in a downtown department store. This happens to be my afternoon off. I . . . you just happened to catch me at home."

"Exactly," Mason said, "and I think it might be well if you didn't mention our visit to anyone."

"How are you going to get the baggage out?"

"We'll arrange for that," Mason said. "Come on, Della. Can you wait about five minutes before you go out, Miss Belan?"

She glanced at her watch. "I'm sorry, I can't. I've got to leave. I'll ride down in the . . . oh, I understand, you must have come up the freight elevator."

Mason nodded.

"Well then," she said, "I . . . oh, I see, and you'll be taking the baggage out the same way . . . well, thanks a lot, Mr. Mason."

She gave him her hand and a cordial smile, shook hands more perfunctorily with Della Street and ushered them out of the apartment.

She went at once toward the passenger elevator. Mason and Della Street walked around the corridor to the freight elevator.

"Think she'll tell the clerk?" Della Street asked.

"Darned if I know," Mason said, "but we have the baggage now. It's evidently Eleanor's baggage and we'll keep it."

Della let out a long sigh. "Lord! My head is still whirling. I was never so surprised in my life to discover that Ethel wasn't Suzanne Granger, or rather—well, you know what I mean. And as for the bluff *you* pulled! I almost gasped out loud when I heard you ask her so casually if that was her raincoat."

"Evidently it was," Mason said. "You see it's the dry season here and when Eleanor packed she certainly didn't put in a raincoat, that is, not a heavy, opaque raincoat like the one she was wearing when the police picked her up. If she'd had a raincoat in her suitcase it would have been one of those transparent plastic types that can be folded into a small, compact bundle."

"But why in the world would Eleanor have wanted to take off her clothes there in the apartment, put on a raincoat, go over to the park and start dancing around in the moonlight, and why would Ethel Belan have given her the raincoat and . . ."

"Let's not overlook one point," Mason said. "She may not have given Eleanor the raincoat. Eleanor may simply have appropriated that. It was evidently Ethel Belan's raincoat, that's all. She didn't tell us anything else."

"Yes, that's right," Della Street said.

"Of course," Mason pointed out, "she acted on the assumption that we knew. Now notice that this receipt covers rent from the sixteenth to the twenty-third. It's the seventeenth now. You can see that Ethel Belan has an eye on the financial end of things, and since the rental was by the week we can assume that the rental started either on the second or the ninth of this month."

"But Eleanor left home on the evening of the second."

"That's right," Mason said, "so probably rental started on the ninth, which leaves her whereabouts from the second to the ninth as a problem."

"And did you notice that Ethel Belan referred to her as Eleanor Corbin, not as Eleanor Hepner?"

"Very definitely," Mason said.

"And what in the world was she doing in that apartment from the ninth to the sixteenth . . . ?"

The freight elevator lumbered to a stop. The door rumbled open.

Mason stood aside for Della to enter, then, carrying the two suitcases, carefully holding them so it could not be told whether they were empty or packed, said to the elevator man, "A job of baggage repair and he sends us to the tradesmen's entrance! The elevators are reserved for *guests!*"

"I know, I know," the janitor sympathized. "They do funny things here. If you'd given the bellboy a dollar to take them down you could have gone down the front way, but . . ."

"*We* should give a bellboy a dollar!" Mason exclaimed. "A dollar for what? A dollar to carry suitcases across the lobby to an automobile . . . ?"

The elevator rattled and swayed on downward, and came to a stop at the ground floor. Mason and Della Street emerged into the corridor, then through the heavy doors into the alley.

Mason said to Della Street, "You walk around and get the car, Della. Drive around here to the alley and pick me up. I'll wait with the baggage."

"Why not you get the car and I'll . . ."

"Someone," Mason said with a grin, "might try to take the baggage away from you."

Mason stood by the three pieces of baggage, all decorated in red and white checkerboards, watching Della Street's trim figure as she hurried down the alley, then

45

turned into the street. Some three minutes later she was back with the car. Mason loaded the baggage into the trunk. Della Street slid over from the driver's seat and Mason got in behind the wheel.

"Where to?" she asked.

"How about your apartment?" Mason asked. "This luggage is rather conspicuous and the office may have some people who would notice. It will probably be described in the press later on."

Della Street nodded.

Mason drove the car through the afternoon traffic, stopped at an intersection and motioned to a boy who was selling newspapers.

Della Street skimmed through the early evening edition while Mason continued to drive the car.

"Well!" she exclaimed.

"Good coverage?" Mason asked.

"I'll say. The newspapermen seem to have taken particular delight in letting you realize that you're persona non grata."

"How come?"

"Evidently they felt that you wanted to avoid publicity so they gave you plenty. Of course it's a nice story. Heiress identified by wealthy family. High-priced attorney retained to control publicity and represent the young woman in any action that may be filed. Chief, when you come right down to it, the family certainly did a strange thing, didn't they?"

Mason nodded.

"Coming in with a retainer of that sort—good Lord, that's the type of retainer you'd expect in a murder case."

Again Mason nodded.

"And this talk about protecting the family from publicity —when you stop to think of it, it was inevitable that the things they did would *make* publicity, ten times as much publicity as they'd have otherwise received."

Again Mason nodded.

"Well, you're a big help I must say," Della Street said.

"I was simply agreeing with you."

"Well, it just hit me all of a sudden how peculiar it

was for people to come to you and ask you to handle the publicity and . . . well, they said they wanted things minimized, but what has happened has just transformed a small story into a big story.

"Perry Mason, the famous criminal attorney, retained by the family, fires the doctor, spirits the patient to a private sanitarium in an ambulance that uses its siren to go through signals at sixty miles an hour so it can't be followed. Nobody knows where the patient is. The wealthy family, the background, the trips to Europe, picture of the father. Story about an elopement with Douglas Hepner. Good Lord, Chief, it's completely incongruous. The very things that they told you they were doing to control publicity have resulted in smearing the thing all over the front page."

Again Mason nodded.

"I take it," she said, "your thinking is in advance of mine and may I ask when this idea which has now hit me with such terrific impact first occurred to you?"

"When they handed me the twenty-five-hundred-dollar check," Mason said.

"Well," she told him, "I certainly swung late on that one! Why in the world do you suppose they did anything like that?"

"Because, as Olga Jordan so aptly expressed it, judging from the scrapes Eleanor has been in before, this one is a lulu."

"Well," she said, "it'll be interesting to interview Suzanne Granger and see what her connection is. I take it she's a third point in a triangle."

"Could be," Mason said.

Della Street, piqued at the lawyer's reticence, settled back against the cushions and remained silent until they reached her apartment house.

"Want me to call a bellboy?" she asked.

"No," Mason said, "I'll go up with you. In that way people will think you've been out on a case and you're just coming back with your suitcases. Hang it, I wish these things weren't so conspicuous."

"We're pretty likely to find the lobby completely deserted," Della Street said, "and, after all, we dash around on cases so much that people take us more or less for granted."

They parked the car. Mason opened the trunk and said, "You take the overnight bag, I'll take the other two, Della."

They entered the apartment house, found the lobby deserted, and went to Della Street's apartment.

"What should I do with these things?" she asked. "Unpack them and put the clothes on hangers, or just leave them . . . ?"

"Leave them packed," Mason said. "I take it you checked through the articles as you were packing them, Della?"

"Just the clothes you'd expect," Della said. "Some of them hadn't even been unpacked. She has an assortment of dresses, underwear, lots of stockings. I presume her more personal things are in the overnight bag."

"Let's just take a look in there," Mason said. "We'd better see what we have."

"Suppose it's locked?" Della Street asked, regarding the formidable catches.

"If it is," Mason said, "we'll get a locksmith and unlock it. I want to see what's in there."

Della Street tried the catches. They snapped up and she pulled back the lid.

"Oh-oh!" she exclaimed. "What a *beautiful* bag!"

The interior had been carefully designed to hold an array of creams and lotions around the edges in special containers. The inside of the lid held a beautiful beveled mirror, and a small margin between the mirror and the edge of the lid was fitted with loops containing a complete manicure outfit. The space in the center of the bag held some folded stockings, some lingerie and a nightgown.

Della Street held the nightgown up against her shoulders. "Well, well, well," she said.

It was one of the new short nightgowns, not much longer than a pajama top.

"Brevity," Mason said, "is supposed to be the soul of wit."

"You couldn't ask for anything wittier than this then," Della Street said.

"Well, we live and learn," Mason told her, grinning. "Personally I guess I'm getting a bit out of date."

"*You* are!" she exclaimed. "How do you suppose this makes *me* feel?"

Abruptly she laughed to hide her confusion, folded the garments, put them back in the overnight bag. She casually unscrewed the lid from one of the jars and said, "Eleanor evidently gives a great deal of thought to her skin."

"Some skin," Mason said. "You should have seen her in the hospital when she threw back the covers and started to get up."

"Good-looking?"

Mason smiled reminiscently.

"I suppose," Della Street said somewhat bitterly, "she was all unconscious of your presence and just threw back the covers. A girl who is accustomed to wearing night-gowns that short should be a little discreet about tossing covers back."

"While brevity," Mason said, "may be the soul of wit, it isn't supposed to have anything to do with descretion."

Della Street placed an exploring middle finger into the jar of cream, said, "Well, I'll see how this expensive cream works on the skin of a working girl and . . ."

Abruptly she stopped.

"What is it?" Mason asked.

"Something in here," she said, "something hard."

Her middle finger brought out a blob of cream.

"It has a hard interior, Chief. It feels like glass or . . ."

Della Street reached for a package of cleansing tissue, rubbed the object in the tissue and then opened the paper.

"Good Lord!" Mason exclaimed.

The facets of a beautifully cut diamond coruscated in glittering brilliance.

"Anything else?" Mason asked after a moment.

Again Della Street dipped her finger into the cream jar. Again she came up with a hard object. This time the

49

cleansing tissue removed the cream and disclosed the beautiful deep green of an emerald.

"I don't know much about gems," Della Street said, "but those certainly look to me like the cream of the crop."

"No pun intended, I take it," Mason said.

She looked blank for a moment, then smiled and said, "Well, let's see what else is in the cream—or shall we?"

Mason nodded.

By the time Della Street had thoroughly explored the jar of cream they had a collection of fifteen diamonds, three emeralds and two rubies.

"There are," she pointed out, "quite a few jars in here in addition to various bottles and . . ."

"We'll take a look," Mason said.

"And what do you suppose Eleanor will say when she finds out that we have taken liberties with her overnight bag?"

"We'll find out what she says," Mason told her, "but we'll look."

"She may not like it."

"I'm her attorney."

"*She* didn't say so—only the family said so."

Mason was thoughtful for a moment. "That's right," he agreed.

"But do we go ahead?"

"Quite definitely we go ahead, Della."

Twenty minutes later Della Street surveyed the glittering assortment of gems.

"Good Lord, Chief, there's a fortune here. What do we do with them?"

Mason said, "We count them. We make as much of an inventory as we can. We wrap them individually in cleansing tissue so we don't mar them in any way.

"And then what?" Della Street said.

"Then," Mason said, "we put them in a safe place."

"And what's your suggestion of a safe place?"

Mason's eyes narrowed. "Now," he said, "you have asked a highly pertinent question."

"The office safe?"

50

Mason shook his head.

"A safe-deposit box?"

"That's a little awkward."

"What do you mean?"

"We don't know what these gems are. They may be her personal property. They may have been stolen. They may have been smuggled. They may represent very concrete and perhaps very damaging evidence."

"And under those circumstances, what?"

"Under those circumstances," Mason said, "I find myself in a peculiar situation. I am, of course, charged with protecting the interests of my client, Eleanor Corbin or Eleanor Hepner, as the case may be."

"And the good name of the Corbin family," Della Street pointed out. "That, I believe, was considered of paramount importance when the retainer was given."

Mason nodded.

"And so?" she asked.

"So," Mason said, "I'm going to telephone Paul Drake. He'll send an armed detective down here to act as a bodyguard for you. The detective will escort you to one of the best hotels in the city. Pick the one that you like the best and where you'd like to stay if you had an unlimited expense account."

She raised her eyebrows.

"You will," Mason said, "register under your true name so that there will be no question of concealment. You will have your luggage with you, and immediately after you have registered and been shown to a room you will go down to the office and tell the clerk that you have some valuables you want to leave in the hotel safe. In those large hotels they have very fine safes and safe-deposit boxes. They'll give you a box. You'll put the package of gems in the box. The clerk will lock up the box and hand you the key."

"And then what?"

"Then," Mason said, "you will start leading a double life. You will come to work as usual during the daytime, but during the late afternoons and evenings you will be the glamorous and mysterious Miss Street who flutters around the hotel as a paying guest, putting on that tight elastic bathing suit of yours, dipping into the pool, being sedate and reserved but not at all forbidding. And in case any amiable and attractive young chap starts making wolf calls you will be archly amused. You will let him buy you a drink and a dinner and Paul Drake's operatives, who will be keeping you under surveillance, will promptly proceed to find out all about the young man's background and whether he's merely acting the part of a wolf with thoroughly dishonorable intentions, or whether his interest is aroused by things other than your face, figure and personality."

"And the key to the hotel lock box?" she asked.

"The key, just as soon as you get it," Mason said, "will be given to me and I'll see that it is put in a safe place so that in case any slick pickpocket should go through your purse while you're dancing or drinking he would find nothing more than the expense money—which is to be furnished by the Corbins."

"You make it sound very exciting and attractive," Della Street said.

"In that case," Mason told her, "we'll make immediate arrangements for the bodyguard."

Mason stepped to the phone, called Paul Drake's number.

"Perry Mason talking. Put Paul on the line, will you? Is he there? . . . Fine, thanks."

A moment later, when Paul Drake came on the line, Mason said, "Paul, I want a bodyguard. I want someone who is dependable, tough and wide-awake, someone who knows his way around."

"Okay."

"How soon can I have him?"

"Half or three-quarters of an hour if you're in a hurry."

"I'm in a hurry."

"Where do you want him?"

"Della Street's apartment."

"Okay. Who do you want him to bodyguard?"

"Della."

"The devil!"

"I want someone who packs a rod and knows how to use it." Mason said. "Then Della is going to a high-class hotel. I want her kept unostentatiously under surveillance at the hotel."

"Now wait a minute," Drake said, "you said a high-class hotel?"

"The best."

"We can't do it unless it happens to be a place where I know the house detective, and even then . . ."

"What do you mean, you can't do it?" Mason interrupted.

"It isn't being done, that's all. You can't hang around a place like that keeping a woman as good-looking as Della under surveillance without their knowing about it and then they bring you in and . . ."

"Can't you have people register as guests and . . . ?"

"Oh sure, if you want to go that strong. That thing runs into money at a good hotel, but if you want to have them register as guests there's nothing to it."

"Okay," Mason said, "have them register as guests. Have one fellow who is young, who can act as an escort in case it becomes advisable, and one fellow who is old and grizzled and tough and is more interested in the financial section than figures in a bathing suit, someone who will not be hypnotized by the smooth sheen of a nylon stocking, but who will keep his eye on surroundings. And get more men if you have to."

"What's the idea?" Drake asked.

"I can't tell you right now. How are you coming with your homework?"

"Look," Drake said, "things are happening. Did you see the papers?"

"Della told me we'd attracted quite a bit of publicity."

"That's only half of it," Drake said. "Now look, Perry, I'm damned if I can find where Eleanor ever married this Hepner guy. It was supposed to have taken place at Yuma, Arizona. We've combed through the records, we've even figured they might have married under assumed names, and we've checked all of the marriages that were performed on the second and third of August. We've managed to account for everyone. Furthermore we've gone over details in every automobile accident that took place anywhere along the road to Yuma on the night of the second and we can't find anything. We can't get a trace of Douglas Hepner any—"

"What about his mother in Salt Lake?" Mason asked.

"Now there is *really* something."

"What?"

"The so-called mother," Drake said, "turns out to be a beautiful brunette babe about twenty-seven years old with lots of this and that and these and those, who lives in a swank apartment when she's there but who flits around like a robin in the springtime. She catches planes on short notice. She goes hither and yon, and . . ."

"And she poses as Douglas Hepner's mother?" Mason asked.

"Apparently only over the telephone. The registration is Mrs. Sadie Hepner on the apartment."

"Good Lord," Mason said, "another wife?"

"We can't tell."

"What does she say?"

"She doesn't say. Apparently she hung up the telephone after talking with you, and got the hell out of there. In fact it's very possible that she was in the process of packing up when you phoned her. She returned this morning from some mysterious mission, packed up and left the place within about fifteen minutes of the time you called her. She took a flock of suitcases with her, got into her nice, shiny Lincoln automobile, told the garage attendant she was headed for Denver and took off. She had gone by the time my operatives got to her apartment.

"We traced her as far as the garage and ran up against a blank wall. Do you want us to try to pick up her trail along the road?"

"Sure. Try Denver, San Francisco and here."

"It's like a needle in a haystack. We may be able to pick up her trail from her license number when she checks in at one of the California checking stations—but suppose she really is headed for Denver?"

54

"If she said Denver she probably meant California. Give it a try, Paul. What about the wire from Yuma?"

"That wire was phoned in from a pay station. No one knows any more about it than that. Hundreds of wires all reading about the same way flow through the Yuma telegraph office."

"Keep running down any lead you uncover," Mason told him.

"Well," Drake said, "things are being stirred up. I've got men in Las Vegas. We've managed to get some pretty good pictures from those negatives and I rushed a man over to Las Vegas by plane. He'll be inquiring around there. We're also looking for marriage records in Las Vegas. I should have some more stuff for you late tonight."

"Stay with it," Mason said. "Put men on the job."

"Of course," Drake pointed out, "it would help if you'd give me some kind of an inkling what you're working on and what you're looking for."

"I'm looking for information."

"So I gathered," Drake told him dryly.

■ 6 ■

IT WAS NEARLY TEN O'CLOCK WHEN PERRY MASON dropped into Paul Drake's office.

The detective was seated at his desk in his shirt sleeves, sipping coffee and holding a phone to his ear.

He nodded as Mason came in, put down the coffee cup, said, "I've just struck something important out in Las Vegas, Perry. My gosh, I've got an army of operatives on the job. I've told every one of them to phone in the minute he finds anything that may be at all significant. No marriage records in Las Vegas, Nevada. Guess I told you. Can't remember just what I've reported and what I haven't. Things have been coming too fast. My man over in Las Vegas says it's a hundred and fifteen and . . . Hello, hello . . . Hello, yes . . . He did, eh? . . . All right, keep trying . . . All right."

Drake hung up the phone, sighed wearily, said, "What's the idea with Della?"

"Della," Mason said, "is putting on the dog. She's joined the ranks of the idle rich, and is looking around."

"So I gathered. Is she still a working gal?"

"Daytimes she's a working gal," Mason said. "Nighttime she stays at the hotel and your men watch her."

"Bait for a trap?" Drake asked.

"Could be. What's the dope on Doug Hepner?"

"That's a funny thing," Drake said.

"What is?"

Drake pushed the coffee cup to one side.

Drake said, "I flew one of my operatives over to Las Vegas, Nevada. He had a bunch of pictures of Hepner. We had some pretty good enlargements and . . ."

"You told me all that," Mason interrupted impatiently.

"I know, but I wanted you to get the picture. My man picked up some of my associates in Las Vegas and got them all started working. Gosh, Perry, do you have any idea of the number of people who pour through Las Vegas, Nevada, in the course of a week?"

"I suppose it's a lot," Mason said. "What are you leading up to? Do you want to show me some particularly brilliant piece of detective work?"

"Hell, no," Drake said. "On the off-chance that this man Hepner had done some gambling and that might be the answer, we took his photograph and dropped around to a couple of dealers that we knew. Understand, Perry, there wasn't one chance in a thousand, not one chance in a million that anything like that would have paid off, but we took a chance at it just to see what would happen."

"All right, what happened?"

"One of these dealers knew the guy."

"Douglas Hepner?"

"Yes. He hadn't seen the guy for a year, but he knew him, knew all about him, knew what he was doing."

56

"Shoot," Mason said.

"He used to be a gambler, a professional. He free-lanced on poker games for a while. He acted as shill for a house. He ran roulette and twenty-one games, and was pretty fair. He was dependable, sharp, quick, likable, had a nice voice and personality and . . ."

"How long ago?"

"Oh, that was three, four years ago."

"Come on," Mason said impatiently, "get down to the present. What's he doing now?"

"Believe it or not, collecting rewards."

"Collecting rewards?" Mason echoed.

"That's right."

"Who from?"

"The United States Government."

"How come?"

Drake said, "You know what happens when people go to Europe."

"Sure. They send home post cards. They bring home souvenirs. They . . ."

"And one woman out of three does a little smuggling—sometimes it doesn't amount to much, sometimes it's a lot."

"Go ahead," Mason said.

"The United States Customs pays a reward for information that leads to the recovery of smuggled goods. Suppose Mrs. Rearbumper smuggles in a ten-thousand-dollar diamond. She's just as safe as can be unless she happens to have bought that diamond where some spotter on the other side tipped off the Government."

Mason nodded.

"If, however, the Government gets a tip-off they go through all of Mrs. Rearbumper's things. They find the diamond. They confiscate the diamond. They fine her. And then if she wants her diamond back she has to buy it back. There's a nice little bit of sugar for the Government and the Government naturally likes to preserve its sources of information, so it pays off."

"I see," Mason said dryly.

"Now then, that's why I was trying to give you this

57

background of Douglas Hepner. Two years or so ago he went to Europe. He thought he'd do a little gambling on the boat. He found that that was a pretty tough nut to crack. The big steamship companies don't like to have professional gamblers take money from passengers. So Hepner, with his nice manners, his knowledge of the world, his suave approach, started using his eyes and ears. He made friends on the trip over. He kept up with his friends in Europe. He posed as having quite a bit of information about values, particularly in regard to jewelry —and I guess he does know quite a bit about diamonds.

"The result was that within thirty days he knew of a big chunk of gems that had been purchased with no intention on the part of the purchaser of paying any duty to Uncle Sam.

"Hepner's trip paid off. Thereafter he started taking more and more trips."

"And he met Eleanor Corbin on a boat coming back from Europe three months ago," Mason said.

"Exactly," Drake told him.

"Do you suppose Eleanor did a little smuggling?"

"Eleanor is quite capable of doing a lot of smuggling," Drake said. "Eleanor has been in a couple of scrapes. She's a hot wire."

"The point is, did someone turn in information on her and did she get caught smuggling?"

"She didn't get *caught* smuggling," Drake said.

"More and more interesting," Mason pointed out.

"She became very friendly with Douglas Hepner. Now do you suppose Douglas Hepner was merely cultivating her as a contact, or do you suppose Douglas Hepner knew about some jewelry she was bringing into this country and was persuaded by one means or another not to say anything?"

"You open up very interesting vistas," Mason said. "How am I going to find Douglas Hepner?"

"That, of course, is the sixty-four-dollar question," Drake said. "Lots of people are asking that question right at the moment."

"Who, for instance?"

"Newspaper reporters. They'd like to make a nice story out of this. It has some choice angles. A bride who can't remember anything about her wedding night or her honeymoon. That's a nice angle. On the other hand, the daughter of a wealthy family who says she's married to Douglas Hepner, and Douglas Hepner says she isn't. She's sporting a wedding ring and a loss of memory. Nice stuff.

"Or take it from the angle of a girl who goes bye-bye for a week end with a good-looking guy she met on shipboard. A nice juicy little scandal here. Lots of people slip out over week ends. They often wonder what would happen if they got caught. So when they read about someone who does get caught it gives the story a lot of impact."

"This smuggling angle gives the whole situation a new slant, Paul."

"It opens up complications," Drake said. "A man who goes in for that line of work is, of course, interested in the twenty percent. He forms friendships for the purpose of getting information. He becomes sort of a sublimated stool pigeon, no matter how lofty he thinks his motives are. He cultivates middle-aged women who think he's a wonderful dancing partner. . . . They become great friends. She tells him about picking up a present for her sister. It was wonderfully cheap and if she can only get it in without paying duty on it, it will be a lot cheaper. She asks him what he thinks. Of course he advises her to go right ahead and then goes back and enters down the name and the approximate amount in a little notebook.

"Well then, of course, once you start figuring on the twenty percent, another beautiful angle opens up."

"Blackmail?" Mason asked.

"Blackmail," Drake said. "Mrs. Rearbumper simply couldn't stand it to be branded as a criminal. That would be terrible. That would put her right out of circulation in the set to which she belongs."

"There is," Mason said, "also a wonderful opportunity for high-grading. Let's suppose that John K. Bigshot, a big gem importer, has worked out a pretty good system of smuggling in a lot of gems at a clip. The Customs men don't catch him but Douglas Hepner catches him. The gems are concealed in a crutch that's been skillfully hollowed out, or in a wooden leg that . . ."

"Sure," Drake said, "there are lots of possibilities."

"Some of them more possible than others," Mason told him.

"Uh-huh."

"So," Mason said, "suppose Hepner is about to inform the Government in order to collect a twenty percent reward on a bunch of smuggled gems. Suppose word of that gets out. People have different reactions. Some people would want to run to him and pay him off. Some would try to skip the country and wait until things blew over. Some would try first one way and then another to silence him. If he couldn't be silenced and the game happened to be important enough, the shipment big enough, or the information Hepner had vital enough, well . . ." Mason shrugged his shoulders.

Again the phone on Drake's desk rang.

Drake picked it up, said, "Okay, let me have that . . ."

The other phone rang.

Drake said, "Hang on just a moment. I'll see what this is."

Drake said, "Hello . . . that's right. Drake speaking. . . ."

He was silent for a matter of some twenty seconds, listening to what was coming in over the telephone, then he said, "This is important. Keep me posted on everything. Goodby."

Drake slammed up that phone, barked into the other one, "Matter of major emergency. If I don't call you in fifteen minutes call me back in fifteen."

Drake slammed the phone into its cradle, turned to Mason. A faint flush of excitement was stealing over the detective's cheeks.

"Know something?"

"What?"

"The police just discovered a man's body in Sierra

Vista Park. The body was located within a couple of hundred yards of where Eleanor was tripping around in a thin slip and sweet smile."

"What about the body?" Mason interrupted.

"That's darn near all I know and apparently it's darn near all the police know. The body has a very neat bullet hole in the back of the head. Apparently the bullet didn't go through the skull."

"How long ago did it happen?"

"Anywhere from twenty-four to thirty-six hours," Drake said.

"Did police find the body?"

"A necking couple left the car and went smooching into the dark shadows. The body was lying in a thick patch of brush. There was a trail through there and the body was just off the trail."

"It's Hepner?" Mason asked.

"So far there's been no identification. It's just a body with a bullet hole in the back of the head."

Mason grabbed for one of the telephones, said to the girl on Drake's exchange, "Get me outside, fast."

Mason dialed a number, said, "This is Perry Mason. I have to talk with Dr. Ariel. Get me through just as soon as you can. This is a major emergency."

Thirty seconds later Dr. Ariel was on the line.

Mason said, "I'm very much concerned about our mental patient, Doctor."

"Eleanor Hepner?"

"That's right."

"Her progress is very satisfactory."

"As I understand it, in treating a person of that sort it's necessary to avoid any mental shock. Any emotional upset could have disastrous results."

"Well, of course," Dr. Ariel said cautiously, "the patient is rather a peculiar individual. She seems to be well-oriented, with a good sense of humor and . . ."

"As I understand it," Mason said, "an emotional shock could send such a patient off the deep end."

"Well, I wouldn't worry too much. You . . ."

"As I understand it, an emotional shock could be disastrous."

Dr. Ariel thought for a moment, said, "Excuse me, I'm a little dumb tonight. It could be, yes."

"It's to be avoided?"

"Well, it certainly isn't what the doctors call 'indicated.'"

"I have a feeling," Mason said, "that she may be pestered by lots of people."

"No one knows where she is, Perry."

"They don't know, but it might be possible for them to find out."

"You mean newspaper reporters?"

"Perhaps—and others."

"You mean relatives?"

"I was thinking of newspaper reporters—and others."

"You don't mean the police, Perry?"

"Well, of course, one never knows."

"Forget it," Dr. Ariel said. "The police have nothing against her. She was wandering around in the moonlight but she wasn't exactly in the nude. They couldn't even get her on indecent exposure. They can't get an identification, and anyhow, the police have wiped the slate clean."

"That's an interesting expression," Mason said. "You wipe the slate clean. Why do you do that?"

"To get rid of what's written on it," Dr. Ariel said, puzzled.

"No. It's because a slate is meant to be written on," Mason corrected. "You wipe it clean so you can write something else on it. I think our patient should be transferred to some place where no one can find her and disturb her."

Dr. Ariel thought for a moment, then said, "Well, of course, these things are a little tricky. No one can predict just what's going to happen."

"I think we should guard against *any* eventuality," Mason insisted.

"Okay," Dr. Ariel said. "I'll get busy."

"I feel she should be where *no one* can disturb her," Mason went on.

"I got you the first time," Dr. Ariel said. "That is, after I finally tumbled. It's going to take a little doing, but I think it can be done."

"At once," Mason said.

"Oh sure," Dr. Ariel told him. "This is an emergency. Got any news for me?"

"No."

"You mean no news?"

"I mean not for you," Mason said. "You'd better get busy. I'm very much concerned about the health of my client and your patient."

"So am I, now that you mention it," Dr. Ariel said. "Thanks for calling, Perry. Good-by."

Mason hung up the phone, turned to Paul Drake. "Paul, you've got a pipeline into police headquarters—"

"A couple of newspaper reporters are willing to do a little work on the side after they phone the story in to the newspaper—and, of course, lots of times newspapers know things that they don't publish."

"Use all your contacts," Mason said. "Spend money as necessary. Find out everything about the body. Find out if it could have been suicide. What kind of a weapon was used. Where the weapon is. How long the body was dead. Check the identification. Find out where Hepner resided. Locate his automobile. Check back on his movements. . . ."

"The police will be doing all that," Drake said. "We can't compete with the police."

"I didn't ask you to," Mason said. "I told you to get that information. I don't give a damn *how* you get it or who gets it first. I want it."

"Okay," Drake said wearily. "And I was just going home. Where will you be, Perry?"

Mason said, "I'll be where no one can find me until after Eleanor has been moved and after the body has been identified. That means I'll be out of circulation until tomorrow morning. I'll then show up at the office as usual. In the meantime, don't waste time trying to reach me because you can't do it."

■ 7 ■

MASON GLANCED AT HIS WATCH AS HE LEFT PAUL Drake's office. It was eighteen minutes past ten.

Mason drove to a service station, had his car filled with gasoline, and while the attendant was washing the windshield, called the Belinda Apartments.

"I know it's late," he told the girl at the switchboard, "but I'd like to talk with Suzanne in 358—that is Miss Granger. I told her earlier in the day that I'd call her."

"Just a moment, I'll connect you."

A few moments later Mason heard a calm, feminine voice saying, "Yes . . . hello."

"I'm sorry to disturb you at this late hour," Mason said, "but this is about Douglas Hepner."

"Hepner," she said. "Hepner . . . Oh yes. And who are you, please?"

"I wanted to ask you some questions."

"And who are you?"

"The name," he said, "is Mason, Perry Mason, an attorney. I left a note in your box."

"Oh yes."

"Did you get it?"

"Certainly."

Mason said, "I thought you should have an opportunity for rehearsal."

"To rehearse what, Mr. Mason?"

"Your story."

"What story?"

"The story you're going to have to tell police and newspaper reporters later on. You can try it out on me and I can question you and point out any contradictions."

"Mr. Mason, are you trying to threaten me?"

"Not at all."

"Why should *I* be telling a story to the police?"

"You're going to be questioned."

"About Douglas Hepner?"

"Yes."

"Where are you now?"

"Not too far from your apartment house."

She hesitated a moment, then laughed. "You know, Mr. Mason, you interest me. I've read a lot about you and your technique of cross-examination. On second thought, I think it would be rather fun to have you fasten your penetrating eyes on me and try to get me rattled. By all means come out."

"I'll be out right away," Mason told her and hung up the phone.

At the Belinda Apartments Mason smiled reassuringly at the clerk at the desk, a different one from the person he and Della Street had encountered earlier in the day.

"Miss Granger," Mason said, "in 358. She's expecting me."

"Yes, she phoned," the clerk said. "Go right up, Mr. Mason."

Mason went to 358, pressed the buzzer. The door was opened almost instantly by an attractive young woman, who regarded the lawyer with challenging gray eyes.

"I want to congratulate you, Mr. Mason," she said. "Won't you come in?"

Mason entered the apartment.

"Congratulate me on what?"

She indicated a chair.

"On the line you used."

"What?"

"That one about asking if I didn't want to rehearse my story before I was questioned by others."

"Oh," Mason said, noncommittally.

"It's rather effective. Do you use it often?"

"It's one of my favorites," Mason conceded. "It *usually* gets results."

"It's provocative. It's just a little alarming and yet one can't say that it constitutes a definite threat."

"I'm glad you appreciate it," Mason said.

She offered him a cigarette.

"I'll have one of my own, if you don't mind," Mason said, taking out his cigarette case and lighter.

She took a cigarette, leaned forward for Mason's light, took a deep drag, settled back and blew out a cloud of smoke.

"Well, Mr. Mason, do you prefer to engage in a little preliminary sparring while we size each other up, or will you try for a quick knockout?"

"It depends on the adversary."

"You'd better spar then."

"Perhaps we'd better be frank. Suppose you tell your story and then I'll question you on it."

"I don't like that procedure. Suppose *you* ask questions."

"Very well. You knew Douglas Hepner?"

"Yes."

"How long had you known him?"

"I met him three or four months ago on a ship coming from Europe."

"You were friendly with him?"

"On shipboard?"

"Both on shipboard and afterward."

"Let's put it this way. I was friendly with him on shipboard and I was friendly with him afterward, but there was an interval during which I didn't even see the man. Then I happened to run into him one day in an art store, and of course, we renewed our association. He bought me a drink as I remember it and asked for a dinner date. I was engaged that night but I believe I went to dinner with him the following night. Now would you mind telling me why you're asking these questions, Mr. Mason, and why you intimate that the police will be interested."

"I'm representing a young woman who is suffering from temporary amnesia."

"So I understand. A woman who claims to be Mrs. Douglas Hepner. How interesting! Did you think that perhaps I could help her prove her point, make an honest woman out of her, so to speak? You had quite a write-up in the evening papers, Mr. Mason."

"So I've been told," Mason said dryly. "Now I'd like to find out something about your dates. You saw Douglas Hepner recently?"

"Oh yes."

"How recently?"

"Why, I believe . . . I believe the evening of the fifteenth was the last time I saw him."

"Did he tell you he was married?"

"He certainly did not."

"Did he tell you that he was *not* married?"

"Not in so many words, but he . . . I gathered that he . . . well, I don't think I care to discuss that matter, Mr. Mason. You'd better ask those questions of Mr. Hepner. I presume that he'll be somewhat surprised when he reads the papers and finds he's supposed to be married to this young woman who has lost her memory."

"You saw quite a good deal of Hepner after that first dinner date?"

"I saw something of him, yes."

"He was here at the apartment?"

"Yes."

"Could you," Mason asked, "tell me just how that happened?"

Her eyes were mocking. "Why, certainly, Mr. Mason. I invited him in. I pay rent on this apartment, you know."

"How many times was he here?"

"I didn't keep a record."

"Have you any recollection?"

"Only generally. It would take some time for me to go back and check that recollection."

"Would you care to do that?"

"Not now, Mr. Mason."

"Did you know his family?"

"His family? Why, no."

"Is that so," Mason said, his voice showing surprise. "I talked with his mother over the telephone and she told me that she had talked with someone in Barstow who claimed to be . . . However, perhaps there was a misunderstanding."

"So *that's* your knockout punch," she said, her eyes

levelly regarding his. "I was wondering when you'd quit sparring and try for a knockout. All right, I went to Las Vegas with Douglas Hepner. So what? I'm over the age of consent and under the age of indifference. I felt like doing a little gambling and Doug was going to Las Vegas. He invited me to go and I went. So what?"

"So nothing," Mason said.

"And," she went on, "Doug stopped at what should have been the most romantic moment to call his mother in Salt Lake City. It was a new revelation of the Hepner character as far as I was concerned. Frankly, it wasn't anything that I cared for in particular. Parental devotion is always commendable but there are times and circumstances. I had made no promises going to Las Vegas. We were simply going for the trip, but a man in Hepner's position should have been at least speculating as to the possibilities of developments. He should have been making guarded approaches—not definitely burning his bridges behind him, but nevertheless making approaches.

"Instead he stopped at Barstow for gasoline, telephoned his mother in Salt Lake City and told her he was with a very interesting young woman, that he couldn't definitely say that his intentions were serious because he didn't know what *my* intentions were, but that he wanted her to meet me over the telephone, and then without any previous warning he put me on the line."

"And what did you say?" Mason asked.

"I was completely flabbergasted. I wasn't expecting to be called to the telephone, I wasn't expecting to hear Doug Hepner discuss his matrimonial intentions with his mother and then call me to carry on a polite conversation."

"He told her who you were?"

"Told her who I was, gave her my name, my address, a description of my build—rather a flattering description, by the way. He certainly noticed things about height, size, weight, measurements. I felt as though I were being discussed for a beauty contest."

"And you say he gave her your address?" Mason prompted.

"Just about every darned thing about me. And then he put me on the line."

"And what did you say?"

"I said, 'Hello, Mrs. Hepner. I'm very glad to meet you,' and so forth, and she said, 'My son tells me you're on the way to Las Vegas with him,' and I felt angry and embarrassed. I made up my mind right then and there that as far as Doug Hepner was concerned he could take me to Las Vegas and buy me dinner and I'd do a little gambling and he could pay the rent on two motel units, count them, Mr. Mason, *two!*" She held up two fingers.

"In other words, the approach," Mason said, "was unexpected and ineffective."

"Call it that if you want. *I* had a very good time."

"Can you remember the date?"

"I have very definite occasion to remember the date."

Mason raised his eyebrows.

"While I was gone," she said, "my apartment was broken into and acts of vandalism were committed, but I . . . well, I didn't complain to the police. I know who did it and why it was done."

"Vandalism?" Mason asked.

She nodded, her eyes angry at the recollection.

"What happened?" Mason asked.

"I'm an artist. I'm not a creative artist. My hobby is studying certain phases of European art. I'm something of a bungling amateur. I probably never will make any great contributions to the artistic world. But nevertheless I like to study early pigmentation, the use of color and lighting effects. I think that a great deal more can be learned about schools of painting through lighting effects than is generally realized.

"Now you want to talk about romance and evidence and amnesia and if I get started talking about European painting you're going to be bored."

"You mentioned certain acts of vandalism."

"I travel quite a bit. I go to Europe sometimes two or three times a year. I'm writing a book which may never amount to much and yet, on the other hand, it may achieve some recognition in art circles. I have great hopes for it. In any event, I'm trying to get my research work handled in such a manner that the book will at least be recognized as being authoritative.

"I have made a great number of copies of various masterpieces, not the entire paintings but the particular parts that I consider significant in connection with my theories. For instance, it may be just a trick of lighting, the manner in which the shadow is depicted on the interior of a hand which is painted so the palm is away from the painter and in shadow.

"On the original painting this hand may be quite small, but I enlarge it so it will cover the entire page in a book. I flatter myself that I am able to make very good copies. At least I use infinite pains."

"And the vandalism?" Mason asked, interested.

"Someone got in my apartment and deliberately ruined several hundred dollars' worth of painting materials."

"May I ask how?"

"Someone cut the bottoms off the tubes of my paints with a pair of scissors, then squeezed all of the paint out. Some of it was put on a palette. Some of it on my washbowl. Some of it was smeared over my bathtub—the bathtub looked like a rainbow having St. Vitus's dance."

"You didn't call the police?"

"Not as yet," she said, "but I know who did it."

"May I ask who?"

"You may well ask who," she said angrily. "Your client did it! While I don't care for publicity and don't want to drag her into court I feel like wringing her damn neck!"

"Eleanor Hepner did that?" Mason asked incredulously.

"Eleanor Corbin!"

"How do you know that . . . ?"

The phone rang.

She said, "Pardon me a moment," picked up the telephone, said, "Yes . . . hello . . . oh yes. . . ."

She was silent for several seconds listening to the voice "Are you sure? . . . Have they made . . . you think it is?"

Again she was silent for several moments, then said, "I have a guest now . . . thanks . . . good-by," and hung up the telephone.

She didn't return immediately, but sat there at the telephone, looking down at the instrument. Then she sighed, walked back to Mason and said, "Well, Mr. Mason, I guess that's all. You've had your field day and you've learned about the Las Vegas trip."

Abruptly she blinked back tears.

"I'd like to know just what caused you to suspect . . ."

"I dare say you would, Mr. Mason, but I'm finished. I have no further comment."

She got up, walked across to the hall door and held it open.

"Really," Mason said, "I have tried to be considerate, Miss Granger. You're going to have to tell this story at least to the police and . . ."

"You used that approach, Mr. Mason," she said. "It got you the interview. It's been used once and I no longer find it amusing or challenging. Good night."

Mason arose from his chair, but didn't at once leave the apartment.

"Is it," he asked, "in order for me to inquire if I have said something that offended you?"

She said suddenly, "Will you get the hell out of here, Mr. Mason? I want to b-b-b-bawl, and I don't want to have you sitting there looking at me while I do it."

"In other words," Mason said, not unkindly, "the telephone call was to advise you that they have found and identified Douglas Hepner's body."

She drew herself up, said, "So you knew that he was dead when you came here to interview me! You knew . . . Mr. Mason! I think I can hate you for that!"

Mason took a good long look at her face and then walked through the open door, out into the corridor.

The door slammed behind him.

■ 8 ■

Mason was already at the office when Della Street unlocked the office door and, humming a little tune, entered the room, stopping in surprise as she saw Mason at his desk.

"Hello, Della," Mason said. "How's everything coming?"

"What are you doing here?" she asked.

"Checking up on things," Mason said. "There have been ... well, developments."

"Such as what?"

"The papers haven't said anything about it as yet," Mason said, "but the body that was found in Sierra Vista Park has been identified as that of Douglas Hepner."

"He's dead?"

"That's right. Shot in the back of the head with a revolver. There's a wound of entrance but no wound of exit, which means the police will be able to recover the bullet and that means that with proper ballistics examination they can determine what gun fired the bullet—provided, of course, they can find the gun. What happened with you, Della?"

"Well," she said, "I had an interesting evening."

"Any approaches?"

"Lots of them."

"Significant?"

"I don't think so. I think they represented merely the usual wolf on the prowl. Of course in a high-class hotel of that sort the approach is rather guarded, discreet and refined, but it has the same ultimate objective as it would have anywhere else."

"What happened?"

"Oh, I was asked very discreetly if I cared to dance.

72

One of them even made a circumspect approach via the waiter with a note stating that I looked lonely and that if I cared to dance the gentlemen two tables over would be very anxious to dance with me."

"Gentle*men?*" Mason asked.

"Two of them."

"What did you do?"

"I danced."

"What did they do?"

"They danced. They made exploratory remarks."

"Passes?"

"Not passes. Exploratory verbal excursions for the purpose of testing my defenses."

"And how were your defenses?"

"Adequate, but not impregnable. I didn't give them the impression that they were storming a Maginot Line. I let them feel that the territory might be invaded, conquered and occupied but definitely not as the result of one skirmish. In other words, I was sophisticated, amused and— I didn't slam any doors. I take it that was what you wanted."

"That was what I wanted at the time," Mason said, "but I don't know now."

"Why?"

"Because I'm afraid there are certain developments that are going to make for complications."

"Such as what?"

"Eleanor Hepner, or Eleanor Corbin as the case may be, had been out of circulation for some two weeks. She was discovered wandering around in the park without adequate covering. Her skin is very light, very creamy . . ."

"Ah yes, her skin," Della murmured. "I've heard you refer to it several times."

Mason grinned. "It's worth referring to, Della. The point is that if she had been wandering around for any length of time without clothing her skin would very definitely have shown a redness, an irritation, in short, it would have been sunburned, and . . ."

"And, of course," Della Street said, "as a good detective you observed those things."

"One learns by observation."

"So I gather. But go on, tell me more about that delightful creamy skin."

"Well," Mason said, "it wasn't the least bit sunburned. It hadn't been exposed to wind, air, or anything other than . . ."

"The soft lights of a bedroom," Della Street interrupted acidly.

Mason went on without noticing the interruption. "Therefore I knew she must have been staying near where she was picked up in the Sierra Vista Park. So, as you know, I made a bluff and got Ethel Belan to admit the girl had been there, but, of course, we didn't learn why. Perhaps Ethel Belan didn't know why. Now I'm afraid I do know why."

"Why?"

"Suzanne Granger. And that makes it look very much as though Eleanor actually hadn't been married."

"In what way?"

"If she had been married," Mason said, "it is difficult to believe that her husband would have deserted her during the honeymoon and started playing around with Suzanne Granger. If, on the other hand, she had gone away on a week-end trip, become infatuated, and if Hepner hadn't been equally infatuated but had perhaps become somewhat bored . . ."

"With that skin? With those beautiful legs?" Della Street asked.

"A man who travels as much as Hepner might well become surfeited with such things."

"I see. *You* don't travel. Do you mean *he* became bored with Eleanor's charms?"

"It could be."

"My, my," Della Street said, "I'd never have thought it possible from your description."

"And so," Mason said, "Eleanor goes to live with Ethel Belan where she can keep an eye on Suzanne. Then Suzanne goes to Las Vegas for a week end with Douglas Hepner, and while she is gone Eleanor gets into the Granger apartment and commits many acts of vandalism, the

74

type of thing that a woman who is exceedingly catty and exceedingly jealous would do to hurt another woman."

"Such as what?"

"Such as cutting the bottoms off a lot of tubes of expensive oil paints, squeezing out the contents all over the place."

"Did she do that?"

"Suzanne Granger thinks she did."

"Did she tell you why?"

"No. Our conversation was interrupted."

"Well, that's interesting," Della Street said. "Just where does that leave us?"

"It may leave us in a beautiful situation," Mason said. "It sketches Eleanor Hepner . . ."

"Or Eleanor Corbin," Della corrected.

"Or Eleanor Corbin," Mason admitted, "in a very unfavorable light. And then, of course, one wonders."

"Wonders what?"

"Suzanne Granger," Mason said, "is an artist. She's a student of painting and of painting technique. She's very much interested in the old masters. She's writing a book on lighting effects and so forth. She hopes the book . . ."

"How old?"

"Twenty-four, -five or -six."

"That means seven, eight or nine," Della Street said. "Good-looking?"

"Very."

"What about *her* skin?"

"I noticed only her face and hands."

"Well," Della Street said, "I'm glad to see *some* of your contacts are conservative."

"I think," Mason said, "you're missing the point."

"I don't think I missed it with Eleanor."

"One doesn't," Mason said, grinning.

"Go on."

"The point is," Mason said, "that Suzanne Granger positively believes that Eleanor got into her apartment while she was in Las Vegas, cut the bottoms off the tubes of paint and . . ."

"Yes, yes, you told me that," Della Street said. "Pardon

me if I seem out of character as the docile secretary this morning, but remember that I was the mysterious Little Miss Richbitch last night, and I've been bandying repartee with predatory males."

Mason grinned. "It's all right, Della. I like it. The point is, suppose it hadn't been sabotage."

"What do you mean?"

"Suppose Eleanor had a definite objective in mind?"

"Cutting the bottoms off tubes of oil paints, squeezing the contents around the apartment?" Della Street asked. "What in the world would she be doing if . . . ?"

"You don't get the sketch," Mason said. "You're accepting Suzanne Granger's story at face value."

"You don't believe Eleanor did it?"

"I'm not commenting about that at the present time," Mason said, "but here's Suzanne Granger, young, attractive, very much on her toes, writing a serious book which requires a lot of research work, trotting off to Europe two or three times a year, visiting studios, carrying a huge number of tubes of paint.

"She has probably built up a character with Customs officials so that they recognize her as a very serious young woman engaged in copying masterpieces. They say, 'How do you do, Miss Granger? How are you today? And did you buy anything while you were abroad?' and she says, 'Just the usual assortment of lingerie and a little perfume which I have here in this suitcase.'

"So then the Customs officials open the suitcase, riffle their hands down through the folded feminine gearments, check the perfume, say, 'Thank you very much, Miss Granger,' close the suitcase, put on the Customs sticker and Suzanne motions for the porter."

"And all the while," Della Street asked, "concealed within those tubes of paint are various and sundry gems?"

"Now," Mason said, "you're beginning to get the idea. There is, of course, a sequence there that a cold, cynical, skeptical mind can't overlook. On the one hand we have Suzanne Granger, a very serious-minded but attractive young woman who is interested in gathering material for a scholarly book on art. We also have her going to Las

Vegas with Douglas Hepner, who seems to have been exceedingly inept in his approach."

"He got her to go, didn't he?"

"He got her to go, Della, but there again is the pattern. He paused at Barstow to buy gasoline. He was seized with the impulse to telephone his very dear mother in Salt Lake. He telephoned Mother and told her that he was with a Suzanne Granger, that Suzanne Granger was headed for Las Vegas to spend a week end with him."

"What a *nice* approach," Della Street said. "How happy Suzanne must have felt!"

"Exactly," Mason said. "And since we now know that Douglas Hepner's mother was an attractive brunette with a good figure and a mysterious personality, and since we now know that while Suzanne Granger was gone someone got in her apartment and clipped the bottoms off the tubes of paint and squeezed out all the paint, and since we now know that concealed within the lotions and creams of Eleanor was a small fortune in jewels, and since we now know that Suzanne Granger didn't notify the police of what had happened . . . well, there we have the elements of something to think about."

"Darned if we don't," Della Street admitted.

"It begins to look like a pattern."

"And what an *interesting* pattern!" Della said.

"Exactly," Mason said. "Imagine how a young woman must feel. She starts out with Douglas Hepner. The air is surcharged with romance. They're headed out away from the city, away from the conventional environment, away from associating with those who know them. They're going to venture forth as strangers, a young man and a young woman, driving in the same automobile. They're going to be away for one, two or perhaps three days.

"Probably there's been nothing crude in his approach. So far everything is perfectly proper. They are, of course, unchaperoned, but after all a man isn't supposed to take a chaperone in this day and age if the young woman happens to be over the age of consent, free, unattached, sophisticated . . . And then Douglas Hepner stops for gasoline. He says casually, 'I have a call to make. Come on over.'

"Naturally the young woman walks over. She wants to know whether he's calling ahead for reservations and if so what type of reservations he's asking for. She doesn't intend to have him take too much for granted. She wants to have the privilege of reaching a decision rather than have it taken for granted.

"And dear little Douglas calls up 'Mother' and says, 'Mother dear, I just wanted to talk with you. At a time like this a man's thoughts quite naturally turn to his mother. I'm headed out for a week end and I have a cute little trick with me. Her name is so-and-so. She's five foot four, weighs a hundred and twelve pounds, has a bust measurement of thirty-four inches, a waist measurement of twenty-six, and a hip measurement of thirty-six, calf thirteen and a half, thigh nineteen inches. Her address is Apartment 358, The Belinda Apartments, Los Angeles, and you really should get acquainted with her because some day you'll be meeting her, and here she is on the phone, Mother.' "

Della Street made a little face. "I can imagine how *that* would leave a young woman feeling."

"We know how it left Suzanne Granger feeling," Mason said.

"In other words, Mr. Hepner paid for two hotel rooms."

"Two units in a motel," Mason corrected.

"And when Suzanne Granger returned she found her apartment had been broken into and . . . Chief, that was the same approach he used with Eleanor."

Mason nodded.

"So what do you suppose Eleanor found had happened when she returned?"

"She didn't return," Mason said, "not to her residence anyway."

"How very, very interesting," Della said, "and so someone puts a bullet in the back of Mr. Hepner's head. One can well imagine that if Douglas Hepner's romantic adventures followed such a delightful pattern the end was almost inevitable."

Mason said, "All right, Della, your reasoning is sound but the way you put it carries the taint of your stay at a highclass hotel as a single, unattached woman. Let's get into our working clothes and . . ."

She picked up a file of unanswered mail. "And you can dictate some of these letters," she said.

Mason winced.

"I've culled out everything except the important stuff, so . . ."

"Well," Mason said, "I suppose . . ."

They were interrupted by Paul Drake's code knock on the door.

"Let Paul in, Della," Mason said.

She said, "Saved by the bell—but you're going to have to get those letters out of the way some time today, Chief. They're things that are important, things I've been holding here until I'm ashamed to hold them any longer."

She opened the office door, said, "Hi, Paul."

Drake grinned at Della Street and said, "Two operatives submitted reports on your activities last night, young lady. I gather that you were in circulation."

"I was being more circulated against than circulating," Della Street said.

"What's the idea, Perry?" Paul Drake asked. "Come to think it over, I don't want to know."

"It might be a good idea if you didn't," Mason admitted. "What about the body? Has it been positively identified?"

"Yes, it's Hepner. He met his death as a result of one shot with a .38 caliber bullet. Now then, Perry, I'm bringing you bad news."

"How bad?"

"That depends," Drake said. "You know all of the cards in the suit. You know pretty much who is holding them. I don't even know what's trumps. I give you the information. It's a one-way street. Now I *think* I'm bringing you bad news."

"Go ahead," Mason said. "What is it?"

"The Ethel Belan who has apartment 360 at the Belinda Apartments has cracked."

"How bad?"

"All the way."

"To whom?"

"Police."

"I didn't think she'd have the moral stamina to stick it out," Mason said. "What does she know?"

"Now there," Drake said, "you're getting into the top classification of super-secret police archives. Whatever it is, it's causing them to smile and lick their chops like a cat who has just managed to overturn a cream bottle and has its belly full."

"Any chance of talking with her?"

"Just as much chance of talking with her as there is standing on the back porch and shouting a message to the man in the moon. The police have her tied up so tight you can't get within a mile of the hotel where she's staying. They got her to throw some things in a bag. Then they whisked her out of the apartment, rushed her to a hotel where she's in a suite of rooms guarded by a policewoman. Those rooms are at one end of a corridor. The suite of rooms opposite is taken by two deputy district attorneys who are interrogating her in relays. That end of the corridor is blocked off by a police guard. Plain-clothes detectives are scurrying in and out like rats looting a grain bin.

"I'm merely reporting this, since you apparently anticipated it."

"What do you mean I anticipated it?"

"You got Della in the same hotel hours before the police moved in. Della's room is even on the same floor as the suite where they're holding Ethel Belan. *I* don't want to know anything. I'm merely telling you what you know already, but I want to tell you so no one can make a point later on that I didn't tell you."

Drake exchanged glances with Della Street.

"Well," Drake went on, "whatever Ethel Belan has told them is damned important and they're really going to town."

"You don't have any idea what it is?"

"Not the slightest, and, what's more, I'm not to be allowed to have any idea what it is. The D.A. is going to move for an indictment with the grand jury and then he's going to press for an immediate trial."

"He won't file a complaint?"

"No complaint, no information, no preliminary hearing, no chance for you to cross-examine witnesses until you get to court in front of a jury," Drake said. "By that time they'll have it sewed up. They're really going to town on this one, Perry."

Mason thought that over for a minute. "What else?" he asked.

"It seems that Eleanor Corbin had a permit for a .38 caliber revolver. No one can find that revolver. She had it with her a few days before she left home. Presumably she was carrying it with her when she left. Police don't know where it is now."

Mason thought that over.

"Of course, you've got her out of circulation now," Drake said, "but when the grand jury returns an indictment and the police notify you and the doctors in charge, and the general public through the newspapers, that she's under indictment for first-degree murder, she then becomes a fugitive from justice and anyone who conceals her is headed for the hoosegow.

"Temporarily you've outsmarted them and they're conceding that you've won one trick. But by two-thirty or three o'clock this afternoon she'll be a fugitive and then they'll be only too glad to have you conceal her."

Mason's eyes narrowed in thought. "Go on, Paul."

"Now then, police have found Hepner's automobile. It's been pretty badly smashed. Evidently it was in some sort of a head-on collision, but police can't find out where the collision took place, they can't find out where the car came from or anything about it."

"That's strange," Mason said. "Why can't they trace that auto accident?"

"Apparently there's no report of it."

"Where did they find the car?"

"In a garage. It was brought in by a tow car late Sunday night. It was left for repairs. The garage people were told that Hepner would be in within twenty-four hours to check it over and that he wanted it repaired and put in shape."

"What about the tow car? Can't they trace that?"

"No one ever got the license on the tow car. Why should they? It was just an ordinary tow car. It came in and dumped the wrecked car and went on its way."

"That's a garage here in town?"

"That's right. The All Night and Day Emergency Repair Company."

"The police talked with them?"

"The police talked with them and my men talked with them," Drake said. "They're very close-mouthed. Personally, I think they *may* know something they're not telling. What they tell is a straightforward story. This wrecking car came in towing Hepner's Oldsmobile. The front end was all caved in. The rear wheels were okay. They'd hoisted the front end up with a derrick and towed it in.

"It was just another job as far as the garage was concerned. They had the car. They didn't intend to spend any money on it until they'd talked with the owner. They just dumped the wreck out in the back along with a lot of other wrecked vehicles. They didn't even check it over carefully to find out how badly it was injured or whether it was worthwhile repairing. In other words, they did exactly nothing. They let it sit there. They knew that the automobile was worth enough for junk to more than cover any storage bill that would pile up. They were waiting for Hepner. Hepner didn't show up."

"I suppose the police have examined the car," Mason said.

"Have the police examined the car!" Drake exclaimed. "I'll say they *are* examining the car! They're examining it with a microscope. They're working against time and trying to get findings ready for the grand jury by two o'clock this afternoon.

"They've found out that the car with which Hepner's automobile had a collision was painted black. From a

82

chemical analysis of the paint they think it was probably a truck. Police are looking for that truck. They're combing every garage in town."

"Anything else?" Mason asked.

"That seems to be the size of it so far," Drake said. "I'm sorry we don't have more to report, Perry, but we've had lots of people finding out lots of nothing. If you want to find out that marriage licenses *haven't* been issued for two people, or that two people *didn't* stay at a hotel on a certain date as man and wife, you have to comb the records, and use up a lot more manpower than if you struck pay dirt.

"In other words, if they *did* register you may find the register the second or third place you look. But if they didn't register you have to cover the whole doggone outfit."

"I know, I know," Mason interposed.

"I've been up all night," Drake said. "I can stick it out for another twelve or fifteen hours and then I'm going to have to cave in and get some sleep.

"You're in a jam, Perry. Whatever you're going to do you're going to have to do between now and two-thirty or three o'clock. At that time you're going to get a telephone call from your friend, the district attorney, telling you there's an indictment for your client, Eleanor Corbin, alias Eleanor Hepner, and will you please see that she is surrendered; that if she is not surrendered will you please tell them where she is; and if you withhold information you'll be obstructing the interests of justice, compounding a felony and all that sort of legal stuff."

"And if the district attorney can't get hold of me?" Mason asked.

"In that event, by five o'clock the newspapers will proclaim to the world that there's a felony warrant out, that the girl is a fugitive from justice, and your doctor will be put in a spot that he won't want to occupy and you won't want to put him in."

Mason nodded.

"So," Drake said, "what do I do?"

Mason said, "Stay on the job until they issue the indictment, Paul, and then go home and get some sleep. Keep getting what information you can. Have your correspondents in Las Vegas start covering motels. Also see if Suzanne Granger and Douglas Hepner registered under their own names in two separate motel units on the night of the thirteenth—that would be Friday."

"Well, well, Friday the thirteenth," Drake said. *"Two* separate units?"

"That's right."

"He got her to go to Las Vegas with him and then they had two units in a motel," Drake said. "Do I get it right?"

"That's the story," Mason told him. "I want it verified."

"Want to bet that it can't be verified?"

"I have a hunch," Mason said, "that you're going to find it happened exactly that way—that they occupied two separate units."

"I don't want to be crude," Drake said, glancing surreptitiously at Della Street, "but my curiosity is aroused."

Della said, "Mr. Hepner was inept, Paul."

"How soon can you have the information?" Mason asked.

"Perhaps by two o'clock," Drake said. "If you're right we may have it sooner. It's just like I told you, when you're looking . . ."

"I understand," Mason told him. "Get busy."

"Okay," Drake said and left the office.

Della Street looking inquiringly at Mason. "Now what?" she asked.

"We're in a fix," Mason said. "Your hotel is crawling with detectives. The minute you show up they'll pounce on you. They'll make a double check, they'll find out about the 'valuables' in the hotel safe. They'll want to look. They'll get a court order if they have to. They may not have to."

"That would seem to leave us high and dry," she said.

"And you have your clothes there?"

"All my best clothes."

Mason thought for a moment, said, "It's a problem

84

we'll have to solve later, Della. Right now we're metering minutes. See if you can get Dr. Ariel on the phone."

Della Street put through the call. It took her two or three minutes before she was finally able to locate the doctor.

"Hello, Doctor," Mason said. "I'm sorry to have to disturb you. I . . ."

"I was just getting ready to operate," Dr. Ariel said. "What's the trouble now?"

"That patient," Mason said. "You put her some place where she couldn't be found?"

"That's right."

"We're going to have to find her."

"How come?"

"She's going to be indicted for first-degree murder by two-thirty or three o'clock this afternoon. By that time she'll technically become a fugitive from justice. In case you should happen to read a paper and know that she was wanted and didn't communicate information . . ."

"I very seldom read the evening papers," Dr. Ariel interrupted. "Was that what was bothering you?"

"No," Mason said. "I think the going will be pretty tough on this one, Doctor. I don't want you to take a chance."

"I'll do anything I can, Perry."

"No, I think we're going to have to surrender Mrs. Hepner and I think you should be the one to do it. When the papers come out just call the police and tell them that Mrs. Hepner is under your care, that you feel that it is only fair to let the police know where she is, that you think she should not be subjected to any shock and that you want to warn the police that she is under medical psychiatric care and so forth."

"When?"

"As soon as you read about it in the newspapers. In the meantime where is she?"

"The Oak and Pines Rest Home."

"Thanks a lot, Doctor. Remember, as soon as the paper comes out ring up the police—better have someone with you listening to the conversation. If you have a good office nurse you can trust, get her to call the police, tell them that Eleanor Hepner is a patient of yours and that you felt that you should communicate her whereabouts to the police although she is under medical attention and all that. Get it?"

"I get it."

"Okay," Mason said. "Good-by."

Mason hung up, glanced at his watch.

Della Street tossed the file of important mail back on the desk and said, "I take it you can now attend to the mail."

"I think not, Della."

"I thought not."

Mason grinned. "You have a few things to do."

"What?"

"You have to call up your hotel, tell the clerk that you're expecting to go to Mexico City with friends on a plane, that you want to keep your room while you're gone, that you don't want to have any misunderstanding about the bill and that you'll mail two hundred and fifty dollars on account."

"And the two hundred and fifty dollars?" Della Street asked.

"You draw it out of the account as a business expense," Mason said. "You charge it to the Corbins. We certainly were unfortunate in our choice of hotels. Now you can't go back there and you don't dare to check out."

"Well," Della Street said somewhat wistfully, "that terminates my very interesting night life. I am going to be missed this evening. Some guests are going to be making discreet inquiries."

"When they find you have gone to Mexico City with friends," Mason said, "they won't fly to Mexico City after you, will they, Della?"

"Oh no, but they'll reproach themselves for not having been a little more persistent in their approach last night. Going to Mexico City 'with friends' has interesting connotations in the mind of the young predatory male who is busily engaged in planning a campaign."

"Yes, I see your point. However, at the moment there's no help for it."

"Isn't it fortunate," Della Street said, "that Eleanor has such a considerate family. Here she finds herself with an attorney all ready to represent her on a murder charge, a lawyer who was retained even before the corpse was discovered."

"It is," Mason said, "a singularly interesting coincidence."

■ 9 ■

DELLA STREET BROUGHT PERRY MASON THE MORNING newspapers. Mason tilted back in his swivel chair, opened the newspapers and studied them.

"Paul Drake phoned," she said. "His men found that Suzanne Granger and Douglas Hepner did have two motel units in Las Vegas just as she told you they did. The date was Friday the thirteenth."

Mason pursed his lips. "Well, we know what we have to work with now," he said.

"She takes a nice photograph." Della Street pointed out the picture in the newspaper, showing Eleanor flanked by a police matron on one side, a detective on the other.

"Yes, Olga evidently got some other clothes out of her closet."

"She wears them well," Della Street commented.

"Nice figure," Mason said.

"And the creamy skin, remember?"

"Oh yes," Mason said, smiling. "How could I ever forget?"

"So she still can't remember what happened," Della Street said.

"That's it," Mason told her. "It's all spread out in

choice newspaper jargon. Beautiful heiress—the lost week end—is she a kissless bride or did she settle for a week end at Las Vegas?—'My mind is a perfect blank ever since that horrible accident,' heiress tells officers, choking back sobs."

"What do they say about the gun?" Della asked.

"She did have a gun once. It's been missing for some time. She had occasion to look for it when she was packing to run away with Hepner—not that she wanted to take the gun but in going through the articles in the drawer where she usually kept the gun she had occasion to notice that it was missing. And she hasn't the faintest idea where her luggage is now."

"I wonder if the police know?" Della Street asked.

Mason said, "According to Paul Drake, Ethel Belan has 'told all.'"

"Do you suppose she has?"

"The police haven't as yet asked any questions about luggage."

"And Ethel Belan must have told them . . ."

The telephone rang.

Della Street picked it up, said, "Hello . . . Yes, Gertie. . . . Put her on."

Della Street turned to Perry Mason and said, "A personal call for me, Chief. Some woman says it's very important."

Della Street turned back to the telephone. "Hello, yes . . . I see. Go ahead. Give me the details. . . ."

Della Street hung on to the telephone for nearly a minute, making rapid shorthand notes. Then she put down the pen, said, "All right, Mrs. Fremont. There was nothing else you could have done. It's all right. Yes, thank you very much and thank you for letting me know."

Della Street hung up, turned to Perry Mason and said, "Well, Ethel Belan talked all right."

Mason raised his eyebrows in silent interrogation.

"That was Mrs. Fremont, manager of the apartment house. Lieutenant Tragg showed up there with a search warrant issued by a court granting permission to search my apartment to look for three articles of red and white checkered baggage, the property of Eleanor Corbin, alias Eleanor Hepner, who is accused of murder. They delivered a copy of the search warrant to the manager, demanded a passkey, entered my apartment and found the articles. They left a receipt for the three articles with the manager."

"Very considerate," Mason said, "very nice. All in accordance with the law in such cases made and provided."

"Well?" Della Street asked.

"And what about the gems?" Della asked.

"There," Mason said, "you have a question."

"Well, what's the answer?"

"I don't know."

"If you don't, who does?"

"Probably no one."

"Chief, if those gems are evidence, isn't it illegal for you to withhold that evidence?"

"Evidence of what?" Mason asked.

"Well, evidence of . . . I don't know—evidence of smuggling perhaps."

"What makes you think the stones were smuggled?"

"How about murder?"

"What makes you think the stones have anything to do with the murder? I have a duty to my client. If the police can tie those gems in with a murder case and make them important evidence that's different, but those gems are in my possession as an attorney. They may be evidence of something else. They might be evidence of blackmail. How do I know? I certainly am not going to take it on myself to assume that they're connected in any way with the death of Douglas Hepner and turn them over to the police, who will promptly call in the newspaper reporters. It'll be bad enough the way it is. They'll go through those bags and inventory the stuff that's in there. They'll have a cute little model demonstrate Eleanor's nighty. You can figure out what's going to happen."

"And you intend to sit tight with those gems?"

"As things now stand I intend to sit tight."

"Suppose they catch you?"

"I'll cross that bridge when I come to it, too."

"Chief, Paul Drake says that the police are absolutely jubilant over this case, that Hamilton Burger, the district attorney, is walking on air, that they're prepared to lower the boom on you on this one."

"So what?"

"Can't you duck it?"

Mason shook his head. "Not now. I'm stuck with it."

"I wish you wouldn't hang on to those gems."

"What do you want me to do? Call up the police?"

"No."

"What?"

"You can talk with your client and ask her about them and find out . . ."

"My client says she can't remember what happened," Mason interposed.

"Your client is a damn liar!" Della Street said. "You know it, she knows it, and she knows you know it."

"But," Mason said, "if she should change her story now and say that she *could* remember and tell me about those gems, give me some story about where they came from and tell me what I was to do with them, *then* the probabilities are I'd be charged with notice that the gems were evidence of something. As it is, I don't know anything about them."

"Well," Della Street said, "I suppose it had to happen sooner or later, but I hate to think of Hamilton Burger being so smugly triumphant."

"So do I," Mason told her. "But don't forget he hasn't won his case yet. He's trying to jockey things so he can get an immediate trial and that's going to suit me fine."

"Wouldn't it be better for you to wait and see what develops?"

Mason shook his head. "Hamilton Burger isn't a fast thinker and he isn't a thorough thinker. If he rushes into court he's pretty apt to have a weak spot in his armor somewhere. If I give him time that battery of assistants he keeps up there will put him in an impregnable position. As matters now stand we'll let him start charging forward with the arc light of publicity full upon his portly figure."

"You think he may stumble?" Della Street asked.

"Well," Mason said, "I'll put it this way—he *could*."

■ 10 ■

PERRY MASON SURVEYED THE CROWDED COURTROOM, taking mental inventory of the situation.

Behind him and slightly to one side sat his client, officially described as Eleanor Corbin, alias Eleanor Hepner.

In the front row of the courtroom was her father, Homer Corbin, a quietly dressed, well-groomed individual whose very appearance lent an air of respectability to the defendant's case.

But Homer Corbin was in the wholesale jewelry business. The decedent, Douglas Hepner, had been a freelance Government informer who made it his business to track down illicit shipments of jewels and turn that information over to the Government. Did the district attorney know that?

If Homer Corbin should take the stand to testify to the good character of his daughter, or to testify to any event leading up to the crime, Mason could visualize Hamilton Burger, the district attorney, asking:

"And did you know, Mr. Corbin, that the decedent, Douglas Hepner, was engaged in this business of detecting smuggled shipments of jewelry, reporting those shipments to the Customs authorities, and receiving a twenty-percent reward therefor; that that was the way he made his living?"

Hamilton Burger would slightly incline his head as if anxious to miss no syllable of the answer, then he would say:

91

"And I believe, Mr. Corbin, that *you* first met the decedent on a ship returning from Europe?"

Then the district attorney would step back a few paces, smile at the harassed witness and say almost casually:

"I believe, Mr. Corbin, that you are in the wholesale jewelry business and that your trip to Europe was a business trip, was it not?"

The insinuation would be there, implanted in the minds of the jury. None of those questions would be objectionable from a legal standpoint. They would merely sketch the background of the witness, his possible bias, his occupation, his knowledge of the decedent, but the cumulative impact would be deadly.

Seated beside her father was Olga Jordan, a thin-mouthed, clever woman, who somehow managed to give the impression of putting on a false front. Not only was it the manner in which she tried to disguise the thin line of her lips with heavy lipstick, but it was something about her manner itself, the alert, intent way with which she regarded everything that took place as though searching for an opportunity to turn every event to her own personal advantage.

Beside his wife, Bill Jordan, a sunburned playboy, was not likely to create a good impression with the jury. He was too young to have retired, too bronzed by sun-swept hours on the golf course to appeal to a jury of men and women who had worked and worked hard during their entire lifetime.

Those were the only people on whom Mason could count to counteract whatever case the district attorney was about to present, and try as he might Mason had no inkling of the ace that the district attorney had in the hole.

The testimony given before the grand jury and on which the indictment had been based showed that the defendant, Eleanor Corbin, had been friendly with Douglas Hepner, that she had left her home with Douglas Hepner, that she had sent a telegram from Yuma stating that they were married, that two weeks later the body of Douglas Hepner had been found, that he had been shot in the back of the head with a .38 caliber bullet, that the defendant owned a .38 caliber revolver, that the defendant had stated to Ethel Belan she considered Douglas Hepner her boy friend and that Suzanne Granger had insinuated herself into the picture; that the defendant had stated that she would kill Douglas Hepner if he tried to throw her overboard, that at the time the defendant made that statement she had in her possession and exhibited a .38 caliber revolver, that the defendant was then living with Ethel Belan who had an apartment adjoining that of Suzanne Granger, a young woman who had attracted the attention of Douglas Hepner and who was going out with him.

This created a web of circumstantial evidence which had been sufficient to bring about an indictment at the hands of a friendly grand jury. It would hardly be sufficient to warrant a conviction before a trial jury. Therefore Mason knew that Hamilton Burger undoubtedly had some evidence which would, in his mind, be determinative, but neither Perry Mason nor the Drake Detective Agency had been able to find out what that evidence was.

And so Perry Mason found himself for once in his life entering upon a trial of a case where he knew that he would inevitably be confronted with evidence which would be disastrous to the defendant, where he had been unable to learn from the defendant the true story of what had happened, where he must rely entirely on his powers of observation and cross-examination, where he would have to get the facts of the case from the mouths of hostile witnesses.

Hamilton Burger, the district attorney, flushed and triumphant in the face of apparent victory, made an opening statement to the jury. After outlining a few preliminary facts by way of background, he said:

"We expect to show you, ladies and gentlemen, that the defendant in this case, actuated by jealousy, armed herself with a .38 caliber revolver; that she made financial arrangements with Ethel Belan to share apartment 360 so that she could spy upon Suzanne Granger who lived in apartment 358; that the purpose of so doing was to catch the man who she claimed was her husband, Douglas

93

Hepner, the decedent, in a compromising position with Suzanne Granger; that she threatened that if she couldn't have Douglas Hepner no one else would ever have him.

"And so, ladies and gentlemen of the jury, we find Douglas Hepner, the decedent, dead, with a bullet from the defendant's gun in his brain, and the defendant making elaborate preparations to have it appear she was mentally irresponsible, that she had amnesia, what we might term a synthetic amnesia, carefully cultivated to shield her from being forced to answer embarrassing questions, an amnesia which psychiatrists will testify is completely simulated."

"Just a moment, Your Honor," Mason said. "I dislike to interrupt the district attorney's opening statement, but the defense will challenge the testimony of any psychiatrist who attempts to qualify as a mind reader. The science of psychiatry is not so far advanced that any man can tell with certainty . . ."

Hamilton Burger interrupted with affable good nature. "This is conceded, ladies and gentlemen of the jury. I withdraw any statement I made about the psychiatrist. We'll put the psychiatrists on the stand. We'll qualify them. We'll let them testify. We'll let counsel for the defense object and we'll let the Court rule on the admissibility of the evidence. But for the present time I withdraw any reference I have made to any psychiatric testimony.

"And that, ladies and gentlemen, is in a general way the picture that we expect to develop before you. Since some of the evidence may be controversial, and since we want to expedite matters, I won't go into all of the details at this time."

And, using Perry Mason's interruption as an excuse to keep his case outlined in broad generalities, Hamilton Burger thanked the jurors and sat down.

Mason turned to Paul Drake. "Notice, Paul, that he said the bullet in the head of Douglas Hepner had been fired from the defendant's gun."

"Did he say that?" Drake whispered.

Mason nodded. "He slipped it in almost casually."

Judge Moran said, "Does the defendant wish to make any statement at this time?"

"No, Your Honor," Mason said. "We will reserve our opening statement until later. Perhaps we may dispense with it entirely. I think the jurors understand fully that it is incumbent upon the prosecution to prove the guilt of the defendant beyond all reasonable doubt, and if the prosecution fails to do this we will rely upon that failure and will put on no evidence at all."

"Is that an opening statement?" Hamilton Burger asked.

"No," Mason said, "it is a statement to the Court."

"You mean you aren't going to put on any evidence for the defense?"

"Not unless you put on sufficient evidence to raise an issue. The law presumes the defendant innocent."

Judge Moran said, "That will do, gentlemen. I don't want any colloquy between counsel. Please address your remarks to the Court. Mr. Prosecutor, the defendant has waived an opening statement at this time. Put on your first witness."

Hamilton Burger bowed and smiled. Nothing could affect his glowing good humor.

"My first witness," he said, "is Raymond Orla."

Raymond Orla took the oath and disclosed that he was a deputy coroner, that he had been called to Sierra Vista Park when the body of Douglas Hepner had been discovered at about 9:15 P.M. on the night of August seventeenth. He had taken charge of proceedings there at the scene and had had photographs taken. He identified various photographs as showing the position of the body and the location where it had been found. He had made an examination of the body, had not moved it until after photographs had been taken; then the body had been taken to the coroner's laboratory where the clothes had been removed and an autopsy had been performed. Photographs had been taken of the body during the several stages of the autopsy and he had these photographs.

Hamilton Burger announced that the photographs of the autopsy would be subject to inspection by counsel but he thought they were too gruesome to be submitted to the jury who presumably were not as accustomed as counsel to seeing photographs of a body during a post-mortem examination.

Orla testified that there was a bullet hole in the back of the head of the decedent, that aside from a few bruises there were no other injuries or marks of violence, that the autopsy surgeon had recovered the bullet from the head.

"That's all," Hamilton Burger said suavely. "I don't know whether counsel has any desire to cross-examine."

"Oh, just one or two questions," Mason said breezily. "What happened to the clothes the decedent was wearing?"

"They were folded and placed in a locker at the coroner's office. They are still there."

"And those clothes are subject to inspection by counsel for the defense at any time," Hamilton Burger interposed. "I'll instruct the witness to arrange for such an inspection at any hour of the day or night."

And the district attorney even made a little bow as though acknowledging applause for his fairness.

"What about the personal possessions? What things were in the man's pockets?" Mason inquired of the witness, ignoring the district attorney's interpolation.

"I have a list," Orla said.

He whipped a notebook from his pocket. "The following articles were in the possession of the decedent: One notebook, a driving license, one fountain pen, one leather key container containing four keys, one handkerchief, one dollar and ninety-six cents in small change, one silver cigarette case, six cigarettes."

"And that's all?" Mason asked.

"Yes, sir. That's all."

"Where are those articles?"

"At the coroner's office."

"I want them introduced in evidence," Mason said.

"Come, come," Hamilton Burger said. "These articles are purely incidental. They have no bearing on the case."

"How do *you* know they don't have any bearing on the case?" Mason said.

"Well, if you want them introduced in evidence, go ahead and introduce them as part of your case. They're not part of mine."

"Your Honor," Mason said, "I would like to have these articles introduced in evidence. I feel that they may be significant, particularly the notebook."

"The notebook was entirely blank," Orla said.

"You mean there was nothing in it?"

"Absolutely nothing. The pages were entirely blank. The notebook was a leather notebook which contained a compartment for a driving license and a filler which was detachable. Evidently an old filler had been taken out shortly prior to the death of the decedent and a new filler put in. There was not so much as the scratch of a pen on the new filler."

"What about the driving license?" Mason asked.

"It was in the notebook, in a transparent cellophane window compartment designed for such purpose."

"If the Court please," Mason said, "I would like to have these articles introduced. I am perfectly willing to stipulate that they may be considered a part of my case, but I would like to have them introduced now."

Hamilton Burger said, "Your Honor, I feel that the People should be permitted to go ahead and put on its case. The defense can then put on its case. I don't think we should have the cases put on piecemeal."

"Under those circumstances," Mason said, "as part of my cross-examination I am going to insist that these articles be introduced in evidence."

"You can't do that as a part of cross-examination."

"I can ask this witness to bring the articles into court," Mason said.

"Come, come," Judge Moran said. "I don't see any point to be gained in becoming technical over these articles. They were in the possession of the decedent, Mr. Witness?"

"That's right. Yes, sir."

"They were in his pockets?"

"Yes, sir."

"And you personally removed them from his pockets?"

"I did. Yes, sir."

"Those articles may be placed in the custody of the Court and marked 'Defendant's Exhibits for Identification.' At this time the articles will be marked for identification only and defense counsel can cross-examine the witness on any of those articles that he wishes. Later on, if defendant wishes, those articles may be received in evidence."

"Thank you, Your Honor," Mason said. "And the defense would like a set of the photographs showing the autopsy of the decedent."

"I have a set of photographs for defense counsel," Hamilton Burger said, presenting a whole sheaf of 8 x 10 glossy photographs with a courtesy so elaborate that it was again obviously designed to impress the jury with his complete fairness.

"Thank you," Mason said. "No further questions."

Dr. Julius Oberon was called as a witness. He gave his qualifications as a forensic pathologist and coroner's physician. He stated that he had performed the autopsy on the body of the decedent, that he had recovered a .38 caliber bullet from the head of the decedent, that the discharge of the bullet into the man's head had resulted in almost instant death. He pointed out the location of the wound of entrance, described generally the damage to the brain, stated that there were no other injuries which could have caused death, and that in his opinion the victim on which he performed the autopsy had been dead for approximately twenty-four to thirty-six hours. He could not fix the time of death any closer than that.

"And what did you do with this bullet after you removed it from the head of the decedent?" Hamilton Burger asked.

"I turned it over to a ballistics expert."

"You may cross-examine," Hamilton Burger said.

Mason glanced at the doctor, who was settling himself firmly in the witness chair as though bracing himself to resist a verbal attack.

"You say death was virtually instantaneous, Doctor?"

"Yes, sir."

"On what do you base that opinion?"

"The nature of the wound, the damage to the brain."

"That wound would have produced complete, instantaneous unconsciousness?"

"Yes, sir."

"But not necessarily death?"

"What do you mean?"

"Aren't you familiar, Doctor, with cases where there is extensive hemorrhage from a head wound, in other words, haven't you had many cases in your own experience where the brain tissue has been damaged and there has been extensive hemorrhage?"

"Yes, indeed. I have seen cases of massive hemorrhage."

"What causes such cases, Doctor?"

"Why, the blood in the body drains out through the damaged blood vessels."

"It is pumped out by the heart, isn't it?"

"Yes, sir."

"So that in those cases, while the person may be completely unconscious, there is nevertheless life for some considerable period of time, a life which manifests itself through the activity of the heart pumping blood into the blood vessels?"

"Yes, sir, that is right."

"Was that the case in this instance, Doctor?"

"Definitely not. There was very little bleeding."

"Did you notice any blood clot on the ground near the head of the decedent?"

"Yes, sir. There was *some* external bleeding, not much."

"And some internal?"

"Yes, sir, but the bleeding was not extensive."

"And predicating your opinion on that lack of bleeding you decided that death was virtually instantaneous, is that right?"

"Not on the lack of bleeding alone, but on the position of the wound and the extent of the brain damage."

"You have seen similar wounds with equally extensive damage where there had been considerable hemorrhage and where the decedent had therefore lived for some time although completely unconscious?"

"Yes, sir."

"Now then, Doctor, did you take into consideration the possibility that the decedent might have been killed at some other place and the body transported to the place where it was found?"

"I did. Yes, sir."

"Did you negate such a possibility?"

"In my own mind, yes."

"May I ask for your process of reasoning, Doctor?"

"The nature and extent of the wound, the damage to the brain, the nature of the hemorrhage, the position of the blood clot, the absence of vertical blood smears, the position of the body—things of that sort."

Mason said, "It is then your opinion, Doctor, that someone stood behind the decedent, shot him in the back of the head with a .38 caliber revolver, and that death was instantaneous, or virtually instantaneous?"

"That is correct, except as to one matter."

"What is that?"

"The decedent may have been seated at the time of his death. I am inclined to think he was. From the position in which the body was found I am inclined to think the decedent was seated on the grass with his legs doubled to the right, his left hand resting on the ground. In that case, since the course of the bullet wound was not downward, the person who shot him was also seated on the ground somewhat behind him. Or was so stooped or crouched that the gun was on a level with the back of the decedent's head."

"Thank you," Mason said. "That is all, Doctor."

"No further questions on redirect," Hamilton Burger said. "I now wish to call Merton C. Bosler to the stand."

Mason, watching Hamilton Burger, saw the district attorney glance at the clock as though carefully timing the course of events.

Merton C. Bosler qualified himself as a ballistics expert. He had, he said, been present at the time the autopsy was performed, he had seen Dr. Oberon remove the fatal bullet from the skull of the decedent, he had seen Dr. Oberon mark that bullet. The bullet had then been turned over to him as a ballistics expert.

In fifteen minutes, led by Hamilton Burger's skillful questioning, Merton C. Bosler proved conclusively that the bullet he produced was correctly identified and that it had been discharged through the barrel of a .38 caliber Smith & Wesson revolver. The bullet and a series of enlarged photographs were received in evidence. The jurors in turn examined the fatal bullet gravely as though by so doing they were able to determine the issues in the case.

"Now then," Hamilton Burger continued, "did you make any search of the vicinity where the body was found for the purpose of determining whether any weapon was lying nearby?"

"I assisted in such a search."

"Did you find such a weapon nearby?"

"Not at the time."

"Now then," Hamilton Burger said triumphantly, "did you subsequently make a search using any mechanical or electronic device?"

"I did. Yes, sir."

"What device?"

"I used what is known as a mine detector."

"And what is that?"

"That is an electronic device so designed that when it is moved over the surface of the ground it will give a peculiar squeal when it is moved over a metallic object."

"And what did you find?"

"Well, we found several metallic objects which were not significant. We found an old rusted penknife. We found the metallic lever key which had been used to open a can of sardines with the tin top of the sardine can still around it, and . . ."

"Yes, yes," Hamilton Burger interrupted. "Never mind these insignificant objects. What else, if anything, did you find that you consider a significant object?"

"We found a .38 caliber Smith & Wesson revolver with one discharged shell. The number of the revolver was C-48809."

"Indeed," Hamilton Burger said triumphantly. "And did you make any ballistics tests with that weapon?"

"I did. Yes, sir."

"Did you fire test bullets through that weapon?"

"Yes, sir."

"And what was the result of that test?"

"The result was that the two sets of individual characteristics—those on the fatal bullet and those on the one fired in the laboratory—exactly matched."

"Did you photograph that matching?"

"I did."

"Will you produce that photograph, please?"

The witness produced a big 8 x 10 photograph. It was placed in evidence and carefully explained to the jury.

"Where did you find this weapon?"

"The weapon was buried about eight inches beneath the ground. It had been thrust into a hole which had evidently been made by some burrowing animal and then the hole had been plugged up with dirt. Over the surface of the ground dry leaves and twigs had been scattered so that it was virtually impossible to notice any disturbance of the ground."

"But you located this with a mine detector, and then did what?"

"Then we carefully examined the ground, carefully moved away the dry leaves and twigs and were then able to observe the place where earth had been pushed into the hole. We removed this earth and found the weapon in the hole."

"And where was this with relation to the place where the body of the decedent was discovered?"

"Fifty-six feet in a northeasterly direction."

"Someone was with you at the time?"

"Oh yes, sir. There were several people."

"Among them was a surveyor?"

"Yes, sir."

"A man who drove a stake at the place where the weapon was discovered and oriented it with the place where the body had been found?"

"That is right. Yes, sir."

"Do you know that surveyor's name?"

"Yes, sir. It was Stephen Escalante."

"Now then, Mr. Bosler, did you subsequently make any examination of the records of firearm purchases on file in this county?"

"I did. Yes, sir."

"And did you find any record of a Smith & Wesson revolver, number C-48809, having been sold in this county?"

"I did. Yes, sir."

"And according to the records, who purchased that weapon?"

"Eleanor Corbin."

"The defendant in this action?"

"Yes, sir."

"And her signature appears upon that record?"

"It does. Yes, sir."

"That is a public record in this county, made such by law?"

"Yes, sir."

"You have a photostatic copy of that record?"

"I do. Yes, sir."

Hamilton Burger was exceedingly unctuous.

"Your Honor, it is approaching the hour for the evening adjournment. I will ask to have this photostatic copy of the record introduced at this time. I have not as yet shown that the signature on this firearms sale registration is the signature of the defendant, Eleanor Corbin, but I expect to produce evidence tomorrow morning, that is, evidence of a handwriting expert, showing that the signature is that of the defendant. However, I believe that the evidence is sufficient in view of the nature of this record to have this photostatic copy introduced in evidence at this time."

"No objection," Mason said, smilingly unconcerned, and giving no sign that this testimony had not been fully anticipated by the defendant. "We will stipulate that this page of the firearms register book may go into evidence, that is, the photostatic copy may, and in order to save the district attorney trouble we will stipulate that the signature appearing on there is actually the signature of the defendant in this case."

Burger showed surprise. "You'll stipulate to that?" he asked.

"Why certainly," Mason said, smiling affably.

"Very well," Judge Moran ruled. "The photostatic copy will be received in evidence with its appropriate numbers, Mr. Clerk, and court will adjourn until ten o'clock tomorrow morning."

As the crowd started shuffling from the courtroom, Della Street and Paul Drake headed through the rail toward Perry Mason.

Mason turned to Eleanor. "Was that your gun?" he asked.

"That is my gun."

"And how did it get there, where it was found?"

"Mr. Mason, I give you my word of honor, I cross my heart and hope to die, I have absolutely no recollection. I carried that gun for personal protection. There had been so many instances of women being molested and . . . well, I didn't live exactly a quiet life and quite often I had to carry jewelry from my father's place of business to my home. The police themselves suggested that I should carry that gun. It's one of those weapons with a two-inch barrel that is designed to fit in a pocket or in a woman's purse."

"And when you left home on this so-called honeymoon of yours you had that gun with you?"

"Yes, I carried it with me. I may as well admit it now. I'm trapped."

"And you *didn't* have it with you when you were apprehended by the police?"

"Quite obviously, Mr. Mason," she said, smiling slightly, "I didn't have it with me. I had very little with me. I believe my garments were described in the press as 'a fluttering diaphanous covering.'"

"Dammit," Mason said angrily, "don't joke about it. That gun is going to convict you of murder. You left home with Douglas Hepner. He was murdered and he was murdered with your gun."

104

"But it was two weeks after I'd left home with him. A lot can happen in two weeks."

"It doesn't make any difference what else happened," Mason said angrily. "He was killed on the sixteenth and he was killed with your gun, within a hundred yards of the place where you were seen running around practically naked in the moonlight."

"You're angry with me, aren't you?"

"I just wish you'd tell me what happened," Mason said, "so I'd have a chance to save you from the death penalty or from life imprisonment. If you shot him you could at least give me an opportunity to plead self-defense or justifiable homicide or . . ."

"I'm afraid," she said, "you forget that the bullet was squarely in the back of the man's head. That would seem to negate any theory of self-defense."

A policewoman beckoned for the defendant.

Mason, still angry, said, "I hope you'll do something to recover your memory before ten o'clock tomorrow morning, because if you don't . . ." He broke off as he saw a newspaper reporter coming toward him.

The newspaper reporter pushed forward. "Mr. Mason, I wonder if you'd care to make any statement?"

Mason smiled genially. "No statement at the present time," he said, "other than that the defendant is absolutely innocent."

"Is it true that she has no recollection of what happened on the night of the murder?"

"Amnesia," Mason said, "is a subject for the experts. I am not an expert. You might ask one of the psychiatrists about retrograde amnesia from mental shock. That's all I can tell you at the present time."

"Your defense will include amnesia?"

"My defense," Mason said, smiling, "is not being announced at the present time for reasons which should be quite obvious. However, you may quote me as stating that before the case is finished Hamilton Burger is going to be greatly surprised."

And, smiling confidently, Mason picked up the papers

from the table in front of him, put them in the brief case and snapped the brief case shut.

Mason cupped his hand around Della Street's elbow, nodded to Paul Drake, said in a low voice, "Let's get out of here where we can talk," and led the way across the courtroom through the court reporter's room, down the corridor and into a witness room.

Mason kicked the door shut, said, "Well, there it is out in the open."

"What can you do against a combination like that?" Drake asked.

Mason shrugged his shoulders.

Drake said, "You can see now why Burger was so anxious to get to trial. Good Lord, Perry, you can't beat a case like that."

Mason pushed back his coat, put his thumbs in the armholes of his vest, started pacing the floor. "I wish that girl would tell me the truth," he said.

"She isn't telling you the truth because she can't," Drake said. "She killed him. There isn't one chance in a million that she didn't kill him."

"Chief," Della Street said, "isn't there some way of combating this question of the ownership of the gun? Of course, it's her gun. It was registered to her. But suppose somebody stole it."

"That, of course," Mason said, "is the only defense we have, but you're overlooking the trap that Hamilton Burger is setting for me."

"What's that?"

"He wants me to work some line of cross-examination that will bring out that very point," Mason said. "Then he's going to bring his star witness to the stand."

"Who's that?"

"Ethel Belan."

"What will she swear to?"

"Heaven knows," Mason said, "but probably it will be to the effect that she saw Eleanor Corbin with that gun in her possession within a few hours of the time of the murder. Lord knows what she's going to testify to, but it's something devastating, you can bet your bottom dollar on that. Otherwise Burger would never have put her up at an expensive hotel, given her a bodyguard, kept her in isolation, away from everyone who might tip us off to what her story was going to be."

"That's so," Drake agreed morosely. "How about making a deal with the D.A., Perry?"

"On what?"

"Copping a plea of guilty, taking life imprisonment and saving your client from the death penalty. After all, with her looks and a little luck she'll get out with some of her life left to live."

Mason shook his head. "I can't do that."

"Why?"

"Because she won't tell me that she actually killed the guy. I can't put an innocent woman up against the horror of life imprisonment on a deal of that sort.

"Figure what it means, Paul. She's young. She's attractive. She's got a good figure. She likes to show it. She has been free as the air. She travels around to Europe and South America. She eats in the best restaurants. She has been on top of the world.

"Now put her in the drab confines of a prison life, take away all initiative, all glamour, all variety. It's condemning her to a monotonous procession of days, one day just like another. Lights out at a certain time each night. Up at a certain time each morning. Drab, tasteless breakfast according to a regular schedule. Time slips through her fingers and goes down the drain. She lives on prison grub. It's a diet that will keep her nourished but it consists of starches in place of proteins. She gets fat. Her tissues become water-logged. She loses her figure. She lets her shoulders sag in a dejected droop. And then after fifteen or perhaps twenty years she gets out. What's she going to do? She's no longer attractive to men. She's no longer filled with that devil-may-care spontaneity which now gives her her charm. Her life has gone. She has the stigma of prison surrounding her. She . . ."

"She'd ten thousand times rather walk into the execution chamber," Della Street said, "and so would I."

"There we are," Mason said.

"Well, we have to do *something*," Drake said. "We can't sit back and take this lying down."

"Of course we're going to do something," Mason flared. "I'm just trying to get things organized in my own mind. We've got to find out something about this case that the prosecution doesn't know. We've got to find it out fast and then we've got to prove what actually *did* happen."

"What actually did happen," Drake said, "is that your client killed Hepner. She got jealous because he started two-timing her and she shot him. Why the hell can't she be normal? Why can't she get on the witness stand, cross her legs, show the jury a lot of cheesecake and tell about that night when Douglas taunted her with the fact that he had betrayed her virtue and wasn't going to do anything about it, how she thought she could scare him into marrying her if she took the gun from her purse, intending just to frighten him, and then he taunted her some more and all of a sudden everything went black. And then the next thing she remembers is his body inert and silent in death. And so she lost her mind and went tearing around in the moonlight, putting on the dance of the seven veils."

"It's a goofy defense," Della Street said, "but at least it's a defense, and with her figure and her charm she could get by with it—at least enough so that some of the old goats on the jury would be hypnotized by her nylon stockings and hold out for acquittal. They'd finally compromise on manslaughter."

"You overlook the fact," Mason said, "that a lawyer is an officer of the court. He represents justice. He represents right. I'm not supposed to use my brains and try to stand between a guilty defendant and the law of the land. I'm supposed to see that my clients are protected, that their interests are protected.

"Now then, Paul, let's look at this thing from a logical standpoint. Let's not let ourselves get stampeded and let's not let ourselves get hypnotized. What have you got in your pockets?"

"Me? My pockets?" Drake asked.

Mason nodded.

"A bunch of junk," Drake said.

"Take it out," Mason said. "Put it on the table."

Drake looked at him in surprise.

"Go ahead," Mason said.

Silently Drake started pulling things out of his pockets.

"Well, I'll be darned," Della Street said, watching the collection pile up on the table. "And then you men talk about the stuff that goes in a woman's purse!"

Drake put down pencil, fountain pen, notebook, knife, cigarette case, lighter, keychain, handkerchiefs, wallet, small change, driving license, a couple of opened letters, an airplane time schedule, a package of chewing gum.

Mason surveyed the collection thoughtfully.

"All right," Drake said, "what have I proved?"

"That," Mason told him, "is something that I wish I knew, but you sure have proven something."

"I don't get it," Drake said.

"Contrast what you have in your pockets, which is probably an average collection of the stuff carried by a busy man, and think of the things which the coroner said were in the pockets of Douglas Hepner."

"Well, of course," Drake said, "I . . ."

"Let's look at it this way. Hepner smoked. He had his cigarettes in a cigarette case. Where were his matches? Where was his knife? Nearly every man carries a penknife of some sort. He had a small amount of chicken feed in his pocket but no bills. He had a driving license but no membership cards in anything. No clubs, no addresses, nothing of that sort."

Drake frowned thoughtfully for a moment. "By gosh," he said, "when you come right down to it, Perry, that *was* a very meager assortment of junk."

"Of course it was," Mason said. "Where did Hepner live?"

"Now there," Drake said, "is something that bothers the hell out of the police. Ostensibly he lived at the Dixiecrat Apartments. He had an apartment there but it wasn't really lived in. There was maid service and the maid said there would be days at a time, sometimes a couple of weeks at a stretch, when the beds wouldn't have been slept in, when linen wouldn't have been used in the bathroom. There was never any food in the icebox. He didn't send out his laundry from there, and . . ."

Mason snapped his fingers.

"What?" Drake asked.

"That's it," Mason said. "The laundry! Come on, Paul!"

"Where?"

"Over to the coroner's office," Mason said. "We were invited to inspect the clothes that the decedent was wearing when the body was found. Let's check for a laundry mark. It's a cinch Hepner didn't do his own laundry."

"Okay," Drake said. "We may have something there, but . . . oh shucks, Perry, if there'd been a laundry mark on those clothes the police would have checked it long before this."

"How do we know they haven't?" Mason said.

"Well, if they have you'll learn about it in due time."

"I want to learn about things before they're thrown at me in court," Mason said. "Just suppose that that client of mine *is* telling the truth. Suppose she *can't* remember what happened. Suppose that she's being railroaded on a murder charge and can't . . ."

"The chances of that are just about one in fifty million," Drake said. "The D.A. has had her examined by psychiatrists. They're satisfied she's faking. The minute she gets on the witness stand and claims that she can't remember what happened, the D.A. is going to start throwing a cross-examination at her that will leave her wilted like a hot lettuce leaf. Then he's going to throw on a battery of psychiatrists and just about prove that she's lying."

"All right," Mason said, "if she's lying, I can't let her get on the witness stand and put herself in that position, but I have to prove to myself that she is lying. Do you have any ultraviolet light in your office, Paul?"

"Yes, I've got a little hand lamp that plugs into an AC current and has two types of filter—a long-length violet and . . ."

"Get it," Mason said. "Bring it along. Lots of laundries

110

these days are using fluorescent ink as a laundry mark. That may give us a clue. What about those keys? There were four keys on the key container. Did the police ever find out what locks they fitted?"

"One of them was to that apartment in the Dixiecrat apartment house. I don't know about the others."

"Okay," Mason said. "Take along a block of wax, Paul. While I'm keeping the attention of the authorities focused on something else, make a wax impression of every one of the keys on that key container."

"Are you supposed to have those?" Drake asked dubiously.

"Any law against it?" Mason asked.

"Hell, I don't know, Perry. You know the law."

"Then do what I tell you to. I want an impression of those keys. We've got work to do. We're beginning to find out what we're up against now, and we can gamble that tomorrow Hamilton Burger is going to throw a mountain at us. He'll bury us under an avalanche."

"Ethel Belan?" Drake asked.

Mason nodded. "It's a safe bet that her testimony is really going to throw a harpoon into us.

"Burger has timed this whole thing. Tonight he'll have us worrying about the gun, frantically trying to dig up evidence that will make the jury think it was stolen.

"Then when we're all ready to stake our case on that he'll have Ethel Belan jerk the rug out from under us.

"Then Hamilton Burger is going to smile sweetly and say, 'The prosecution rests,' and toss the case into my lap.

"If I put Eleanor on the witness stand they're going to tear her to pieces. If I don't, she's going to get convicted. Either way it goes we're hooked. Come on, let's go."

◾ 11 ◾

A SOMEWHAT BORED ATTENDANT AT THE CORONER'S office said, "I'll have to call either the D.A. or the police."

"You won't catch the D.A. at this hour," Mason said. "There was a stipulation made in court this afternoon that we could inspect the clothing of Douglas Hepner."

"Oh, I guess it's all right," the attendant said. "There's no reason why you shouldn't. Didn't Raymond Orla testify up there today?"

"That's right."

"Well, I've got a night number. I can get him. He'll be getting home just about this time. You wait here."

The attendant entered another office, carefully closing the door behind him, then, after some five minutes, came back and nodded. "It's okay," he said. "Orla said the D.A. said you could look at them. Right this way."

He led the way down a long corridor, into a room where there were numbered lockers. He took a key from his pocket, opened a locker and said, "There you are. These are the clothes."

"There were some articles of personal property," Mason said. "A fountain pen, notebook, things of that sort."

"Those will be in this little lock box here."

The attendant opened the lock box, placed them all on a table. "I'll have to sort of stick around," he apologized.

"Certainly," Mason said, glancing significantly at Della Street.

"My, what a job you must have here," Della Street said, moving over to inspect some of the other lockers. "You have to keep all of these straight." She laughed. "As a secretary I can appreciate the problem you have."

The attendant began to warm up. He moved over to Della Street's side. "Well, it's quite a job," he admitted.

112

"Of course, you see, things keep changing here. We'll have cases come in and . . . some of them aren't here twenty-four hours. Some of them where there's a court action on are here for weeks. Now over here is our temporary side. Things here run from twenty-four to seventy-two hours. And in this other room over here we keep the bodies. On this temporary side the numbers on the lockers and the numbers on the lockers containing the bodies are both the same so that we can give a body a key-number —take a tag and tie it on his big toe.

"I presume this is all pretty gruesome to you. Most women get the creeps. You can see that tier of files in there looks like oversized filing drawers. Each one of them has a body, kept under just the right amount of refrigeration."

"No, it doesn't frighten me," Della Street said, her voice showing interest. "I'm a realist. I know that death is one logical end of the life stream, just as birth is at the other end. And I know that a certain percentage of deaths are sudden and unexplained. It's up to you people to keep the records straight."

She moved over toward the other room and the attendant, after pausing to glance momentarily over his shoulder, followed her, explaining as he went.

Mason examined the garments. "This is a tailor-made suit, Paul," he said, "but the label has been carefully cut out. Suppose the police did it?"

"I doubt it," Drake said. "You never can tell. It's been cut out all right."

Mason said, "Take this underwear, Paul. Hold the coat over it. Now get your ultraviolet light going."

Paul Drake held the coat over the underwear, making something of a tent of it, then flashed the ultraviolet light on the underwear.

Almost immediately a number flared into brillance.

"This is it," Mason said excitedly. "Get this, Paul."

Mason smoothed out the underwear. Drake held the light.

The number N-4464 flared up brilliantly.

"Quick," Mason said. "Get that light away, Paul. I

113

don't want the attendant to report to the police what we've been doing and give the police any ideas."

"What about the suit?" Drake asked.

"We won't bother with it now," Mason said. "While Della has him over there get the wax impression of those keys. I'll hold the coat up as though I'm looking through the lining and hold it between you and the attendant."

The attendant, looking back at them, had turned and started moving back toward the table. Della Street held him back with one last question. Mason held up the coat on its wire hanger, apparently inspecting the lining.

Della Street veered over toward a locker. "What's this?"

The attendant, suddenly suspicious, broke away, hurried forward. Mason turned the garment on the hanger, apparently completely oblivious of the fact that anyone else was in the room, yet managing to hold the coat in front of the attendant very much as a toreador holds the cape in front of the bull.

"What are you guys doing?" the attendant asked.

Mason said accusingly, "They've cut the label out of this coat. We're going to have to see that label."

"Who's cut it out?" the attendant demanded.

"How should I know?" Mason said. "It's in your custody."

"Well, it wasn't cut out after it came here."

"It wasn't?" Mason asked in surprise. "Didn't the police do it?"

"Heck, I don't know. We just keep the stuff, that's all. But no one here cut any labels out."

"You mean to say you don't cut out the labels in order to check . . . ?"

"We don't touch a thing. You'll have to take that business up with the police. All we're supposed to do is keep the stuff. I have orders to let you look at it, that is, the D.A. said you could look at it, and that's that. As far as I'm concerned, go ahead and look. What's that guy doing over there?"

Drake straightened, holding the key container in his hand. "I've been studying these keys," he said, "trying to find out whether there's any identifying number on them."

The attendant laughed. "That's one thing the police sure worked on. They went over those keys with a magnifying glass. There aren't any numbers on them."

"Oh well," Drake said, tossing the keys back on the table. "I guess there's no need for me to look at them then. How about it, Perry? Have you seen everything you want?"

"I suppose so," Mason said grudgingly. "What about his shoes?"

"I can tell you something about the shoes," the attendant said. "Of course I don't want to be quoted."

"It's confidential if you say it's confidential," Mason told him.

"Well, the shoes were sold by a downtown department store as you can see. Police checked. It was a cash purchase. This guy didn't have any credit there. The shoes were part of a shipment received about three months ago. Police thought they had something for a while but it turned out to be a blind alley."

"Just what were they looking for?" Mason asked.

"Looking for anything they could find. There was something mysterious about the guy's apartment. He wasn't there much of the time. The police are trying to find out where he spent his time."

"Probably in travel," Mason said casually.

"That's the way of it," the attendant said. "It's probably the explanation. The guy was on the move all the time. Well, you folks finished?"

"We're finished."

The attendant returned the articles to the lock box and the filing cabinet, locked the filing cabinet, smiled at Della Street and said, "It was a pleasure. Anything else I can do for you fellows?"

"Not at the moment," Mason told him. "Well, let's go and eat. I just wanted to check on that stuff," he explained to the attendant. "You know how it is. You can hear someone describe a suit of clothes or something but it's hard to tell . . ."

"Yeah, I know," the attendant said. "I guess you've got the picture now."

"I think I have," Mason said.

"Well, good night."

They moved into the fresh air or outdoors, away from the stuffy smell of corpses, pathological specimens and the odor of death.

"Well?" Drake asked.

"You've got your work cut out for you, Paul," Mason said. "You've got to get that laundry mark traced and you've got to do it fast."

"Have a heart, Perry, I'm hungry. We can't get the thing until . . ."

"You've got to get it," Mason said. "In the first place the police have most of these laundry marks filed, that is, the general code and . . ."

"And you know how anxious *they'll* be to help us," Drake said.

"Try the sheriff's office," Mason said. "Dig out some of your contacts. Get hold of the secretary of the laundry association."

Drake groaned. "I can see that I'm going to have a night of it."

"You may get it faster than you think," Mason told him. "Those laundry marks are important. Hamilton Burger was too sure of himself on this case. He thinks he's got a cinch case and has just made a superficial investigation. Some of the police would have known about that laundry number. A lot of laundries are using that ultraviolet device now. They can stamp on a big, easily read number without defacing the garment. Now get busy, Paul. Did you get the wax impression of the keys?"

"I sure did. Just had time to get the last impression when that attendant came back. Thought for a moment he'd caught me."

"It wouldn't have made any difference if he had," Mason said. "We're entitled to inspect those keys, and in order to inspect them we can photograph them or do anything else."

Della Street said, "I can take charge of having the keys made, Paul. There's a locksmith who has his shop near my apartment. He frequently works late, and if he

116

isn't working I know where to find him. I pass the time of day with him every once in a while. You go ahead and chase down the laundry mark. Chief, you go to the office and I'll take the car and go down and get the keys made."

"Okay," Mason said, "but remember he has to keep his mouth shut."

"I think you can trust him all right," Della said. "He's a great fan of yours, follows all of your cases in the newspapers, and if he thought he was doing something to help he'd be tickled to death."

"Well, he can do something all right," Mason said, "and let's hope it will help. Paul, you get busy on that laundry number. Della, as soon as you get the keys made come back to the office and we'll wait for Paul and see if he gets any results."

Mason drove back to the office. Drake started work at once on the telephone. Della Street took the car and went out to get the keys made.

Mason latchkeyed the door of his private office, switched on the lights, and started pacing the floor, taking mental inventory.

Fifteen minutes lengthened into twenty, became a full half hour.

The unlisted telephone rang sharply. Mason picked it up. Drake's voice came over the wire. "Think I'm getting some place, Perry. I managed to locate the secretary of the laundry association. He doesn't have any idea what I'm working on. The number is a code. The 64 means that it's the Utility Twenty-four-hour Laundry Service, and the N-44 is the individual mark. The secretary tells me that the name of the patron whose laundry mark is registered probably begins with an N and that he's forty-fourth on the list. He's given me the name of the manager of the laundry and I'm trying to locate him now. I hope I'll have something for you within a short time. When do we eat?"

"When we get this thing buttoned up."

"Look, Perry. I can have a hamburger sent up from

downstairs. It's not much, but a hamburger and a good mug of coffee will help a lot."

"When Della gets back," Mason said. "If we haven't had a break by that time we'll have something sent in while you're working."

"Okay," Drake said. "I just thought I'd let you know that we're striking pay dirt. But why would the thing be listed under N? Do you suppose Hepner was using an alias?"

"He could have," Mason said. "There's something pretty damn mysterious about Hepner's whole background."

"Okay," Drake said. "I'll let you know."

Another ten minutes passed, then Della Street came in jingling a bunch of keys.

"Okay?" Mason asked.

"Okay, Chief. I had two of each made so that in case we were fortunate enough to find the locks they fitted we would have two strings to our bow. Sometimes in making up keys from a wax impression some little imperfection or other will throw them off. I have a file here. The key man gave it to me and suggested that if the keys didn't work we start filing the edges, just touching them up a bit."

"And he's going to keep quiet about it?" Mason asked.

"He's having the time of his life," Della Street said. "He told me to pass the word on to you that any time he could help you in any way on a case to just let him know and that you could trust him to be the soul of discretion."

"Well, that helps," Mason said, grinning. "You and the locksmith seem to think that once we find the locks that these keys fit we're going to walk right in."

"Well," Della Street asked, "what's the object of having keys if you aren't going to use them?"

"That, of course," Mason said, "is a question. Let's go on down to Drake's office and see how he's coming. He thought maybe he'd have something for us in a short time and suggested that we might celebrate by having hamburgers and coffee sent up to the office."

"I could use some of that," Della Street said. "Let's go."

They switched off the lights, walked down the corridor to Drake's office. The night telephone operator motioned for them to go in.

"Paul's on the phone," she said. "He's been on the phone almost constantly. Go on in. I won't need to announce you."

Mason held open the wooden gate and Della Street preceded him down the long, narrow corridor, flanked by the doors of small offices on each side where Drake's operatives interviewed witnesses, prepared reports and at times conducted polygraph tests.

Drake was talking on the telephone, making notes, as Mason and Della Street entered. He waved his hand at them, nodded his head exultantly and said, "Just a minute, let me get that down. Now, let's see. That's Frank Ormsby Newberg at the Titterington Apartments on Elmwood Place. . . . Can you tell us how long he's been a customer? . . . I see . . . kept the same laundry mark, eh? . . . All right, thanks. . . . No, no this is just a routine check trying to trace a lost suitcase. Question of whether or not there's a twenty-five dollar limit on liability for loss of a suitcase and trying to prove the identity of garments. Nothing except a routine matter and I'm sorry I bothered you after office hours but I'm working against rather a tight schedule. . . . That's right. This is the Drake Detective Agency. . . . Sure, look me up. Perhaps *we* can give *you* a helping hand some time. Okay, good-by."

Drake hung up the telephone, said, "Well, we have it. Frank Ormsby Newberg, Titterington Apartments, Elmwood Place."

"Okay," Mason said, "let's go."

"Eats?" Drake asked.

Mason shook his head, glanced at his wrist watch, said, "Not yet."

"It would only take a minute to . . ."

"We don't know how many minutes we have left,"

119

Mason said. "You can't tell what we're going to run into. We're working against time and against the police. That attendant at the coroner's laboratory *may* not have been as preoccupied as he seemed."

■ **12** ■

THE TITTERINGTON APARTMENTS TURNED OUT TO BE A narrow-fronted, three-story, brick building, more than a hundred feet deep, with no clerk on duty. The names of the tenants of the apartments were listed in a long directory to the right of the locked front door. There was a speaking tube by each name and a call button.

"Old-fashioned joint," Paul Drake said. "What do we do?"

Mason found the name of Frank Ormsby Newberg listed opposite apartment 220, and pressed the button.

There was no answer.

Mason waited a while, then pressed the button the second time.

Mason turned to Della Street.

Wordlessly she handed him the set of four keys.

Mason tried the first one in the front door. Nothing happened.

The second one fitted smoothly in the lock and clicked back the bolt.

Mason held the key between his thumb and forefinger, said, "This looks like the key. Let's go."

Drake said, "Are we apt to get into trouble over this, Perry?"

"Of course," Mason said, "but all I'm doing at the moment is trying to find out if the keys fit."

"Are you going into the apartment?"

"That," Mason said, "depends."

120

There was a little cubbyhole lobby in the front of the building and a sign reading "Manager—Apt. 101," with an arrow pointing to the apartment.

Mason led the way down the corridor to the lighted elevator shaft. The automatic elevator wheezed upward to the second floor. Apartment 220 was designated by a number on the door in a poorly lit corridor. There was a fairly good-sized crack at the bottom of the door and no light came through from this crack although other apartment doors on the same floor showed well-defined ribbons of light.

There was a doorbell to the right of the door. Mason pressed this and could hear a buzzer sounding on the inside of the apartment.

Drake said, "Perry, this thing gives me the creeps. Let's go talk with the manager. Let's keep our noses clean."

"Before I talk with the manager," Mason said, "I want to be sure what I'm talking about."

"I don't want to go in," Drake said.

"You don't mind if we demonstrate that the key fits, do you?"

"I don't like any part of this," Drake said.

"I don't like it myself," Mason told him, "but I'm trying to find evidence."

They stood there waiting.

The corridor was poorly ventilated. There was a warm aroma of cooking odors mingled with the feel of human tenancy. Down the corridor someone was listening to a television show and the words were plainly audible through the thin door of the apartment.

"An old dump made over," Drake said.

Mason nodded, then gently inserted the key which had opened the front door, and which he had been holding in his thumb and forefinger.

"I'm just going to try this," he said.

The lawyer twisted the key. Nothing happened.

He moved the key slightly back and forth in the lock, exerted pressure, but the key refused to turn.

Della Street said, "How about the file, Chief? The locksmith said perhaps we'd have to dress off a high spot."

Mason withdrew the key, looked at it for a moment, then tried another key on the key container. That key didn't even fit the lock. Nor did a third key. But the fourth key slid smoothly into the lock.

Again Mason twisted the key and this time the bolt on the door slid quietly back.

"Oh-oh!" Drake said.

Mason, placing a handkerchief over the palm of his hand and the tips of his fingers, gently turned the knob and opened the apartment door.

"Now this," Drake said, "is where I came in. I don't want any part of this."

Mason stood in the doorway for a second or two, then reached in and groped for the light switch. He found it and pressed the light button.

The interior of the apartment looked as though it had been visited by a cyclone. Drawers had been pulled out, cupboards had been opened, dishes had been piled on the floor, clothing was stacked in a heap, papers had been strewn about indiscriminately.

"I guess someone beat us to it," Della Street said.

The elevator door clanged open. Someone started down the corridor.

"Inside," Mason said, and led the way into the apartment.

Della Street followed him immediately. Drake hesitated, then reluctantly entered.

Mason kicked the door shut.

"Don't touch anything," the lawyer warned.

"Now look, Perry," Paul Drake said. "We're sitting in on a game. We don't know what's trumps. The only thing we know for sure is that *we* don't have *any*."

As they stood there waiting they could hear steps in the corridor and voices.

Paul Drake whispered, "Perry, this is carrying things too far. If anything should happen and we were seen and recognized as we go out . . ."

Della Street put her finger to her lips. "Shhhhh, Paul!"

The voices came closer.

Abruptly they could recognize the voice of Sergeant

Holcomb of Homicide Squad saying, "Now as I understand it, Madam, you think you recognized his picture."

The steps paused in front of the door.

"That's right," a woman's voice said. "I'm satisfied from the picture in the paper that he's the one who rented this apartment, under the name of Frank Ormsby Newberg."

"Well," Sergeant Holcomb said, "an identification from a picture is a tricky thing. We'll see if there's anybody home."

The buzzer sounded.

Paul Drake looked desperately around him. "There must be a back way out somewhere," he whispered.

"We haven't time to find it," Mason whispered in reply. "They have a passkey. Della, do you have a notebook?"

She nodded.

"Get it out," Mason said.

The buzzer sounded again.

Mason said, "Start writing, Della, anything."

Della Street starting writing shorthand in the small notebook which she took from her purse.

Knuckles pounded on the door, then Sergeant Holcomb said, "All right, we'll try the passkey."

Mason turned the knob, swung the door open and said, "Well, well. Good evening, Sergeant Holcomb. This *is* a surprise!"

Holcomb's face registered dismayed incredulity.

"What the devil?" he exclaimed as soon as he could find his voice.

Mason said smoothly, "I'm taking inventory."

"*You* are? What the devil right have *you* got to be *here* and what are you taking an inventory of?"

"The assets of the estate, of course," Mason said.

Holcomb stood, groping for words that refused to come.

Mason said, "My client, Eleanor Hepner, is the widow of Douglas Hepner. We are, of course, at the moment engaged in a murder trial but that doesn't affect the estate. As soon as she's acquitted she'll be entitled to inherit all of the property as the surviving widow. In the meantime she's entitled to letters of administration and naturally, as her attorney, I'm taking an inventory."

Mason turned to Della Street and said, "Five dress shirts. One, two, three, four, five, six, seven athletic shorts. One, two, three, four . . ."

"Hey, wait a minute," Sergeant Holcomb bellowed. "What is this? Are you trying to tell me that Frank Ormsby Newberg is an alias of Douglas Hepner?"

"But of course," Mason said. "Didn't you know that?"

"How the devil would we have known it?" Sergeant Holcomb asked. "If it hadn't been for this woman calling the police and insisting that she recognized Douglas Hepner's picture in the paper as that of the tenant of one of her apartments who hadn't shown up for a while, we'd have never got a lead on this apartment."

"Well, well," Mason said indulgently. "Why didn't you simply ask me?"

"Ask *you!*" Holcomb exclaimed.

"Why, certainly," Mason said.

"How did you get in here?" Holcomb demanded.

"With the key," Mason said.

"What key?"

Mason's voice had the quiet patience of an indulgent parent trying to explain a very simple problem to a very dull child. "I have told you, Sergeant, that my client, Eleanor Hepner, or Eleanor Corbin as she is mentioned in the indictment, is the surviving widow of Douglas Hepner. Quite naturally she'd have the key to the apartment where she spent her honeymoon, wouldn't she?"

The woman who was evidently the manager of the apartment house said, "Well, he never told me anything about being married."

Mason smiled at her. "I understand. Rather mysterious, wasn't he?"

"He certainly was," she said. "He'd come here and keep the most irregular hours, then he'd disappear and you wouldn't see him for a while. Then he'd be back and . . . it drove us crazy trying to get in a weekly cleaning of the apartment."

"Yes, I can well understand," Mason said. "Eleanor

told me that . . . however, I think perhaps under the circumstances I'd better wait until she tells her story on the witness stand."

Sergeant Holcomb, completely nonplused, said, "Perhaps you can tell me what this is all about. How did it happen this apartment is wrecked like this? You didn't pull all this stuff out taking an inventory."

"Evidently," Mason said, "someone has been in here, someone who was searching for something. As soon as we had completed our inventory I was going to suggest that the police had better try taking some fingerprints. As you'll perhaps notice, Sergeant, we're not touching anything but are simply standing here in the middle of the floor making an inventory of the things that are readily visible. Now, Della, there are some men's suits in the closet. Try not to leave any fingerprints on the door. Open the door with your foot. That's right. Three business suits, one tuxedo, five pair of shoes, and . . . yes, that's a suitcase in the back of the closet there, and . . ."

"Hey, wait a minute," Holcomb said. "All this stuff is evidence."

"Evidence of what?" Mason asked.

"I don't know, but it's sure evidence. Someone has been in here."

"Elemental, my dear Sergeant," Mason said.

"Dammit, I can get along without any of your humor, Mason. You're willing to admit that Frank Ormsby Newberg was Douglas Hepner?"

"But, of course," Mason said as though this were one of the most obvious facts in the entire case.

"Well, we've been trying to find out where he lived. We were satisfied there was some sort of a hideout like this."

"You could have simplified matters a lot if you'd asked me," Mason said.

"You evidently just got here yourself," Holcomb said.

"That's right. I've been busy, Sergeant."

"Well, we want to investigate this. I'm getting in touch with Headquarters. We're going to have some fingerprint men down here. We're going to go through this thing with a fine-toothed comb looking for evidence. We don't want *anybody* in here messing things up."

Mason hesitated for a moment. "Well," he said at last, "I don't think there's any objection on the part of the widow to that, Sergeant, except that I want you to take great precautions to see that the personal property is conserved. There is, of course, as you know, a mother involved in the case and it may be the mother will make accusations against the widow and . . ."

"If you know where the mother is," Holcomb said, "you can tell us. *We* can't find her."

"Neither could we," Mason said. "She seems to have disappeared. Now wouldn't you consider that as a suspicious circumstance, Sergeant?"

Sergeant Holcomb, gradually recovering his poise, said, "We don't need any wisecracks from you, Mason. Do you know where the mother is?"

"No."

"You have a key to this apartment?"

"That's right."

"I want it."

Mason shook his head. "No. The manager can let you in with the passkey. The key that I have I want to return to . . . well, you can understand my position, Sergeant."

"I'm not sure that I can," Holcomb said. "There's something fishy as hell about this whole business."

"There certainly is," Mason agreed good-naturedly. "Someone has been in here searching for something. I had assumed it was the police until you told me that this whole thing came as a surprise to you. Of course, Sergeant, I'm willing to take your word. I won't question *your* statement for a minute, although there are times when you seem to be a little reluctant to return the courtesy."

Sergeant Holcomb turned to Della Street. "How long have you folks been here?"

Mason said patiently, "For a little while. I've been busy in court and I've been busy with the preparation for trial. I haven't had an opportunity to look into the civil aspects of the case because of the criminal charge that has been pending against my client. I do, however, expect to file an application for letters of administration and . . ."

"Now listen," Holcomb interrupted. "You don't need to go over that again. I asked a question of your secretary."

"I'm trying to give you the information you wanted," Mason said.

"Oh hell, what's the use!" Holcomb exclaimed disgustedly. "Get out of here. I'm telephoning Headquarters for some fingerprint men. Now get the hell out of here and don't come back until I tell you you can."

"That's rather a highhanded attitude," Mason said, "in view of the fact that . . ."

"Come on. Out!" Holcomb said. "Just get the hell out of here."

He turned to the manager of the apartment house, a rather fleshy woman, in the late forties, who was standing in the doorway with eyes and ears that missed nothing. "We're going to seal up this apartment," he said. "We're going to see that no unauthorized person enters it. Now if you'll just step out in the corridor we'll get these three people out of here, then I'll be the last to leave the apartment. You can give me the duplicate key and I'll telephone Headquarters."

The woman stepped out into the corridor.

"Go on," Holcomb said to Mason. "Out."

Paul Drake moved out into the corridor with alacrity. Della Street followed, and Mason brought up the rear, saying, "You can make a note, Della, that the taking of inventory was interrupted by the arrival of the police who wished to investigate an apparent burglary. Make a note of the date and the exact time. And now," Mason said urbanely to Sergeant Holcomb, "we'll hold the police responsible. I take it that you'll notify me when you've finished with your investigation so we can continue with our inventory. Good night, Sergeant." And Mason, nodding to Della Street, led the way down the corridor to the elevator.

As they entered the cage and closed the door, Drake leaned back, supporting himself in a corner of the elevator, and, taking a handkerchief from his pocket, made elaborate motions of wiping his brow.

"You can do the damnedest things, Perry," he said.

Della Street, voice apprehensive, said, "*Now* how are you going to explain the fact that Eleanor, who has previously told the police she can't remember a thing about where she spent the time or what happened after she started on her honeymoon, has disclosed to you the apartment where Douglas Hepner lived and given you a key to that apartment?"

Mason said, "I'll cross that bridge when I come to it."

"The hell of it is," Drake groaned, "there isn't any bridge. There's only a chasm, and when you come to it you're going to have to jump."

■ 13 ■

As court convened the next morning an unusual situation was commented on by courtroom attachés.

Usually a trial in which Perry Mason appeared would fill every seat in the courtroom. Now there was but a sprinkling of spectators, a sinister indication of the fact that in the mind of the public the case against Eleanor Hepner was so dead open-and-shut that the contest was too one-sided to be dramatic and that even the ingenuity of Perry Mason couldn't keep the case from being a run-of-the-mill conviction.

Hamilton Burger, the district attorney, noticed the vacant rows of seats with annoyance. Cases where he had met humiliating defeat at the hands of Perry Mason had made newspaper headlines and had resulted in packed courtrooms. Now that he was in a position to win a case hands down it appeared he would have but a small audience.

Hamilton Burger said, "Your Honor, I now wish to call Ethel Belan to the stand."

"Very well," Judge Moran said. "Come forward and be sworn, Miss Belan."

Ethel Belan, carefully groomed for her appearance on the stand, her manner radiating self-confidence and an eager desire to match wits with Perry Mason, held up her hand, was sworn, took the witness stand, answered the usual preliminary questions as to occupation and residence, then glanced expectantly at Hamilton Burger.

Burger, with the manner of a magician about to perform a trick which will leave the audience speechless, said. "You live in apartment 360 at the Belinda Apartments, Miss Belan?"

"That's right. Yes, sir."

"Who has the adjoining apartment on the south?"

"Miss Suzanne Granger has apartment 358."

"You are acquainted with Miss Granger?"

"Oh, yes."

"How long has she lived in that apartment?"

"Some two years, to my knowledge."

"And how long have you lived there in apartment 360?"

"Just a little over two years."

"Are you acquainted with the defendant, Eleanor Corbin?"

"I am. Yes, sir."

"When did you first meet her?"

"On the ninth of August."

"Of this year?"

"Yes."

"And how did you happen to meet the defendant?"

"She came to see me. She said she had a proposition to make to me."

"And did she make such a proposition?"

"Yes."

"This was in writing or in a conversation?"

"In a conversation."

"Where did that conversation take place?"

"In my apartment."

"And who was present at that conversation?"

"Just the defendant and me."

"And what did the defendant say at the time, as nearly as you can give us her exact words?"

"The defendant told me that she was interested in Suzanne Granger in the adjoining apartment."

"Did she say why?"

"She said Miss Grainger had stolen her boy friend."

"Did she use the word husband or the expression boy friend?"

"She said boy friend."

"Did she give you the name of the boy friend?"

"Yes, sir."

"What was that name?"

"Douglas Hepner."

"And what was the proposition the defendant made to you?"

"She wanted to come and live with me in my apartment. She wanted to see whether Douglas Hepner was actually calling on Suzanne Granger. She said that Douglas Hepner had told her it was purely a business relationship, that she felt certain he was two-timing her with Suzanne Granger, that she wanted to find out. She offered to pay me two hundred dollars as a bonus and a rental of eighty-five dollars a week for two weeks."

"And what did you do in relation to this proposition that she made?"

"Naturally I jumped at the chance. The apartment had been rather expensive, my roommate had left and I was a little lonely. I had a roommate for some eighteen months, then she left and I have been carrying the apartment alone because I wanted to find someone who was completely congenial. That hadn't been as easy as I had hoped. This offer was one I could hardly afford to reject."

"So the defendant moved in with you?"

"That is right."

"Now I have here a sketch map of the arrangement of your apartment and the arrangement of the adjoining apartment, that of Suzanne Granger. I am going to ask you if this correctly shows your apartment?"

"It shows the arrangement of my apartment, but I have never been in Miss Granger's apartment."

"That's right. I am going to identify it as Miss Granger's apartment by another witness. I am asking you only to tell us whether this correctly shows the arrangement of your apartment."

"It does. Yes, sir."

"It represents a correct delineation of the general plan of your apartment?"

"Yes, sir."

"Now did the defendant designate any particular place where she was to stay in the apartment?"

"She did indeed. My bedroom was the one with the larger closet. It was next to the bedroom occupied by Miss Granger in 358. The defendant insisted that I should move my bedroom to the other one with the smaller closet so she could move in this bedroom which was next to the Granger apartment."

"Now then," Hamilton Burger said, rising from his chair with ponderous grace, and with something of a verbal flourish in his voice, "I show you People's Exhibit G, a .38 caliber Smith & Wesson revolver, number C-48809, and ask you if you have ever seen that gun before?"

"Just a moment, Your Honor," Mason said. "That question is objected to as leading and suggestive."

"It can be answered yes or no," Hamilton Burger said.

"Certainly it can," Mason said, "but you have indicated the answer that you desire. If you want to ask this witness about *any* gun, go ahead and ask the witness, but don't shove the weapon in her face, don't designate it, don't describe it by number. If she saw a .38 caliber revolver, let her testify to that fact."

"Oh, it's so obvious, Your Honor," Hamilton Burger said. "This objection is merely for the purpose of . . ."

"Technically the objection is well taken," Judge Moran said.

"Very well," Hamilton Burger said, tossing the revolver back on the clerk's desk with a gesture of disgust. "Did the defendant have any weapon in her possession?"

"Yes, sir."

"What?"

"A .38 caliber revolver."

"Can you describe that revolver?"

"It had a short barrel. It was blued steel. It looked just like that revolver you picked up just now."

Burger turned and let the jury see his triumphant grin as he looked at Perry Mason.

"Did she show you that revolver?"

"I saw it in her overnight bag."

"I am coming to that," Hamilton Burger said. "What luggage did the defendant have with her when she moved in?"

"She had an overnight bag, a suitcase and a two-suiter. They were all very distinctive, a red and white checkerboard pattern."

"And what became of this luggage?"

"She telephoned me about it."

"Who did?"

"The defendant."

"You talked with her on the phone?"

"Yes, sir."

"Did you recognize her voice?"

"Yes, sir."

"Did you call her by name?"

"Yes, sir."

"Did she call you by name?"

"Yes, sir."

"What was the date of this conversation?"

"The seventeenth of August."

"And what did she say?"

"She said, 'Ethel, you're going to have to stand back of me. I'm pretending I have amnesia. Don't say anything to anyone about my staying with you. Don't communicate with the police or newspaper reporters. Just sit tight. I'll send for my luggage when I think it's safe to do so.'"

"You're certain about that conversation?" Hamilton Burger asked.

"Why, of course. Yes, sir."

"And the defendant said she was feigning amnesia?"

132

"Yes, sir."

"And this was on the seventeenth?"

"Yes, sir."

"At what time?"

"About eight-thirty in the morning."

"Now then," Hamilton Burger said, his manner showing that this was the dramatic highlight of the entire case, "did you ask the defendant why the necessity for all this secrecy, why she was feigning amnesia?"

"Yes, sir."

"And did the defendant answer you?"

"Yes, sir."

"Did the defendant make any explanation, give any reason that would account for her conduct?"

"Yes, sir."

"And what was that reason?"

"The defendant said, and I can give you her exact words because they seared themselves into my memory, she said, 'Ethel, I'm in a scrape, and I've got to protect myself.'"

Hamilton Burger stood facing the jury, his hands slightly outspread, prolonged the dramatic effect of that moment by a significant silence.

Judge Moran, finally realizing the tactics of the district attorney, his voice showing irritation, said, "Well, proceed with your questioning, Mr. District Attorney, unless you have finished with the witness, and if you have, kindly advise counsel for the defense so he may cross-examine."

"No, Your Honor," Hamilton Burger said, still facing the jury, "I am by no means finished with this witness. I was merely collecting my thoughts as to further questions."

"Well, get them collected and proceed," Judge Moran said testily.

"Yes, Your Honor."

Hamilton Burger turned to the witness. "At the time she told you this, the body of Douglas Hepner had not been discovered. Is that right?"

"Objected to as calling for a conclusion of the witness, as argumentative, as leading and suggestive," Mason said.

"Sustained," Judge Moran snapped.

Burger tried another tack. "Now what did you do with the luggage belonging to the defendant and which you said you had in your possession?"

"That was given to her attorney."

"By her attorney you mean Perry Mason, the lawyer seated here at the defendant's counsel table?"

"Yes, sir."

"And when did you give that baggage to him?"

"On the seventeenth day of August. In the afternoon."

"And how did you happen to give it to him?"

"Well, he came to see me. He was accompanied by his secretary, Della Street. He knew that the defendant had been staying with me and from what he said I gathered that . . . well, he wanted the luggage and I let him have it."

"And that luggage which you gave Perry Mason was the same which the defendant had left with you?"

"It was."

Hamilton Burger said, "I now hand you an overnight bag bearing the initials E.C. and ask you if you have ever seen that bag before?"

"Yes, sir."

"Where did you see it before?"

"In my apartment."

"When?"

"When Eleanor brought it to my apartment and again when I gave it to Perry Mason."

"Do you wish the Court and the jury to understand that this is one of the articles of baggage that you gave Mr. Perry Mason?"

"It is. Yes, sir."

"And it is the same bag that the defendant brought to your apartment?"

"Yes, sir."

"I show you a suitcase. Do you recognize it?"

"Yes, sir, that is the suitcase she brought with her to the apartment and one of the articles I gave Mr. Mason."

"And this two-suiter?"

"The same."

"I ask they be introduced in evidence, Your Honor."

"Any objection?" Judge Moran asked of Mason.

"Not to the bags, Your Honor. The contents have not been identified."

"The bags are now empty," Burger said with a smile. "I anticipated this objection by the defense."

"Then I have no objection to the bags being received in evidence," Mason said. "I feel certain they are the same bags the witness gave me."

Burger whirled suddenly to Perry Mason and said, "And now you may cross-examine, sir."

The district attorney walked over to the plaintiff's counsel table and flung himself into his seat, grinning at the smiling faces of two assistant district attorneys who flanked him on each side.

"Did you," Mason asked the district attorney, "intend to introduce that diagram in evidence?"

"I did."

"You mentioned that there was another witness who would identify it as to the Granger apartment."

"That is true."

"If you have that witness here," Mason said, "I would suggest that I defer my cross-examination of this witness until you have put this other witness on the stand, identified this diagram, and then I will be in a position to cross-examine the witness intelligently as to the position of the various rooms in the apartment."

"Very well," Hamilton Burger said. "Call Webley Richey. You may step down from the witness stand for a moment, Miss Belan. The testimony of Mr. Richey will be quite brief, and then you may resume the witness stand for cross-examination."

"Yes, sir," the witness said.

"Sit right here inside the rail," Judge Moran instructed. "Mr. Mason will want to proceed with his cross-examination as soon as Mr. Richey has been asked a few questions, which I take it, Mr. District Attorney, are in the nature of routine."

"That is right."

"Come forward and be sworn, Mr. Richey," Judge Moran said.

Mason, turning to look at the witness who was coming forward, said under his breath to Della Street, who was seated slightly behind him and to the right of the defendant, "Well, well, well, see who's here. The supercilious clerk who high-hatted us."

Richey came forward, was sworn, and gave his name, age, address and occupation to the court reporter, then looked up expectantly at the district attorney.

Hamilton Burger, his voice indicating to the jury that this was merely a matter of red tape brought about because of the annoying persistence of the defendant's counsel, said, "Now as I understand it your name is Webley Richey and you are employed as a clerk at the Belinda Apartments."

"Yes, sir."

"How long have you been so employed?"

"Something over two years."

"Are you familiar with the apartments on the third floor?"

"I am. Yes, sir."

"Do you know the tenant of apartment 358, Miss Suzanne Granger?"

"I do. Yes, sir."

"And Ethel Belan, the witness who has just testified?"

"Yes, sir."

"Are you familiar with the floor plan of the various apartments occupied by Suzanne Granger and by Ethel Belan?"

"I am. Yes, sir."

"I show you a diagram and ask you whether or not that diagram correctly designates the position of the various rooms in apartment 358 and in apartment 360?"

The witness glanced at the diagram and said, "It does. Yes, sir. The two apartments are identical except that the closet in one of the bedrooms in 360 is three and a half feet shorter than the other closets shown in this sketch map, otherwise the apartments are identical in plan."

"This map is a floor plan. Is it made to scale?"

"It is. Yes, sir."

"Who made it?"

"I did."

"At whose request?"

"At yours, sir."

"And it is a full, true and accurate descriptive diagram?"

"It is. Yes, sir."

"I ask that it be introduced in evidence," Hamilton Burger said. "That's all."

"Oh, just a moment," Mason said. "I have a few questions on cross-examination."

"But there can't be any objection to the diagram," Hamilton Burger said.

"I just want to find out a few things about the witness's background," Mason retorted.

"Very well, cross-examine," Judge Moran said, his voice indicating that he would consider any lengthy cross-examination an imposition on the time of the Court and the jury.

Richey faced Mason with the same supercilious, somewhat patronizing manner which he had displayed when he was behind the desk at the Belinda Apartments.

"Do you remember when you first saw me in August of this year?" Mason asked.

"Yes, sir. Very well."

"I asked for Miss Suzanne Granger, did I not?"

"Yes, sir."

"And you told me that she was out and could not be reached?"

"That is correct."

"I told you who I was and I told you I wanted to leave a message for her?"

"Yes, sir."

"Oh, just a moment, Your Honor," Hamilton Burger said. "This is hardly proper cross-examination. This witness was produced only for the purpose of testifying to a floor plan of an apartment. That floor plan is quite obviously correct. Counsel has made no objection to it. This cross-examination is incompetent, irrelevant and immaterial. It calls for matters not covered on the direct examination, and it is entirely out of order. It is simply consuming time."

"So it would seem," Judge Moran said. "I am inclined to agree with the prosecution, Mr. Mason."

"The object of this cross-examination," Mason said, "is simply to show bias on the part of the witness."

"But what good will that do since apparently there is no question as to the accuracy of the . . ."

Judge Moran caught himself just in time to keep from commenting on the evidence. He said somewhat testily, "Very well. Technically I believe you're within your rights, Counselor. Proceed. The objection is overruled."

"Let me ask this one question," Mason said. "As soon as I asked for Suzanne Granger didn't you step into a private glass-enclosed office, pick up a telephone and ring the apartment of Ethel Belan?"

Mason was unprepared for the expression of consternation which appeared on Richey's face.

"I . . . I have occasion to call many of the apartments."

Mason, suddenly realizing he had struck pay dirt, pressed on quickly. "I'm asking you did you or did you not at that particular time retire to your private office and call the apartment of Ethel Belan?"

"I . . . after all, Mr. Mason, I can't be expected to remember every apartment that I call. I . . ."

"I am asking you," Mason thundered, "whether or not at that particular time you did not retire to a glass-enclosed, private office and call the apartment of Ethel Belan? You can answer that question yes or no."

"Provided, of course, he remembers the occasion and what he did on that occasion," Hamilton Burger said, rushing to the witness's rescue.

"I can't remember," Richey said, flashing a grateful glance at the district attorney.

Mason smiled. "You might have remembered," he asked the witness, "if it hadn't been for the prompting by the district attorney?"

"Your Honor," Hamilton Burger protested, "I object to that question. It's not proper cross-examination."

"Well, I think the witness may answer it," Judge Moran said. "The jury, of course, saw the demeanor of the witness, heard the question and answer. You may answer that question, Mr. Richey."

"I . . . I can't remember calling Ethel Belan's apartment."

"You can't remember ever calling Ethel Belan's apartment?" Mason asked.

"Oh, yes. Naturally I call many of the apartments. I guess I have called many of the apartments many times."

"Then what do you mean by saying you can't remember?"

"I can't remember calling it on that particular occasion."

"Do you remember stepping into the glass-enclosed office?"

"No."

"Do you remember your conversation with me?"

"Yes."

"Do you remember what you did immediately following that conversation?"

"No."

"I will ask you," Mason said, "if at any time on that day you talked with Ethel Belan on the telephone and told her that Mr. Perry Mason, an attorney, was in the building and that he was asking for Suzanne Granger? Now you can remember if you did that. Answer yes or no. Did you or didn't you?"

"I . . . I don't think I did."

"Or did you use words having substantially that same meaning or effect?"

"I . . . I . . . I simply can't remember, Mr. Mason."

"Thank you," Mason said. "That's all. I will stipulate the diagram may be received in evidence. Now, as I understand it, Miss Belan is to take the stand for cross-examination."

Richey left the stand. Ethel Belan returned to the stand, settled herself and glanced at Perry Mason as much as to say, "All right. Come on. See what you can do with *me*."

"You're absolutely certain that the defendant had a revolver while she was in your apartment?"

"Absolutely certain."

"That it was a blued-steel revolver?"

"Yes."

"That it was a .38 caliber revolver?"

"Yes."

"In how many calibers are revolvers manufactured?" Mason asked.

"Why, I . . . I'm not an expert on guns. I don't know."

"What is the meaning of .38 caliber?" Mason asked. "What does it have reference to?"

"It's the way they describe a gun."

"Certainly it's the way they describe a gun," Mason said, "but what does it relate to? What does caliber mean?"

"It has something to do with the weight of the shells, doesn't it?"

"With the weight of the bullet?"

"Yes."

"In other words, a long, slender bullet would have a higher caliber than a short, thicker bullet if it weighed more?"

"Oh, Your Honor," Hamilton Burger said, "I object to this as an attempt to mislead the witness. This is not proper cross-examination. The witness has not qualified as an expert, and . . ."

"The objection is overruled," Judge Moran snapped. "The witness has described the revolver in the possession of the defendant as a .38 caliber revolver. Counsel is certainly entitled to find out what she means by .38 caliber."

"Go ahead," Mason said. "Answer the question."

"Why, if the bullet, if the long, slender bullet weighs more, why, it is a bigger caliber, that is, I think it is."

"That's what you mean by caliber?" Mason said.

"Yes, sir."

"So when you described the .38 caliber revolver, you

referred to a revolver shooting a bullet of a certain weight. Is that right?"

"Oh, Your Honor, this is certainly assuming facts not in evidence," Hamilton Burger said. "It is not proper cross-examination. It is an attempt to mislead the witness."

"Overruled," Judge Moran snapped. "Answer the question."

The witness glanced dubiously at the district attorney, then after some hesitancy, said, "Yes, sir. I believe so. Yes, sir."

"When you used the words .38 caliber you were describing only the weight of the bullet?"

"Yes, sir."

"Did you mean that the bullet weighed 38 grains?"

"I believe that is it. Yes, sir."

"You don't know whether the gun was a .38 caliber, a .32 caliber, or a .44 caliber, do you?"

"Well, it was described to me as a .38 caliber revolver," the witness said, obviously becoming confused.

"So you simply repeated the words that had been used to you. Is that right?"

"Yes, sir."

"And when you said it was a .38 caliber revolver you didn't know whether it was a .38 caliber revolver or a .32 caliber revolver or a .44 caliber revolver, did you?"

"Well, the district attorney told me . . ."

"Not what someone told you but what you know of your own knowledge," Mason said. "Do you know?"

"Well, I guess, if you want to come right down to it, I'm a little hazy about what caliber means."

"Then you don't know whether the defendant had a .38 caliber revolver, a .32 caliber revolver or a .44 caliber revolver, do you?"

"Well, if you want to put it that way, I don't," the witness snapped.

Mason said, "That's the way I want to put it. And now we'll see if your recollection is any better than that of Webley Richey. Do you remember the occasion when Mr. Richey telephoned you and said that Perry Mason, the lawyer, was in the building, asking questions, that he

141

was inquiring for Suzanne Granger but that there was a possibility he might be very suspicious of the facts, but that he, Richey, had got rid of Mason and you wouldn't be bothered with him? Now those may not be the exact words, but I will express it as having been in words to that effect purely for the purpose of identifying the conversation. Do you remember the occasion of that conversation?"

She tilted her head back. Her chin came up. For a moment her eyes were defiant. Then, as she met the steady gaze of Mason's eyes, saw the granite-hard lines of his face, she wavered, lowered her eyes and said, "Yes, I remember it."

"Do you remember the date and the hour?"

"It was on the seventeenth day of August, sometime in the afternoon. I don't remember exactly what time."

"But you can place the time with reference to the time when I called on you," Mason said. "It was immediately before, wasn't it?"

"That depends on what you mean by immediately."

"If you want to quibble," Mason said, "we'll say that it was within approximately ten or fifteen minutes of the time I called on you."

"Well . . . oh, all right, have it your own way."

"It isn't my way, or your way, or Richey's way," Mason said. "It's a question of what is the truth. That's what the judge and the jury want to know."

"Well, he called me and said something along those lines. Yes."

"What is the connection between you and Richey?" Mason asked.

"Your Honor, I object to that as incompetent, irrelevant and immaterial, not proper cross-examination."

Judge Moran hesitated for a moment, then said, "The objection is sustained."

Mason, looking surprised and hurt so that the jury would be sure to note the expression on his face, sat down and turned to Della Street.

"I want to quit this cross-examination at a point where the jurors feel that my hands are being tied by Hamilton

Burger's objections and the Court's rulings. I want them to feel that there is something important in this case that is being withheld from them, some sinister something in the background. I think this is a good time to quit. I'm whispering to you now so they'll think I'm conferring with you on a point where we have a lot at stake."

Della Street nodded.

"Now shake your head gravely," Mason said.

She did as he instructed.

Mason sighed, made a little gesture of weary dismissal with his hands, said, "Well, of course, Your Honor, this is a part of the case which the defendant considered vital."

He glanced down at Della Street again, shrugged his shoulders, said, "Very well, if that is the ruling of the Court I have no further questions."

"The Court doesn't intend to close any doors," Judge Moran said, suddenly suspicious that Mason had jockeyed him into a position where there was error in the record. "You are at liberty to reframe the question."

"Did you tell Webley Richey all about your agreement with the defendant?" Mason asked.

"Objected to as calling for hearsay evidence, as not proper cross-examination, as calling for matter which is incompetent, irrelevant and immaterial," Burger said.

"I will permit the question on the ground that it may be preliminary as to the bias of the witness," Judge Moran ruled.

"Answer the question," Mason said.

"Well, in a way, yes."

"And did he advise you?"

"Same objection," Burger snapped.

Judge Moran's fingertips moved slowly along the angle of his jaw. "What a third person may have told this witness is something else. You may answer the question yes or no —only as to whether he did advise you."

"Yes."

"What did he tell you?"

"Objected to, Your Honor. This is plainly hearsay, incompetent . . ."

"I think so. The objection is sustained," Judge Moran said.

"Did you ask for and receive his advice prior to the date when the defendant was first taken into custody?"

Burger said doggedly, "I object on the ground that it is incompetent, irrelevant and immaterial, that the question is vague and indefinite and it is not proper cross-examination."

Judge Moran debated the matter in his own mind. "Can you reframe your question, Mr. Mason?"

"No, Your Honor."

Judge Moran glanced somewhat dubiously at the district attorney.

"I feel that my objection is well taken, Your Honor," Hamilton Burger said. "I think it is quite obvious that counsel is merely on a fishing expedition. If there is any agreement in connection with the testimony in this case, any agreement in connection with the facts in this case, he can so specify."

"My question is broad enough to include all of those things," Mason said.

"Too broad," Hamilton Burger retorted. "It covers everything. I contend, Your Honor, that the question is not proper cross-examination. I am quite willing to accept a ruling to that effect for the record."

"Very well," Judge Moran ruled. "The Court will sustain the objection."

"That's all," Mason said.

"That's all," Hamilton Burger snapped.

The witness started to leave the stand, then Burger, with every appearance of sudden recollection, said, "Oh, no, it isn't either. There's one other matter. I should have brought this out on my direct examination. I beg pardon of Court and counsel. I overlooked the matter. One of my assistants has just called my attention to the oversight."

"Very well, you may ask your question," Judge Moran ruled.

Hamilton Burger faced the witness. "Did you at any time see the defendant in the possession of any articles

144

other than this revolver—articles of some extraordinary value?"

"Yes."

"What?"

"She had a large number of precious stones."

Hamilton Burger appeared excited. "Precious stones, did you say?"

"That's right."

The jurors were now sitting forward on their chairs, watching the witness with fascination.

"Where were you when you saw these?" Burger asked.

"I had started to go into her bedroom. The door was slightly ajar. The hinges had been well oiled. She didn't hear me."

"And what was she doing?"

"She had a pile of gem stones on some paper tissues on the bed. She was kneeling by the bed. Her back was to me. She was counting the gems."

"How many gems?"

"Quite a number."

"Did she know you had seen her?"

"No, sir. I backed out as soon as I realized I was intruding. I gently closed the door and she never realized . . ."

"Never mind what she did or didn't realize," Burger interrupted. "You're not a mind reader. You saw those stones?"

"Yes, sir."

"You don't know what became of those gems?"

"No, sir."

"But you did see them in the defendant's possession?"

"Yes, sir."

"And for all you know these stones could have been contained in the luggage you delivered to Perry Mason?"

"Objected to as argumentative, assuming a fact not in evidence, leading and suggestive and utterly incompetent, irrelevant and immaterial," Mason said.

"Sustained."

"Cross-examine," Hamilton Burger snapped.

Mason hesitated a long moment, said to Della Street,

"There's a trap here, Della, but I'm going to have to face it. He's making it appear I am afraid to have the facts brought out about those gems, that *I'm* keeping things from the jury. Well, here we go."

Mason slowly rose from his seat at the counsel table, walked over to the corner of the table and stood looking at the witness.

"You stood in the door of the room?" he asked.

"Yes."

"And saw these gems on the bed?"

"Yes."

"A distance of how many feet?"

"Perhaps ten feet."

"You saw they were gems?"

"Yes, sir."

"What kind?"

"Diamonds and emeralds and a few rubies."

"How many real gems have you ever owned in your life?" Mason asked.

"I . . . well, I have some chip diamonds."

"Were these chip diamonds?"

"No."

"How many full-cut diamonds have you ever owned?"

The witness averted her eyes.

"How many?" Mason asked.

"None," she confessed.

"How many genuine rubies have you ever owned?"

"One. That is, it was given to me. I . . . I supposed it was genuine."

"How long did you have it in your possession?"

"I still have it."

"When was it given to you?"

"Ten years ago."

"Is it genuine?"

"I have assumed that it is. I tell you, Mr. Mason, that it was given to me and so I don't know. I have assumed it is a genuine ruby."

"How about these rubies on the bed," Mason asked, "were they genuine rubies, costume jewelry or imitations?"

"They were rubies."

"Genuine?"

"Yes, sir. At least that is my impression. I am testifying now to the best of my ability."

"Exactly," Mason said. "And you have gone over your testimony many times with the district attorney?"

"I have told him what happened. I haven't gone over my testimony."

"You have told him what you expected to testify to?"

"Well, in a way."

"You have told him *everything* that happened, haven't you?"

"Yes."

"And you have told him that those were genuine rubies?"

"Yes."

"You were within ten feet of them?"

"Yes."

"No closer than that?"

"No, I suppose not."

"How long were you standing in the door?"

"Perhaps for ten seconds."

"Now this ruby that you own. How is that mounted? Is it in a ring?"

"Yes."

"The ruby is perhaps your birthstone?"

"Yes."

"And there is a certain sentimental attachment in connection with that particular ruby?"

"Yes."

"And you have worn it and looked at it many times?"

"Yes."

"Within a matter of inches from your eyes?"

"Yes."

"And yet," Mason said, "you still don't know whether *that* ruby is genuine. Yet you want this jury to believe that you could stand ten feet away and look at an assortment of gems for not more than ten seconds and unhesitatingly testify that each and every one of the gems was genuine. Is that right?"

"Well, I . . . of course, when you put it that way it sounds absurd."

"It sounds absurd because it is absurd," Mason said. "You aren't an expert on gems."

"No, but you can tell whether gems are genuine or not."

"How?"

"Well, you know instinctively. You can tell from the way they sparkle."

"But you didn't know instinctively about this ruby that you've possessed for ten years. You simply assume it's genuine. You don't know whether it's a synthetic ruby or an imitation ruby or what it is."

"Well, I . . . it was different from the rubies that I saw there."

"In what way?"

"Those rubies had more fire."

"Then you assume that this gem you have been familiar with for ten years is not genuine, that it is an imitation of some sort, a synthetic?"

"I don't know."

"How many gems were there on the bed?"

"I would say, oh, perhaps fifty."

"There could have been more?"

"There certainly could. There might have been as many as seventy-five."

"If you had seventy-five gems to inspect in ten seconds you must have inspected them at the rate of better than seven a second. Isn't that true?"

"I suppose so."

"You know, do you not, that it takes an expert jeweler many seconds of examination with a magnifying glass to tell whether a gem is genuine or not?"

"Well, I suppose so."

"Yet you, without any knowledge of gems, without ever having possessed genuine gems, with the exception of one ruby that you don't know is genuine, want to put yourself in the position of swearing absolutely that you looked at from fifty to seventy-five stones ten feet away in a period of ten seconds, and are willing to pronounce each and every one of them genuine?"

"I didn't say that. I can't pronounce each and every one of them genuine."

"How many of them were spurious?"

"I don't know."

"What percentage of them was spurious?"

"I don't know."

"How many of them were genuine?"

"I don't know."

"Was one of them genuine?"

"Yes, of course."

"Were two of them genuine?"

"I tell you I don't know."

"Exactly," Mason said. "You don't know whether any of them was genuine or not, do you?"

"I think they were."

"You knew instinctively, is that right?"

"Yes."

"You simply saw them as a glittering pile of gems?"

"Yes."

"That's all," Mason said, smiling at the jury.

Hamilton Burger came forward, a triumphant smirk on his face.

"Now assuming for the sake of this question that Douglas Hepner was killed on the sixteenth of August at about five o'clock in the afternoon, did you see these gems before or after his death?"

"Objected to as incompetent, irrelevant and immaterial, argumentative evidence," Mason said angrily. "I assign the asking of that question as prejudicial misconduct and ask the Court to advise the jury to disregard it."

Judge Moran's face was stern. "The objection is sustained. The jury will disregard the question."

"Very well," Hamilton Burger said. "*When* did you see these gems?"

"On the sixteenth of August."

"At what time?"

"At about six o'clock in the evening."

"That's all."

"No further questions," Mason said.

"That's all," Hamilton Burger said. "We will now call Miss Suzanne Granger to the stand."

Suzanne Granger came forward and was sworn.

"You are the Suzanne Granger who occupies apartment 358 in the Belinda Apartments?"

"Yes, sir."

"Is that Mrs. or Miss Granger?"

"Miss."

"You are living alone in an apartment there?"

"Yes."

"You have been to Europe on several occasions?"

"I am interested in art. I spend what time and what money I can afford in European museums studying pigmentation, the work of the old masters, and gathering data which I do not care to reveal in advance of the book I am writing on the subject."

"You recently returned from Europe?"

"I did."

"And while you were on shipboard did you meet Douglas Hepner?"

"That is right."

"Now you became friendly with Douglas Hepner?"

"There was a shipboard friendship, yes."

"And then what happened?"

"Then I didn't see Douglas for . . . oh, a few weeks and then I happened to run into him and he asked me for a date and . . ."

"Now when was this that he asked you for a date?"

"That was during the latter part of July."

"And then what?"

"I went out to dinner with him two or three times and he told me . . ."

"Now I don't think we're entitled to have his conversation introduced in evidence," Hamilton Burger said with a great show of legal virtue, "but I think you can testify as to the relationship which developed."

"Well, he became friendly to the extent of confiding in me."

"You were out with him several times?"

150

"That's right."

"And at times he returned with you to your apartment?"

"Naturally he saw me home."

"And came into your apartment for a nightcap?"

"That's right. I invited him in as a matter of common courtesy and he always accepted."

"Now then," Hamilton Burger said, "we are somewhat handicapped by not being able to show the conversations which took place, but I will ask you if on occasion Douglas Hepner discussed the defendant, Eleanor Corbin, with you?"

"Indeed he did."

"Now, of course," Hamilton Burger said, "I feel that we are not entitled to bring those conversations into evidence except that I will ask you if at any time during any of those conversations he ever referred to Eleanor Corbin as his wife?"

"Indeed he did not. In fact, on the contrary he . . ."

"Never mind, never mind," Hamilton Burger said, holding up his hand, palm outward, as though he were a traffic officer flagging down oncoming traffic. "I want to keep the examination within strictly legal limits. Since it was claimed that the defendant was his wife I am simply asking you whether he ever referred to her as his wife. You have said he did not. That answers the question. Now then, I am going to ask you about something that *is* proper. Did you ever have a conversation with the defendant about Douglas Hepner?"

"I did. Yes, sir."

"And when was that?"

"That was about the fifteenth of August."

"And what was said?"

"I . . . well, Douglas had been calling on me and then when he left I noticed that the door of apartment 360 opened just a crack so that the defendant could watch him as he walked down the hall and . . ."

"How did you know it was the defendant who was watching?"

"Because . . . well, because I knew she had moved in with Ethel Belan for the purpose of spying . . ."

151

"Never mind the purpose," Burger interrupted, "that's a conclusion of the witness. Your Honor, I ask that the witness be instructed to confine her answers to the question and not volunteer information."

"Very well," the witness said with hostility. "I knew that the defendant had moved in with Ethel Belan. I knew that on almost every occasion that Douglas left my apartment the door would open. Since there would have been no way of knowing exactly when he was going unless she had some means of listening in on conversations I knew what was happening."

"And on this particular occasion what happened?"

"As soon as Douglas had entered the elevator and before she had a chance to close the door I walked over and pushed the door open."

"And who was standing on the other side of the door?"

"Eleanor Corbin."

"You mean the defendant in this action?"

"Yes, sir."

"That is the woman sitting beside Mr. Perry Mason, there at the defense counsel table?"

"Yes."

"Go ahead, tell us what happened."

"I told the defendant she was making a fool of herself. I said, 'You can't hold a man that way. You're just a jealous, frustrated fool, and furthermore I want you to quit listening to what goes on in my apartment. I'm not going to have you or anyone else listening in on my private conversations. I think there's a law against that, and if I have to I'm going to do something about it.'"

"And what did the defendant say?"

"The defendant became furious. She told me that I was a tramp, that I was trying to steal Douglas away from her, that like all men he was an opportunist and that I was deliberately providing an opportunity."

"Did she say anything at that time about being married to Douglas Hepner?"

"She said she wanted to marry him. She said that if she couldn't have him nobody would have him."

"Did she make any threats?"

152

"Oh, I don't remember all that she said. Yes, of course, she made threats. She threatened to kill both him and me. She said that she would kill Douglas if I tried to take him away from her—something to the effect that if she couldn't have him no one else could."

"Was anyone else present at that conversation?"

"Just the two of us were actually present at the time."

"Did the defendant say anything about how she proposed to carry out her threats?"

"Yes, indeed. She opened her purse. She showed me a revolver and said she was a desperate woman and that it wasn't safe to trifle with her, or words to that effect."

"What did she have in her purse?"

"A revolver."

"I call your atention to Plaintiff's Exhibit G and ask you if you have ever seen that revolver before?"

"I don't know. I've seen one that looks very much like it."

"Where?"

"In the defendant's handbag."

"And what happened after this conversation?"

"I turned around and went back into my apartment."

"I think," Hamilton Burger said, "you may now cross-examine this witness, Mr. Mason."

And Burger went back and seated himself at his counsel table, smiling to himself, his face radiating complete self-satisfaction.

Mason said, "You instituted this conversation, did you, Miss Granger?"

"You mean I took the initiative in bringing it about?"

"Yes."

"I most certainly did. I was tired of being spied upon and I intended to put a stop to it."

"Did anyone else hear this conversation? Was Miss Belan present?"

"Miss Belan was away. The defendant was alone in the apartment."

"In other words," Mason said, smiling easily, "it's only your word against hers. You . . ."

"I am not accustomed to having my word doubted," Suzanne Granger said indignantly.

"The point, however, is that no one else heard this conversation," Mason said.

"In that you are wrong," she retorted acidly. "I was the only other person present but Mr. Richey overheard the conversation and later remonstrated with me about it. He said that this was a high-class apartment house and people didn't have brawls . . ."

"Never mind what someone else said to you," Mason said. "That is hearsay. I am asking you if anyone else was present at that conversation."

"Mr. Richey was in an adjoining apartment. The door was open and he heard the entire conversation."

"That's all," Mason said.

"Just a minute," Hamilton Burger said. "You didn't tell me about Mr. Richey having heard the conversation."

"You didn't ask me."

"After all," Mason said, "it's a conclusion as far as this witness is concerned. *She* doesn't know that Richey heard the conversation."

"Well, he certainly came to me afterward and remonstrated with me about . . ."

"There, there, that will do," Hamilton Burger said. "Your Honor, this opens up a very interesting phase of this case that I hadn't known about before. Why didn't you tell me, Miss Granger?"

"Tell you about what?"

"About the fact that someone else was present at this conversation?"

"He wasn't present. He only heard it. And besides I'm not accustomed to having my word doubted."

"But this is a court of law," Hamilton Burger said.

She gave her head a little toss and said, "I told you what happened and I told the truth."

"Very well," Hamilton Burger said. "That's all."

The district attorney glanced at the clock, said, "Your Honor, I know it is early but I think the prosecution will rest its case within the next few minutes after court reconvenes. However, there are certain points I would like

154

to check over with my associates to make certain that I have introduced all of the evidence that I desire to produce at this time. I think the Court will agree that the case is moving very expeditiously and, of course, the Court will realize that a prosecutor is always faced with a problem at such a time as to what evidence is legitimately a part of his case in chief and what should be saved for rebuttal. I feel, therefore, that I am justified in asking the Court to recess at this time until two o'clock this afternoon so that I may check over my evidence. I feel certain that the prosecution will rest its case not later than two-thirty."

"Very well," Judge Moran ruled. "Court will take a recess until two o'clock this afternoon, predicated on the statement of the district attorney that he expects to rest his case by two-thirty."

Mason turned to the policewoman who was approaching to take charge of the defendant. "I want to talk with the defendant a little while," he said. "I would like to go into the witness room."

"Very well, Mr. Mason," she said. "It's early, so I can give you fifteen or twenty minutes."

"I think that will be enough," Mason said.

He nodded to Della Street, and said to Eleanor, "Please step this way, Mrs. Hepner."

Eleanor followed him into the witness room.

Mason kicked the door closed.

"All right," he said, "this is it."

"What is?"

"Quit stalling," Mason said. "They've jerked the rug out from under you. Now I'm not a magician. This is the time when I have to know what happened. The district attorney is going to rest his case at two-thirty this afternoon. He has a perfect case of first-degree murder. If you don't go on the stand you're licked. If you do go on the stand and testify to this amnesia business they'll rip you wide open. If you admit that telephone conversation with Ethel Belan you're a gone goose. It shows your amnesia is just a dodge.

"If you deny that conversation the district attorney probably has switchboard records from the hospital to show that you called Ethel Belan's number. You must have slipped the call through while the nurse was out of the room.

"He also has a bunch of psychiatrists who have examined you and will swear your loss of memory is merely a defensive pose. Now then. I have to know the truth."

She avoided his eyes. "Why did he want an adjournment at this time?" she asked.

"Because," he said, "he wants to check with Richey and see if Richey overheard that conversation. If Richey did and if his recollection coincides with that of Suzanne Granger's he's going to put Richey on the stand. Otherwise, he'll fumble around with a few platitudes and state that after checking with his associates he feels that they have introduced all of the evidence they care to in chief and that the balance of evidence will be saved for rebuttal, that therefore the prosecution rests its case."

"You think I'm not telling the truh about not being able to remember, don't you, Mr. Mason?"

Mason shrugged his shoulders and said, "It's your funeral, and," he added, "I mean that literally. It will be your funeral. They can return a verdict that will mean you're strapped into the little steel chair in a small, glass-windowed cubbyhole. Then everyone will withdraw. The door will clang shut and you'll hear the clank of an iron gate as the cyanide pellets are dropped into the acid. Then you'll hear a little hissing and . . ."

"Don't!" she screamed. "Don't do that to me. Good God, don't you suppose I've sweated through this thing in a nightmare night after night?"

"I'm telling you now," Mason said, "because this is the last time. This is the last opportunity anyone has to help you. Now then, you go ahead. It's your move."

Eleanor glanced at Della Street. Her glance was that of a trapped animal.

"Want a cigarette?" Della asked.

Eleanor nodded.

Della gave her a cigarette and lit it for her. Eleanor took in a deep breath. She exhaled a cloud of smoke, said, "It's so damn bad, Mr. Mason, that if I tell it to you you'll walk out on me."

"Tell it to me," Mason said.

"It's the truth," she said.

"What is?"

"What they've been saying."

"The story the witnesses have been telling?"

She nodded.

"You killed him?" Mason asked.

"I didn't kill him, but what good is it going to do for me to say so?"

"Suppose," Mason said kindly, "you start at the beginning and tell me the truth, but condense it into a capsule because we aren't going to have much time. I'll ask you questions about the parts I want you to elaborate."

She said, "I've always been rather wild. I've been in a few scrapes in my time. My father is conservative. He values his good name, his standing in the community and things of that sort.

"Coming over from Europe I met Douglas Hepner. Father didn't like him. One thing led to another. Father told me that if I married Doug Hepner I was finished as far as any financial connection with the family was concerned. He had been paying me a rather generous allowance but he'd threatened to stop it several times, and this time he really meant business."

"Go on," Mason said. "What happened?"

"Doug and I were in love—not so much on shipboard, that was one of those shipboard affairs. He was pretty much in demand as a dancing partner and . . . well, I thought it was a shipboard crush, but it wasn't. It was the real thing as far as I'm concerned and I supposed it was with him."

"Go on," Mason said.

"All right, it began to be serious and we talked a lot about getting married. Dad told me that if I married Doug I might just as well wash my hands of the family."

"Did Hepner tell you what his occupation was—how he made a living?"

"Yes."

"When?"

"The last few weeks—when we were talking about getting married. He told me a lot of things about himself. He'd been a rolling stone. He was an adventurer and an opportunist. He'd gone in for this stuff that he called being a free-lance detective. He was finding out about smuggled stones and getting a reward."

"Go on," Mason said.

"Well, this Suzanne Granger—I hate that woman."

"Never mind that," Mason said. "You haven't time for that. Go on, tell me what happened."

"Well, anyhow, Doug got the idea that Suzanne Granger was the head of a huge smuggling ring. Don't ask me how he got the idea because I don't know. I don't know what evidence he had."

"Did he work hand in glove with the Customs people?" Mason asked. "Perhaps they tipped him off."

"No, I don't think so. The Customs people had absolutely no suspicion of Suzanne Granger. They let her breeze through Customs with as much deference as though she'd been a visiting potentate. She's one of those queenly, aristocratic women who always want to be better than the other person, want to get the other person on the defensive."

Mason said, "Try and forget how much you hate her and give me the facts and give them to me fast."

"Well, Doug said that if he could break up that smuggling ring Suzanne was in he could make enough from the reward to buy an interest in an importing company. He knew of one he could pick up cheap from a friend of his, and with his knowledge and connections he could build it up to something really big."

"He thought Suzanne Granger was a smuggler?"

"Either she was the big smuggler or she had the contact. I think he thought she was the big smuggler."

"So what did he do?"

"He told me that he'd have to be free to date Suzanne. He said he wouldn't get too involved with her, he'd just date her and sound her out so he could get access to her apartment. He told me that he was going to have associates search her apartment. In order to do that he had to be sure. He wanted to be where he could listen to what went on in her apartment. He had a listening device, some sort of a microphone with electronic amplification that he could press against the wall of the bedroom in Ethel's apartment and hear everything that went on in Suzanne Granger's apartment.

"So he and I worked out this plan. I was to pose as a jealous, frustrated woman. I made a deal with Ethel Belan to get into her apartment.

"Well, somehow something happened and Suzanne Granger learned that I was in the adjoining apartment. I don't know how, but Doug knew. I guess she must have told Doug I was in there snooping."

"So then what?"

"So then Doug told me to plan on leaving the apartment for long periods of time. In that way Suzanne Granger would think the coast was clear and she would go on making her plans to dispose of the smuggled stones.

"The man who runs the freight elevator hates the snobs in the front office and Doug bribed him. In that way Doug could ride up in the freight elevator without anyone knowing about it.

.. "So what would happen, Ethel would leave and go to work. She works as some sort of a buyer in a department store. After she'd gone I'd put on my things and go out in the hallway, making a lot of noise, then I'd take the elevator down and walk right past the desk. I was there as a guest, not as a tenant, but I'd contrive to let the girl at the switchboard know I expected to be out all day. Then I'd go out and usually stay out."

"And Douglas would move in?"

She nodded. "He'd go up in the freight elevator and take over."

"But he *could* have gone to Suzanne Granger's apartment."

"If he wanted to he could have."

"And for all you know, he did."

"Well, if he'd been doing that why would he have

159

asked me to get in Ethel Belan's apartment in the first place?"

Mason thought that over.

"He had a key?" he asked.

"Of course he had a key. I gave him my key long enough to have a duplicate key made. If you'll examine the keys that he had on him at the time of his death I'm certain you'll find that one of the keys fits Ethel Belan's apartment."

"The police don't know that?" Mason asked.

"Apparently so far the police don't know it."

"And, of course, Ethel Belan had no idea that Doug was using her apartment as a listening post to monitor what went on in Suzanne Granger's apartment."

"No, of course not, that's why Douglas was supposed to be hot and heavy after Suzanne and I was supposed to be there eating my heart out and listening and trying to catch them out.

"We had to play it that way because Ethel's a rattle-brained little biddy who would have spilled the beans if she'd had any inkling of what was going on.

"Even as it was, Ethel Belan began to be a little suspicious. She thought that Doug had been visiting me in the apartment while she was out and wondered if my jealousy wasn't an act trying to cover up something. She talked a little bit to Suzanne Granger and Doug got terribly afraid that Suzanne was smart enough to put two and two together.

"So Doug told me to arrange a scene where I was to goad Suzanne into saying something to me, then I was to open my purse and show her my gun and make threats against everybody and everything and put on the act of a jealous woman, the neurotic type who can be dangerous.

"Well, I did that and it worked. I don't know just what happened because within half an hour of the time we had that scene Doug doubled back to the apartment and put the listening device on and listened and seemed to be tickled to death with what he heard. He told me that he thought he knew the answer. He told me to let him have my gun and go out and that he'd get in touch with me later on."

"And you gave him your gun?"

"Of course," she said. "I'd give him anything he asked for."

"You weren't married, were you?"

"We were going to be married as soon as . . ."

"But you *weren't* married!"

"Doug said we'd have to wait, but on that trip to Yuma and Las Vegas we traveled as man and wife."

"Why did you say you were married?"

"Doug said it was like a common law marriage and he told me to wire the family from Yuma. We didn't want any fuss."

"And the car wreck?" Mason asked.

"That was a fib. I made that up."

"But his car was smashed."

"I know. That's where I got the idea of the wreck. I had to have something to use for an excuse to account for my loss of memory."

"When did his car get smashed?"

"Sunday evening—the night before he died. A big truck rounded a curve and came straight for him. It's a wonder Doug wasn't killed. That's what the truck driver was trying to do.

"You see, this is a regular smuggling gang and . . . well, they play dirty. I wanted Doug to quit then because it showed they were after him. That's when I gave him the gun. He promised he would if he couldn't crack the case within a couple more days, but he thought he was on the point of making a big stake that would get us started in this new business."

"You gave him your gun when he asked for it and what did you do?"

"I went out."

"And when did you come back?"

She lowered her eyes. "Later."

"How much later?"

"Quite a bit later."

"Was Doug there when you came back?"

"No."

"Was Ethel Belan?"

"No, she was away for the week end and wasn't coming back until Monday."

"Now what about those gems?" Mason asked. "How did you get them?"

"Mr. Mason, you've got to believe me. That story about the gems is absolutely completely cockeyed. I never had any gems. I never saw any gems. She's lying when she says she saw me with those gems."

Mason's eyes were cold. "You didn't conceal them anywhere in your baggage?"

"Don't be silly, Mr. Mason. I'm telling you the truth now."

"You've told me that before."

"On my word of honor."

"You've said that before too."

"You just have to believe me."

"I can't believe you," Mason said. "There's too much corroborative evidence against you. I've got to fight this case through. They've got you dead to rights. They've caught you in a whole series of lies. They have proven that Doug Hepner was killed with your gun, that within a very short time prior to his death you had stated that he was your boy friend, that Suzanne Granger was stealing him, that if you couldn't have him nobody else could, and that you'd kill him rather than give him up."

"I know," she said, "but I've tried to tell you . . . that was what Doug told me to say, that was an act I was putting on at his request."

"There's only one person who can save you from the death cell by corroborating your story on that," Mason said.

"Who's that?"

"Doug Hepner, and he's dead. If you're telling the truth you put yourself in the power of fate when you told that story, and if you're not telling the truth . . ."

"But I am, Mr. Mason. I'm telling you the absolute truth."

"You're lying about those gems."

162

"I'm not, Mr. Mason."

"But suppose they should find those gems—perhaps in your baggage?"

"Well, I guess I'd be on my way to the gas chamber. It would be the final corroboration of Ethel Belan's story that would . . . it would make people think that Doug had recovered gems and I'd stolen them from Doug and . . . well, it would just be a mess that nobody could get out of."

"You're in a mess now," Mason said, "and I don't see how anyone can get you out of it."

"Can't I tell them the truth? Can't I tell them that Doug told me to put on that act? Can't I tell them that Doug was sort of a detective for the Customs officials? Can't we bring on the Customs officials to corroborate that? Can't we at least insinuate that Suzanne Granger was a smuggler?

"I understand that while she was gone on a trip to Las Vegas her apartment was broken into and all the tubes of paint were cut open. Couldn't she have had gems in the tubes of paint?"

"She could have," Mason said. "Who accompanied Suzanne to Las Vegas?"

"That's something I don't know."

"But if we do that," Mason said, "and if we should by any strange chance get anyone on the jury to believe us, then that story told by Ethel Belan about you having that assortment of gems in your possession would make it appear that *you* were the one who had gone into the apartment and cut open the tubes of paint, that *you* were the one who had recovered the gems, that *you* had tried to hold out on Douglas Hepner, and that had resulted in a fight and that you had killed Hepner."

"But she's lying about the gems."

"All right, let's pass that for a moment," Mason said wearily. "Now I want the real story of why you were running around in the park in the moonlight, making come-hither gestures to masculine motorists . . ."

"But I wasn't, Mr. Mason. I was appealing for help. I was trying to get the *woman* to follow me."

"It didn't look that way," Mason said. "When the woman followed you, you started screaming and . . ."

"She didn't follow me, she was chasing me. She was chasing me with a jack handle."

"Well, why did you want her to follow you?" Mason asked.

"I wanted her to find Doug's body."

"You what?" Mason asked, his voice showing his utter incredulity.

"I wanted her to find Doug's body. I was going to lead her to it."

"You knew that Doug was there, dead?"

"Yes, of course."

"How did you know that?"

"Because Doug and I had a rendezvous there in the park. Whenever anything happened and we got signals mixed or we wanted to communicate with each other we'd meet there at that place in the park.

"When I went there this night, Doug was lying there dead and my gun was right there beside him."

"Well," she said, "of course it was a terrific shock to me, but . . . well, instantly I saw the spot I was in, Mr. Mason. I had been trapped into making that statement to Suzanne only the day before—understand, when I say I was trapped, I mean that events had trapped me. I don't mean that Doug had anything to do with it.

"But there I was. I'd sworn that I was going to kill Doug and that if I couldn't have him no one else would and all of that stuff and I'd exhibited my gun—and, of course, it *was* my gun. I'd had it in my possession and then I'd given it to Doug when he asked for it. Someone must have followed him there to the park where he went to meet me, overpowered him, pulled the gun out of his pocket and shot him in the back of the head.

"There was his body lying there, with my gun beside it. I simply didn't know what to do."

"I can well imagine," Mason said dryly. "Now tell us what you did do, and for once try telling the truth."

"I picked up the gun and carried it over to where I could bury it. I was terribly afraid that they'd pick me up while I had the gun in my possession. I knew that every minute, every second that I had that gun in my possession I was in a very, very vulnerable position.

"I finally found a place where I could bury it where a ground squirrel or something had dug down in the ground. I shoved it way down in this hole and then kicked dirt in on top of it and put dry leaves and sticks over the top of the ground so I didn't think there was one chance in a million anyone could find it."

"And then?" Mason asked.

"Then I knew that I was in a spot. I didn't know what to do and I was in a panic. When you get in a panic like that you just can't think clearly."

"What did you think you were trying to do?"

"Well, I felt that if I should be found out there in the park without any clothes on, I could tell a story about having been out there with Doug and having been assaulted by a strange man who killed Doug and attempted to rape me, that I fought my way clear and was wandering around in a semi-dazed condition."

"Go on," Mason said.

"So I rushed back to the apartment," she said, "took my clothes and literally tore them off of me. Then I borrowed one of Ethel's raincoats and walked over to the park. I kicked up a bunch of the ground as though there'd been a struggle and left the clothes scattered around. Then I hid the raincoat and went out across the park until I saw a car that was parked. Then I came toward it, making motions to the woman. I felt that I should act as though I were too modest to come out where the man could see me. I was appealing for feminine help and . . . well, you know what happened. The woman started after me with a jack handle thinking I was being promiscuous and trying to vamp her boy friend. I ran, and I guess I was screaming, and managed to get away from her.

"Then I realized I was in a devil of a mess. I couldn't make the same approach again and I thought I'd just better go back to the apartment and try something else. So I picked up my clothes and wadded them into a small

165

bundle and stuffed them down another ground squirrel hole and put earth on them and . . . ."

"Where are they now?" Mason asked.

"As far as I know they're in that same ground squirrel hole."

"Then what?"

"Then I picked up this raincoat where I'd hidden it, where I felt certain it wouldn't be found, put it on and started back to Ethel's apartment and . . . well, that's when fate started taking a hand in the game. That's when everything I did went wrong. Police picked me up and I just didn't know what to say. I certainly was in a position where I needed time to stall.

"I'd been in a jam once before and had pulled this business about a loss of memory and a friendly doctor had helped me along with it and I'd got by very nicely. I felt that that would establish something in the way of a precedent, that I could show I had these attacks of amnesia and . . . well, that's what I did."

Mason said, "Eleanor, do you expect anyone on earth to believe that story?"

She avoided his eyes for a moment, then looked at him.

"No," she admitted, "not now."

"If you get on the stand and try to tell that story to the jury," Mason said, "the district attorney will rip you up with cross-examination, he'll show that you've lied before, time and time again, he'll show the utter, weird improbability of that story, and he'll convict you of first-degree murder."

"As I see it," she said, looking him squarely in the eyes, "it's all a question of whether we can shake Ethel Belan's story about me having those gems. If I had them then, of course, people will think that I recovered the gems while Suzanne Granger was in Las Vegas, and that because I was having a fight with Doug or something of that sort I tried to keep them all and Doug and I quarreled."

"Exactly," Mason said dryly. "On rebuttal or cross-examination it's going to come out what Doug Hepner actually did for a living. The district attorney has been

166

holding back on that. If you take the stand he'll crucify you with it on cross-examination. If you don't take the stand he'll bring it out if I put on any evidence at all."

"But if you don't put on any evidence at all then he can't bring it out, can he?"

"If I don't put on any evidence at all," Mason said, "he won't need to."

"Well, I've told you the truth. That's all I can do."

"This is your last chance to tell the whole truth."

"I've told it."

Mason got to his feet. "Come on, Della," he said.

At the door he nodded to the policewoman. "That's all."

■ **14** ■

MASON, DELLA STREET AND PAUL DRAKE SAT HUDDLED in the restaurant booth, engaged in low-voiced conversation.

"What are you going to do?" Drake asked.

"I'm damned if I know," Mason said, "but I've got to do something and I've got to do it fast. The way things stand right now there isn't a whisper of a chance."

The waiter came and presented the check. "Everything all right?" he asked.

"Everything was fine," Mason said.

"To look at you you'd never know you were going to have to go into court and let Hamilton Burger cut your throat," Paul Drake said.

"And it didn't affect your appetite any," Della Street observed.

"I didn't dare to let it affect my appetite," Mason said. "Food makes energy. I didn't eat heavy food but I ate food that will furnish me with a little fuel to last through the afternoon—and it's going to be *some* afternoon."

"Can't you let Eleanor go on the stand and tell her story no matter how utterly incredible it sounds?" Paul Drake asked.

Mason shook his head.

"Well then, couldn't you work a razzle-dazzle that would sound plausible? Couldn't you sketch Suzanne Granger as a sinister character? Couldn't you cast her in the role of a smuggler who had paint tubes full of gems?

"Suppose Eleanor got those gems? Then Suzanne would do anything to get them back. Suppose Eleanor gave them to Doug Hepner? Well, there you have motive and opportunity. Hell's bells, Perry, give this Granger dame a working over on cross-examination, sneer at her, question her great love of art, insinuate she's a smuggler. Ask her why she didn't report this vandalism to the police. Give her hell."

Mason shook his head.

"Why not?" Drake asked.

"Because," Mason said, "it isn't the truth."

"Don't be naïve," Drake said. "A lot of criminal lawyers I know don't pay much attention to the truth. Often when the truth would get a client stuck a good lawyer has to resort to something else."

"I'm afraid of anything that isn't the truth," Mason said. "My client tells me a story that's almost impossible to believe, but it's her story. If I, as her attorney, adhere to that story I at least am being true to the ideals of my profession. I may think it's a lie, but I don't know it's a lie.

"If, however, I think up some synthetic story, then I *know* it's false and I'm afraid of anything that's false. A lawyer should seek the truth."

"But your client's story, from what I gather about it, *can't* be true," Drake said.

"Then," Mason said, "it's up to me to seek out the truth."

"But the reason she's lying is that the truth is something she can't face."

"You mean she killed him?"

168

"It could be that. Or it may be she's trapped by a whole series of events so that the truth would betray her."

"If she killed him, that's her funeral. If she didn't then only the truth can save her. Her fear of the truth is that a jury won't believe it. It's my duty to uncover the truth and then see that the jury knows it is the truth and believes it."

"Yes," Drake said sarcastically. "It's up to you to try to cast Ethel Belan in the role of a liar and Suzanne Granger in the role of a smuggler, with Eleanor taking the part of a pure maiden who is being persecuted. Look where that leaves you."

"There's something about the way Eleanor does things that destroys all confidence in her. The Granger woman radiates truth and integrity on the witness stand. She's proud and aristocratic. She scorns subterfuge and her record is as clean as a hound's tooth.

"On the other hand, there's Eleanor who pulled all this stuff of flashing guns around, who lied about being married, who made statements that she was going to kill the man she loved so that nobody else could have him in case she couldn't have him, and betraying herself every time she opened her mouth. Then the minute she goes on the stand and admits that she knew Doug had been killed with her own gun and . . . well, there you are."

Paul Drake looked at his watch. "Well, Perry," he said, "I guess we're going to have to shuffle on up to the execution chamber. I certainly hate to see Hamilton Burger hand you one, but this is the time he's really done it."

"A made-to-order case," Mason admitted. "No wonder Hamilton Burger was so damned happy. He's been laying for this for years. This is the time he has everything his way."

"But what *are* you going to do, Chief?" Della Street asked.

"I don't know," Mason admitted. "Eleanor is my client and I'm going to do the best I can for her. Burger has been putting in the noon hour talking with Webley Richey. If Miss Granger's story isn't true, naturally Richey won't be in a position to corroborate it. Therefore, Burger will rest his case right after he walks into court. If it develops that he's got a corroborating witness he'll put Richey on the stand."

"But you can't cross-examine Richey on that conversation for more than a minute or two," Drake said.

"I've got to find a loophole somewhere," Mason said. "Our only hope is that Burger rests his case without recalling Richey. If he does that I'll know something's wrong with Suzanne Granger's story. If he recalls Richey I'll know Eleanor's case is hopeless. Richey is the barometer."

They entered the Hall of Justice, were whisked upward in an elevator and walked into the courtroom.

It was quite evident that Eleanor had been crying during the noon hour. Her swollen, red-rimmed eyes were definitely no help as far as Mason's task was concerned.

Della Street, sizing up the grim, hard faces of the jurors as they gazed in unsympathetic appraisal at the defendant, leaned toward Perry Mason and said, "Gosh, Chief, I feel like bawling myself. Look at the faces on the jurors."

"I know," Mason said.

A smiling Hamilton Burger, flanked by his assistant district attorneys, made something of a triumphant entry into the courtroom, and a few moments later Judge Moran took the bench and court was called to order.

"Are the People ready to proceed?" Judge Moran asked.

"This tells the story," Mason whispered.

Hamilton Burger got to his feet. "Your Honor," he said, "we have one more witness, a witness whom I didn't realize could corroborate the story of Miss Granger until Miss Granger's statement on the stand took me completely by surprise. Because I hadn't anticipated such a situation, I hadn't asked Miss Granger or Mr. Richey about the conversation. Miss Granger had told me, as she stated on the stand, that just she and the defendant were present at the time of this conversation and I had let it go at that. I simply hadn't thought to ask her if some other person who hadn't been present might nevertheless have overheard the conversation.

"I mention this in order to show the Court and counsel my good faith in the matter.

"Mr. Webley Richey, will you come forward, please? You have already been sworn. Just take your position there on the witness stand, please."

Richey walked forward with studied dignity. He seated himself on the witness stand, glanced patronizingly at Perry Mason, then raised his eyebrows in silent interrogation as he looked at Hamilton Burger. His manner said louder than words that he was graciously granting permission to the district attorney to question him.

"Did you," Hamilton Burger asked, "hear a conversation on or about the fifteenth day of August of this year between the defendant and Suzanne Granger?"

"I did. Yes, sir."

"Where did that conversation take place?"

"At the door of apartment 360."

"And who was present at that conversation?"

"Just Miss Granger and the defendant."

"Tell us what was said," Hamilton Burger said.

"Just a moment," Mason said. "I would like to ask a preliminary question."

"I don't think you're entitled to," Hamilton Burger said. "You can object if you want to."

"Very well," Mason said. "I object on the ground that the question calls for a conclusion of the witness. If the Court please the witness has testified that only two people were present. Therefore he wasn't present."

"But he certainly can testify to what he heard," Judge Moran ruled.

"Provided he can identify the voices," Mason said, "but there has as yet been no proper foundation laid."

"Oh, very well," Hamilton Burger said. "You know the defendant, do you, Mr. Richey?"

"I do. Yes, sir."

"Have you talked with her?"

"Well . . . on occasion."

"Do you know her voice?"

"Well . . . yes. I know her voice very well."

"And was she one of the persons who participated in the conversation?"

"Yes, sir."

"And how about the other person?"

"That was Miss Granger."

"Do you know her voice?"

"Very well."

"Go on. Tell us what was said."

"Well, Miss Granger said that she didn't propose to have anyone spying on her, that she didn't like it, that she was independent, paid her own bills and intended to live her own life and she wasn't going to have anyone keeping watch on her."

"And what did the defendant say to that?"

"The defendant said that she was trying to steal her boy friend."

"Boy friend or husband?" Hamilton Burger asked.

"Boy friend."

"Go ahead."

"And the defendant said that she wasn't going to stand idly by and let anyone steal her boy friend, that if Suzanne Granger interfered she would shoot Suzanne Granger, and if she couldn't get her boy friend back by any other means she certainly would see to it that no one else had him."

"Did she say how she proposed to see that no one else had him?"

"She said that she would kill him."

"And did she at that time exhibit a weapon?"

"Well, of course," Richey said, "I couldn't see what was going on. I could only hear. But I gathered from the conversation that she was showing a weapon to Miss Granger. She said something about, 'You can see that I'm prepared to make good my promise,' or something of that sort."

"You may inquire," Hamilton Burger said smugly.

Mason glanced at the clock. Somehow he had to think up a strategy by which this rather routine corroborating witness could become a pivotal controversial figure so that the case would drag on until the next day.

172

"Subsequently," Mason asked, "you remonstrated with the parties about this scene?"

"I spoke to Miss Granger about it, yes."

"That was in your official capacity?"

"Certainly."

"You were the clerk on duty at the apartment house and as such felt that you had the duty of maintaining order and the dignity of the apartment?"

"Absolutely."

"And in that capacity you spoke to Miss Granger, I believe remonstrated was the word she used?"

"Yes, sir."

"And what did you say?"

"I told her that the Belinda Apartments was a high-class apartment house, that we didn't believe in having brawls."

"What did you say to the defendant?"

"I didn't talk to her. She went out right after the altercation with Miss Granger."

"Why didn't you talk to her later?"

"Well, I . . . officially, you understand, I hadn't been advised the defendant was a tenant. She was there as a guest of a tenant. Actually she had made financial arrangements with Miss Belan to share her apartment, but that was supposed to be confidential. No one was supposed to know that Miss Belan had a subtenant in the apartment. The defendant was supposed to be a guest. In that way it wasn't necessary for her to register."

"I see. Who told you about the arrangements?"

"Miss Belan."

"Not the defendant?"

"No."

"Then you had never talked with the defendant personally?"

"I saw her from time to time."

"But you hadn't talked with her?"

"I tried to take no official notice of the fact that she was a paying tenant in the house."

"Then you hadn't talked with her?"

"Not in that sense of the word."

173

"Then how," Mason asked, "could you be familiar with the sound of her voice?"

The witness hesitated. "I . . . I had heard it."

"How had you heard it?"

"Why, by hearing her speak."

"When had you heard her speak?"

"I don't know—from time to time, I guess."

"Over the telephone?"

"Yes, over the telephone."

"Do you sometimes monitor the switchboard?"

"Well, I . . . sometimes I check on calls."

"You don't actually manipulate the switchboard yourself?"

"No."

"Do you know how to do so?"

"I'm afraid I do not."

"Then when you say you monitor calls does that mean you listen in on calls?"

The witness became embarrassed. "I wouldn't use that term, Mr. Mason. It sometimes is necessary to make decisions in regard to the lines."

"What do you mean by that?"

"If, for instance, a person has placed a long-distance call and then is engaged in some rather trivial telephone conversation when the long-distance call comes in, I have to give the operator a signal as to whether the local conversation should be interrupted so that the long-distance call can come across the board."

"I see. That takes a certain amount of judgment?"

"A very great deal of discretion."

"It means that you have to know the habits of the people?"

"Oh yes, definitely."

"I mean their telephone habits."

"Yes, sir."

"And have some idea as to the importance of the long-distance call?"

"Well, yes."

"And the only way you can get that is by monitoring the conversations from time to time?"

174

"Well, I wouldn't say that."

"How else would you get the information?"

"I wouldn't know. Perhaps intuitively."

"You do monitor conversations, don't you?"

"I have."

"You make a habit of it, don't you?"

"Definitely not."

"When you're not busy with something else?"

"Well, sometimes I listen in on the line, that is, I . . . well, I have monitored conversations when I felt there was some reason for it."

"And the switchboard is so constructed that any conversation can be monitored from your office. In other words, your phone can be plugged in on any line going across the switchboard?"

"Well, of course, the switchboard is one of those . . ."

"Answer the question," Mason said. "Isn't it a fact that the switchboard is so constructed that your telephone can be plugged in on any line so that you can monitor any conversation that's going through the switchboard?"

"Well, you see . . ."

"I want an answer to that question," Mason thundered. "Is that a fact?"

"Yes."

"Well now," Mason said, smiling, "was there any reason why you couldn't have answered that question directly? Were you ashamed of what you did in monitoring the conversations?"

"No, definitely not."

"I'm sorry if I got that impression from your continued evasions," Mason said.

Hamilton Burger jumped to his feet. "That remark is uncalled for, Your Honor. The witness didn't continually evade the question."

Mason smiled at the judge. "I won't argue the point, Your Honor. I'll leave it entirely to the jury."

"But I don't like that insinuation in the record," Hamilton Burger protested.

"I didn't think you would."

Judge Moran said, "Come, come, gentlemen. We'll have

no more personalities. Go on with your cross-examination, Mr. Mason."

"Now according to your version of this conversation," Mason said, "Miss Granger was a perfect lady. She made no threats."

"No, sir."

"*She* didn't pull a gun on the defendant?"

"Definitely not."

"*She* didn't threaten to shoot the defendant?"

"No, sir."

"*She* didn't threaten to shoot Douglas Hepner?"

"Definitely not."

"*She* comported herself in a respectable manner throughout?"

"Yes, sir."

"Then why did you deem it necessary to remonstrate with *her?*"

"I . . . well, of course, she was the one who initiated proceedings. It was she who opened the door and told the defendant she didn't propose to have anyone spying on her."

"You were there, you said, in an adjoining apartment?"

"Yes, sir."

"How could you hear so clearly what was being said?"

"The door of the apartment was open."

"And you were there in your official capacity?"

"Yes, sir."

"Then why didn't you step out into the hallway and put a stop to the altercation then and there?"

The witness hesitated.

"Go on," Mason said. "Why didn't you? What was holding you back?"

"Well, of course, in many years of employment in high-class apartment houses one learns a certain amount of discretion. When one interferes in a quarrel between two angry women . . ."

"*Two* angry women?" Mason asked.

"Well, yes, sir."

"I thought you said it was one angry woman and one dignified one? Were both women angry?"

"Well, I think Miss Granger was angry when she started the conversation."

"She pushed the door open and confronted the defendant?"

"Well, I . . . I don't know about pushing the door open. I couldn't see. I could only hear."

"And she was angry?"

"I think her feelings were outraged."

Mason said, "You draw a very nice line of distinction, Mr. Richey. One woman was angry and the other woman's feelings were outraged. Yet when you said you didn't interfere you said that you didn't want to get mixed up in an altercation between *two* angry women."

"Oh, have it your way," Richey said. "I'm not going to quibble with you, Mr. Mason."

"You're not quibbling with me," Mason said. "I'm trying to get the exact picture of what happened."

"After all, is it that important?" Hamilton Burger asked somewhat sneeringly.

"It's important because it shows the attitude of this witness," Mason said.

"An absolutely unbiased, impartial witness," Hamilton Burger retorted with feeling.

"Is that so?" Mason said. "Now, Mr. Richey, you have testified that you were in an adjoining apartment at the time?"

"Yes, sir."

"And the door was open?"

"Yes, sir."

"That is, the door from the apartment to the corridor?"

"Yes, sir."

"And you could hear the sounds of the altercation?"

"Yes, sir."

"What apartment were you in?" Mason asked, getting to his feet and raising his voice. "Tell us, what apartment were you in?"

"Why, I . . . I was in an adjoining apartment."

"Adjoining what?"

"Adjoining . . . well, it was a nearby apartment."

Mason said, "You've used the word adjoining a dozen

177

different times. Now was it an adjoining apartment or wasn't it?"

"It was a nearby apartment."

"Was it an adjoining apartment?"

"At this time, Mr. Mason, it would be difficult for me to tell you what apartment I was in."

"So you can remember the conversation almost verbatim," Mason said, "and yet you can't remember what apartment you were in."

"Well, I haven't given that matter much thought."

"Let's give it some thought now. What apartment were you in?"

"I . . . I'm sure I can't . . . it would be very difficult . . ."

"Was it an adjoining apartment?"

"Adjoining what?"

"You've used the word," Mason said. "What did you mean by it?"

"Well, I . . . I don't know what I meant by it."

"In other words, you were using words without knowing their meaning?"

"I know the meaning of the word adjoining."

"And you used that word?"

"Yes, sir."

"All right, what did you mean when you used it?"

"Well, there, of course . . . I wasn't thinking."

"You're under oath?"

"Of course."

"You knew you were testifying under oath?"

"Yes, sir."

"And yet when you said adjoining and knew the meaning of the word you didn't think of the meaning at the time you used it?"

"Well, that's not expressing it very fairly."

"Express it in your words then," Mason said. "Express it fairly."

"Oh, Your Honor," Hamilton Burger said, "this is browbeating the witness."

"I'm not browbeating him," Mason said. "Here's a witness who has an air of supercilious superiority. Here's a witness who has testified a dozen times that he was in an adjoining apartment. Now I'm trying to find out whether he actually was in an adjoining apartment."

"Well, of course, if you want to be technical about it, there could actually be only two adjoining apartments, one on each side," Richey blurted.

"That's exactly what I'm trying to get at," Mason said. "You understand the meaning of the word adjoining?"

"Yes, sir."

"What is it?"

"It means immediately contiguous to."

"All right. Were you in an apartment that was immediately contiguous to apartment 360?"

"It would be difficult for me to tell you at this time, Mr. Mason."

"I think, if the Court please, that question has been asked and answered half a dozen times," Hamilton Burger said. "The witness has stated he can't remember."

"He didn't state any such thing," Mason said. "He said that it would be difficult for him to tell me. *Were* you in one of the adjoining apartments?"

"Well, I . . . I may have been."

"You said so a dozen times, didn't you?"

"I don't know how many times."

"You used the word adjoining?"

"I believe I did. I used it without thinking."

"Were you testifying without thinking?"

"No, I simply used the word without thinking."

"Exactly," Mason said. "You were betraying yourself by the use of the word. There was only one adjoining apartment that had the door open and that was apartment 358. That was the apartment of Suzanne Granger. She had gone out, in fact she had stormed out when she found the defendant watching Douglas Hepner's departure down the elevator. She stormed out and left the door open. You therefore heard the conversation. You were in Suzanne Granger's apartment, weren't you?"

"I . . . I can't remember."

"You can't remember whether you were in the apart-

179

ment of Suzanne Granger at the time this conversation took place?"

"I . . . I . . . well . . . come to think of it, I remember now that I was."

"Oh, you were in there?"

"Yes, sir."

"On official business?"

"I was in there in connection with my employment. Yes, sir."

"And you were there in that apartment when Suzanne Granger stormed out of the apartment and left the door open?"

"Yes, sir."

"Now when Douglas Hepner departed he had left by that door and gone to the elevator, had he not?"

"Yes, sir."

"And Suzanne Granger had stepped to the door and was watching to see if the door of apartment 360 opened a crack. Isn't that right?"

"I don't know what was in her mind."

"But she did step to the door, didn't she?"

"Yes, sir."

"And then while you were standing there you heard the clang of the elevator door as Douglas Hepner went down?"

"Yes, sir."

"And then saw Suzanne Granger storm out into the corridor?"

"Well, I don't know what you mean by storming. She went out into the corridor."

"Hurriedly?"

"Yes."

"Angrily?"

"Yes."

"And you stood there in the apartment behind this open door and heard the conversation?"

"Yes, sir."

"Now why," Mason said, pointing his finger at Richey, "why did you try to conceal the fact that you were in Suzanne Granger's apartment?"

180

"I didn't. I said I was in an adjoining apartment."

"Then when you said you were in an adjoining apartment you meant that you were in the apartment adjoining that of Ethel Belan, in other words in Suzanne Granger's apartment?"

"Certainly."

"Then why did you tell us it would be difficult for you to tell me what apartment you were in?"

"Well, I didn't want to come out and mention it in so many words."

"Didn't you try to convey the effect that you couldn't remember what apartment you were in?"

"Certainly not. I said that it would be difficult for me to tell you. I was very careful in choosing my language."

"Yet you noticed that the learned district attorney became confused by your language and stated to the Court that you had testified half a dozen times that you couldn't remember. Didn't you hear him say that?"

"Yes, sir."

"And you didn't try to straighten him out or tell him that it would be difficult for you to say?"

"Well, I . . . I feel that the district attorney can take care of himself."

"You don't have to do his thinking for him, is that it?"

"Well, you can put it that way if you want."

"And then, later on, you did say you couldn't remember and then said you had remembered, isn't that right?"

"I may have. I was confused."

"Actually you did remember?"

"I remembered until I became confused and then I forgot. When I remembered I told you so. When I said it would be difficult for me to tell you, I meant just that."

"Yet at one time you said you couldn't remember?"

"I may have."

"That was a lie?"

"Not a lie. I was confused."

"You said you couldn't remember?"

"You got me so rattled I didn't know what I was saying."

"Now why was it difficult for you to tell us that you were in Suzanne Granger's apartment?"

"Because I suddenly realized that under the circumstances it might be . . . it might be embarrassing."

"To whom?"

"To Miss Granger."

"So you were willing to quibble and avoid answering the question in order to spare Suzanne Granger's feelings?"

"I try to be a gentleman."

"Was there any reason why you shouldn't have been in Suzanne Granger's apartment?"

"Not in my official capacity, no."

"And you were there in your official capacity?"

"Yes, sir."

"What were you doing?"

"I . . . I was discussing a matter with Miss Granger."

"A matter which had to do with her position as a tenant and your position as the clerk?"

"It was in my official capacity. Yes, sir."

"What were you discussing?"

"Oh, if the Court please," Hamilton Burger said, "I object to that. It's incompetent, irrelevant and immaterial. It's not proper cross-examination."

"On the other hand," Mason said, "it goes to the very gist of the motivation and the bias of this witness. It is an important question."

Judge Moran frowned thoughtfully. "Under certain circumstances," he said, "I would think that it would be rather remote, but in view of the situation that has developed with the examination of this witness it . . . I think I will overrule the objection."

"What were you discussing?" Mason said.

"I can't remember."

"Now this time you don't mean that it would be difficult for you to say, you mean that you can't remember?"

"I mean that I can't remember."

"You remember the conversation that took place between Miss Granger and the defendant?"

"Yes, sir."

"You remember that almost word for word?"

"I remember what was said. Yes, sir."

"But you can't remember the conversation which took place immediately before that, the conversation on an official matter between you and Miss Granger?"

"No, sir, I can't."

"Then how do you know it was on an official matter?" Mason asked.

"Because otherwise I wouldn't have been there."

"You're certain of that?"

"Definitely."

"You have never been in the apartment of Suzanne Granger except upon an official matter?"

The witness hesitated, glanced appealingly at Hamilton Burger.

"Oh, Your Honor," Hamilton Burger said, "now we are getting far afield. This is an attempt to discredit the witness, to besmirch the reputation of another witness and . . ."

"This shows the bias of the witness," Mason said, "and I furthermore fail to see how the fact that he was in the apartment of Miss Granger on a matter other than official business is going to besmirch her reputation."

"Of course," Judge Moran said thoughtfully, "this cross-examination has taken a most peculiar turn."

"The reason it has taken a most peculiar turn," Hamilton Burger said, "is very simple. The defense, in desperation, is sparring for time. He's trying to introduce every possible technicality that he can in order to try and appraise the case which has been made by the People so that he will know what sort of a defense to put on."

"I think that remark is uncalled for," Judge Moran said. "The jury will disregard that. Any remark made by counsel for either side is not to be taken as evidence. And I consider, Mr. District Attorney, that in your position you should realize that a statement of that sort in front of the jury might well become prejudicial misconduct."

"I'm sorry, Your Honor, I withdraw the statement. I made it in the heat of . . . well, of exasperation."

"Now then," Judge Moran said, "I want to repeat that this cross-examination has taken a peculiar turn. Yet it is a logical turn in view of the testimony of the witness. I don't care to comment on that testimony because that is not my function. I am here to rule on legal question. However, I think that under the circumstances I will give the defense the utmost latitude in cross-examination. The objection is overruled."

"Were you ever there on matters other than business?" Mason asked.

"Well, I may have dropped in from time to time just to pass the time of day."

"If," Mason said, "some tenant of a neighboring apartment, not an adjoining apartment but a neighboring apartment, should say that you had been in there dozens of times, would that testimony be incorrect?"

"Now just a minute, Your Honor," Hamilton Burger said, "I object to that question as argumentative, as not proper cross-examination, as assuming facts not in evidence."

"It's argumentative," Judge Moran said. "The objection is sustained."

"Were you in there dozens of times?" Mason asked.

The witness, plainly rattled, shifted his position on the witness stand, cleared his throat, reached for a handkerchief, blew his nose.

"Any time you're finished with your stalling," Mason said, "just answer the question."

"I . . . it depends on what you mean by dozens of times."

"In what way?" Mason asked.

"How many dozens?"

"I'll leave it to you," Mason said. "How many dozens of times have you been in there on matters that were not official?"

"I . . . I can't remember."

"Five dozen times?"

"Oh, I don't think so."

"Four dozen times?"

"Hardly."

"Three dozen times?"

"Well . . . perhaps."

"Then what did you mean by telling us that you wouldn't have been in there except on an official matter?"

The witness hesitated for a moment, then with his face suddenly lighting in a triumphant leer, he said, "I mean on the day in question, Mr. Mason. Your question related to a conversation on the fifteenth day of August of this year, and I told you I wouldn't have been in there at that time except on an official matter."

"You mean on that day?"

"Yes, sir."

"And what was there about that day that was different from the three dozen odd times that you had been in there when it wasn't on official business?"

"Well, I . . . I didn't say it was three dozen."

"I thought you did."

"I said it might have been three dozen."

"All right," Mason said. "What was different about this fifteenth day of August of this year? Was there anything different?"

"Well . . . there had been events which made the day unusual."

"Now how long had you been in that apartment at the time of the conversation?" Mason asked.

"For a . . . well, there again I . . . I can't remember."

"You didn't enter *after* Hepner entered?" Mason said.

"No, sir."

"Then you must have been in there *before* Hepner entered?"

"Yes, sir."

"Did you see Douglas Hepner in there?"

"I . . . I heard him."

"That's what I thought," Mason said. "Let's be frank about this now."

Mason reached over to the counsel table, grabbed up a sheaf of documents, turned the pages rapidly as though looking for some statement that he had, then, apparently finding it, marched forward to confront the witness and said, "You were hidden in that apartment listening to what Douglas Hepner said, weren't you?"

The witness twisted and turned uncomfortably.

Mason glanced at the paper as though reading, then looked back at the witness and said, "Now you're under oath. Let's have it straight. Were you concealed in that apartment, listening, or not?"

"Yes, sir. I was."

"That's better," Mason said, folding the papers and tossing them back on the counsel table with a dramatic gesture. "Now why were you in there listening?"

"Because I felt that matters had reached a point where . . . where I should know what was going on."

"Between Miss Granger and Douglas Hepner?"

"Well, I wanted to know what was going on. I wanted to know what all the facts actually were. I wanted to know what the defendant was doing up there and how far . . ."

Suzanne Granger jumped to her feet, her face flaming with indignation, and shouted, "This man is lying. He wasn't in my apartment. He . . ."

"Just a moment, just a moment," Hamilton Burger exclaimed angrily, turning to face Suzanne Granger.

"Be seated, Miss Granger," Judge Moran said not unkindly. "We can't tolerate a disturbance in the court. The witness is testifying."

"He's testifying to falsehoods, Your Honor."

Judge Moran said, more sternly this time, "There is no occasion for you to comment on the testimony of the witness. If you have anything to say concerning it you can talk to the district attorney or, for that matter, you're at liberty to talk to counsel for the defense, but we can't have proceedings interrupted in this manner. If you can't control yourself I will have to eject you. Now do you understand?"

"I understand, but I don't feel called upon to sit here and listen to statements that reflect upon my good name. The witness told *me* he was in an adjoining apartment. That was my testimony this morning and . . ."

"You won't engage in an argument with the Court in front of the jury," Judge Moran ruled. "Now, Miss Granger, sit down."

She seated herself.

"Now reman quiet," Judge Moran said. "If you want to communicate with counsel for either side you may do so during the recess. We will have no more interruptions."

Judge Moran turned to Perry Mason. "Go on with your cross-examination, Mr. Mason."

"Is it possible," Mason asked, "that you were in Miss Granger's apartment without her knowledge?"

"I . . . I . . ."

"Just a moment," Hamilton Burger said, lunging to his feet. "This witness can't testify to what Miss Granger knows or what she didn't know. That question calls for a conclusion of the witness."

"Sustained," Judge Moran said, smiling slightly.

"Is it possible," Mason said, "that *you* took precautions to see that Miss Granger *didn't* know that you were in her apartment?"

"I . . . I . . . I can hardly say."

"You mean you can't remember, or that it's difficult for you to say?"

"Well, I . . . of course I can't say as to what she knew."

"How did you get in that apartment?"

"I used a master key."

"Was Miss Granger in the apartment when you entered?"

"No, sir."

"Miss Granger came in later?"

"Yes, sir."

"Was Mr. Hepner in there when you entered?"

"No, sir."

"Did you go there to meet Miss Granger?"

"No, sir."

"Did you go at Miss Granger's request?"

"No, sir."

"Why did you go there?"

"I went there to . . . to make an investigation."

"An investigation of what?"

"Miss Granger had reported that there had been acts of sabotage committed in her apartment."

"What sort of sabotage?" Mason asked.

187

"Objected to as incompetent, irrelevant and immaterial, and not proper cross-examination," Hamilton Burger said.

"Overruled," Judge Moran snapped. "I'm going to give counsel latitude to find out the true situation here. It's been brought in on direct evidence and I think counsel is entitled to clarify it fully on cross-examination. Answer the question."

"Well, Miss Granger reported that while she was away on a week-end trip someone had broken into the apartment and had . . . well, had clipped the ends off the tubes of her oil paints and then had squeezed all of the oil paints out on the . . ."

"Oh, if the Court please," Hamilton Burger said, "that is very plainly hearsay. I submit that any statement as to what had happened made by Miss Granger to this witness and not under oath is hearsay and that this is not proper cross-examination."

Judge Moran hesitated. "I think we are trying to determine what was said in a conversation," he said, "not to establish a fact by evidence of that conversation. However . . . I will ask the witness a few questions."

Judge Moran swung around so as to look at Richey's profile. "Look up here, Mr. Richey."

Richey reluctantly raised his eyes to meet those of the magistrate.

"Did you personally go up to the apartment to inspect this act of sabotage?"

"Yes, sir."

"Did you personally see the paints from these tubes of oil paint spread around the apartment?"

"Yes, sir. They were spread all over the bathtub and the washbowl and . . . it was quite a mess."

"How many tubes of paint?" Judge Moran asked.

"Heavens, I don't know. There must have been . . . well, there were dozens of them. It was a terrible mess."

"Who cleaned up the apartment?"

"The janitor."

"Was this reported to the police?"

"I don't believe so."

"Why?"

Hamilton Burger said, "Just a moment, Your Honor. I'm trying to protect the record here so that we don't drag in a lot of extraneous matters and get lost in a maze of confusing side issues. After all, it seems to me that it has no bearing on the case which we are now trying as to whether an act of sabotage was committed in the apartment of the witness, Suzanne Granger, or not.

"I don't wish to be placed in the embarrassing position of objecting to the Court's question, but I do wish to point out to the Court that there is a limit of pertinency and relevancy."

"Yes, I suppose so," Judge Moran ruled, somewhat reluctantly. "I guess perhaps we *are* getting this inquiry rather far afield, but it is impossible not to believe that there is some connection . . . however, I won't comment on the evidence. I think perhaps that it is better if the Court withdraws that last question."

"On the other hand, Your Honor," Mason said, "I feel that the defense should be permitted to explore this matter. I feel that there is a very definite connection between what happened in the apartment of Miss Granger and what was happening in the apartment of Ethel Belan, and, since the prosecution has been permitted to show what happened in Ethel Belan's apartment, it seems to me that the defense should be permitted to explore the unusual and bizarre circumstances which it is now apparent were taking place in the apartment of Suzanne Granger."

Suzanne Granger started to get to her feet.

"Just a moment," Judge Moran snapped. "Now Miss Granger, be seated and remain seated. Don't open your mouth. Don't address the Court. Don't say a word. You either remain in that seat and keep silent or I'll have a bailiff eject you. Do you understand that?"

She subsided in tight-lipped indignation.

"Very well," Judge Moran said. "Now let's try and get this situation straightened out. I think under the circumstances the Court will refrain from asking further questions. Mr. Mason, you were cross-examining the witness. You ask your questions. The district attorney can object to those questions and the Court will rule on the objections."

Hamilton Burger, badly flustered, glanced at the clock and the confused witness, and realized that his carefully planned schedule of procedure was going awry.

"Your Honor," he said, "I feel that the Court can rule at this time as to this entire matter, that questions concerning it are improper and . . ."

"I don't," Judge Moran snapped. "Go ahead with your examination, Mr. Mason."

Mason said to the witness, "Now let's get this straight. You went to the apartment of Suzanne Granger. You let yourself in with your passkey. Was that in an official capacity?"

"I considered it so. Yes."

"You wanted to make certain inspections?"

"Yes."

"And this was on the fifteenth?"

"Yes."

"That was Sunday?"

"Yes."

"There had previously been an act of sabotage reported in the apartment, an act of vandalism?"

"Yes."

"At what time was this reported?"

"At about one o'clock in the afternoon."

"Of that same day?"

"Yes."

"That act was reported to you?"

"Yes."

"By whom?"

"By Miss Granger."

"And what had she said?"

"She said that she had been on a week-end trip in Las Vegas and . . ."

"Did she say with whom she had made that trip?"

"I object. Incompetent, irrelevant, immaterial, not proper cross-examination," Hamilton Burger shouted.

"Sustained," Judge Moran said. "I think this entire conversation may be improper."

"Then I object to it."

"The objection is sustained."

"You went to Miss Granger's apartment on the fifteenth?"

"Yes, sir."

"You let yourself in with a passkey?"

"Yes, sir."

"Was that the first time you had gone to that apartment that day?"

"No, sir."

"When had you been there earlier?"

"When Miss Granger took me up to the apartment to show me what had happened during her absence."

"That was when you saw the tubes of paint cut open and the paint smeared on the bathtub?"

"Yes, sir."

"Now can you describe generally the condition of the apartment at that time?"

"Oh, Your Honor," Hamilton Burger said, "this thing is getting all out of hand. We have a murder case. The People are about ready to rest their case. It's a clean-cut case. In fact, I may say it's a dead open-and-shut case. Now we've gone far afield with acts of vandalism that . . ."

"However, in view of the fact that this witness was called to the stand to corroborate a conversation taking place between Miss Granger and the defendant on that day," Judge Moran said, "I think counsel is entitled to explore the rather unusual fact that this witness was apparently by his own admission concealed in the Granger apartment without the knowledge of the tenant."

"I think the Court shouldn't comment on the evidence," Hamilton Burger said.

"I'm not commenting on it," Judge Moran said. "I'm simply telling you what the witness testified to. Your objection is overruled. Go on with your examination, Mr. Mason."

"Answer the question," Mason said. "Describe the condition of the apartment."

"Well, it was a wreck."

"What do you mean by that?"

"A search had been made."

"What sort of a search?"

"A very thorough search. Things had been dumped from the drawers and . . ."

"I object," Hamilton Burger said. "The witness isn't entitled to state that a search had been made. That's a conclusion."

"It's too late for an objection now," Judge Moran ruled, his manner plainly showing his interest in this entire line of testimony. "The witness has answered the question. Now go ahead. Let's get this situation clarified if we can."

"You were called in there by Suzanne Granger as the official representative of the apartment house?"

"Yes, sir."

"And you ordered it cleaned up?"

"Yes, sir."

"Did you summon the police?"

"No, sir."

"Did Miss Granger summon the police?"

"Objected to as calling for a conclusion of the witness," Hamilton Burger said.

"Sustained."

"Did Miss Granger say anything to you about not calling the police?"

"Same objection."

"Overruled."

"Yes, sir, she did."

"What did she say?"

"I asked her if we should call the police and she said no, that she knew who was responsible for the damage and that she didn't care to have the police called."

"So then you summoned the janitor?"

"Yes, sir."

"And ordered the janitor to clean up the mess?"

"That is, to clean up the bathtub and the washbowl. It was something of a job. He had to use turpentine and then, of course, the maids came in and cleaned off the turpentine, the washbowl and the bathtub."

"Then you left?"

"I had left before the maids came in."

"And then after the maids and the janitor left, and while Miss Granger was out, you sneaked back to the apartment?"

"I went back to the apartment."

"Miss Granger was not there?"

"I have told you several times she wasn't there."

"You knew she wasn't there?"

"Well, I . . . I had seen her go out."

"And when you went back there what did you do?"

"I started looking around."

"Checking the damage?"

"Yes, sir."

"But the damage had all been cleaned up by that time, hadn't it?"

"Well, I guess it had."

"Then why did you go there?"

"To see that the damage had been cleaned up."

"And then Miss Granger returned?"

"Yes, sir."

"Did you let her know that you were in the apartment?"

"No, sir, I didn't."

"What did you do?"

"When I heard her returning I slipped into a closet."

"And remained there?"

"Yes, sir."

"And what did Miss Granger do?"

"She was in something of a hurry. She hurriedly disrobed and took a shower. Then she stood in front of a dressing table . . ."

"*Stood* in front of a dressing table?"

"Yes, sir."

"Then you must have been watching?"

"I had opened the door of the closet a crack."

"So you could see?"

"Yes."

"Why did you do that?"

"I had been trapped in there and I wanted an opportunity to escape."

"So you were watching Miss Granger standing there

in front of the dressing table so that you could find an
portunity to escape."

"Yes."

"How was she clothed?"

"She was just out of the shower."

"You mean she was in the nude?"

"I . . . I believe so, sir."

"What do you mean, you believe so? You were watching, weren't you?"

"Well, yes."

"Was she clothed?"

"No."

"And you were watching simply in order to find a
favorable opportunity to make your escape?"

"Yes, sir."

"Well, why didn't you make your escape while she was
in the shower?"

"I . . . I was confused at the time."

"Yes, so it would seem," Mason commented dryly.

"It was an embarrassing situation."

"And you become confused when you're embarrassed?"

"Quite naturally, yes."

"And you're embarrassed now?"

"In a way."

"Then you are confused?"

"That doesn't follow. I'm telling the truth."

"That," Mason said, "is all."

Hamilton Burger heaved a very audible sigh of relief.

"That's all, Mr. Richey. You may leave the stand.
that, Your Honor, is the People's case."

"Just a moment," Mason said. "I desire to ask some
additional questions on cross-examination of some of the
People's witnesses."

"I object," Hamilton Burger said. "The defense had
every opportunity to cross-examine every witness."

"But," Mason said, "the district attorney was given an
opportunity to put the witness Richey back on the
stand for the second time after previously calling the witness and not asking him about this conversation."

"That's because the prosecution was taken by surprise, Your Honor," Hamilton Burger said.

"And so was the defense," Mason said. "I feel that under the circumstances I'm entitled to ask some more questions of Miss Granger on cross-examination. I also have some further questions to ask Dr. Oberon."

Hamilton Burger, fighting desperately to keep control of the situation, said, "The prosecution has no objection to further questions on cross-examination of Dr. Oberon, but the prosecution definitely objects to any cross-examination of Miss Granger at this time."

"Well," Judge Moran said, "If you have no objection to further cross-examination of Dr. Oberon, let's let him resume the stand and then the Court will reserve its ruling on the matter of further cross-examination of Miss Granger."

"It will take a few minutes to get Dr. Oberon here," Hamilton Burger said.

"Very well, the Court will take a five-minute recess," Judge Moran said.

The judge had hardly left the bench when Suzanne Granger, bristling defiance, came striding down the aisle.

Hamilton Burger rushed toward her.

"Now, Miss Granger," he said, "just a moment. Let's be reasonable, please."

Mason raised his voice. "Did you wish to talk with me, Miss Granger?"

She hesitated, looking at Perry Mason, then at Hamilton Burger.

"No, no," Burger protested. "You're the People's witness. Now we'll give you every opportunity to get the facts straight, Miss Granger. Just be calm, please."

Mason moved down the aisle. "If Hamilton Burger is going to put you on the stand so you can tell the true story of what happened I won't have to do it, Miss Granger, but otherwise if you want to protect your reputation I'll be only too glad to . . ."

An officer interposed himself between Mason and the witness.

Hamilton Burger swung Suzanne Granger away from

195

Mason and toward the witness room. Another officer helped block Mason's way.

Mason turned to Paul Drake and winked. He walked dejectedly back to the counsel table where a policewoman was keeping the defendant in custody.

He leaned over and whispered in Eleanor's ear. "What's this all about? Why was Richey in that apartment?"

"I don't know. I think he's in love with her," she whispered.

Mason grinned. "You think then that he was jealous of Douglas Hepner?"

"Doug," she said with dignity, "was not making love to Suzanne Granger. He was simply trying to get information. He was dating her and taking her out, but that's all."

"That's what you think," Mason said.

"That's what Doug told me and Doug wouldn't lie—not to me."

Mason returned once more to where Paul Drake was standing.

"Paul," he said, "cover the door of the witness room where Burger took Suzanne Granger. I want to see if the conversation is friendly. I want to get the expression on her face when she comes out."

"I'll see what I can do," Drake said, "but I can't get near the door. They've got a bunch of gorillas covering the district attorney and he isn't in the happiest of moods this afternoon."

"I know, but get out in the corridor if you have to. Look around. See what happens when she comes out. See whether they are smiling and friendly, or how they act."

Drake nodded and left the courtroom.

A few minutes later Dr. Oberon, carrying a brief case, came hurrying into the courtroom. The bailiff called for the jury and Judge Moran returned to the bench.

"Where's the prosecutor?" Judge Moran asked.

One of the deputy district attorneys looked toward the door of the witness room. His manner was somewhat harassed, somewhat anxious.

"The district attorney," he said, "has been detained

momentarily but as I understand it this is a situation where counsel for the defense desires to ask additional questions on cross-examination of Dr. Oberon. In the absence of the district attorney my associate and I will represent the prosecution."

"Very well," Judge Moran said. "I take it there is no objection to this further cross-examination of Dr. Oberon."

"None whatever," the deputy said with smug virtue. "If there is any fact in the case that Dr. Oberon has testified to which the defense wishes cleared up we will be only too glad to co-operate to the extent of our ability."

"Thank you," Mason said affably. "That attitude is appreciated and I trust you will be equally broad-minded in regard to clearing up any situation with Miss Granger."

The deputy district attorney, suddenly taken aback, blurted, "Well, I don't know about that . . . you'll have to ask the chief . . . that question is in Mr. Burger's province."

Judge Moran smiled slightly. "We'll cross that bridge when we come to it, Mr. Mason. You may now proceed with further cross-examination of Dr. Oberon."

Mason faced Dr. Oberon.

"Doctor, as I understand it, you have stated that the cause of death was a .38 caliber bullet which lodged in the brain?"

"That is correct. Yes, sir."

"Did you examine the body to determine if there was any contributing cause of death?"

"What do you mean?"

"I direct your attention to a photograph which was taken at the time of the autopsy. It shows the right arm of the decedent, and I call your attention to two little spots on that right arm."

"Yes, sir."

"Why was that photograph taken?"

"Because of those spots."

"You directed that that photograph be taken?"

"Yes, sir."

"And why?"

"Well, the spots were . . . I thought we should have

the photograph. I believe that every evidence of any abnormality should be photographed in any autopsy, particularly in cases of homicide."

"And what was abnormal about these blemishes?"

"Well, they are some sort of puncture."

"In other words, Doctor, you thought they might have been made by a hypodermic needle, didn't you?"

"Well, there was always that possibility."

"And why didn't you mention that in your direct testimony, Doctor?"

"Well, I wasn't asked about it, either on direct or cross-examination."

"But why didn't you mention it?"

"I didn't feel called upon to mention it unless I was asked."

"But you considered it highly significant?"

"I considered it significant."

"How significant?"

"I took a picture of the arm, that is, I asked to have a picture taken of the punctures."

"That are in the right arm?"

"Yes, sir."

"A right-handed man administering a hypodermic would be inclined to puncture the left arm, would he not?"

"Either the left arm or the left leg."

"You thought these were the marks of a hypodermic?"

"They could have been."

Burger came tiptoeing into the courtroom and took his seat at the counsel table between the two deputies. His face was flushed and angry.

"And did you test the body for morphia?" Mason asked, when the district attorney had settled himself.

"No."

"Did you test it for any drugs?"

"No. I determined the cause of death."

"Was there anything in the evidence that made you feel that at the time the bullet was fired the decedent might have been under the influence of drugs?"

"Objected to as incompetent, irrelevant and immaterial, not proper cross-examination," Hamilton Burger said.

"Overruled," Judge Moran snapped, his eyes on the doctor.

"Well . . . I . . . no, I can't say that."

"The body was subsequently embalmed?"

"I believe so, yes."

"And buried?"

"Yes."

"Doctor, would embalming destroy the evidence of poison?"

"Of some poisons, very definitely. Cyanide of potassium would be completely neutralized by the embalming."

"What about morphia?"

"Morphine is an alkaloid. It would be possible to get evidence in the system for a period of . . . well, several weeks."

"If the body should be exhumed at the present time and there was morphine present, could that be determined?"

"Let's see, when was the murder? . . . I think there might be a good chance, yes."

Mason turned to the Court. "Your Honor," he said, "I ask that this body be exhumed. I believe that at the time of death Douglas Hepner was under the influence of morphine which had been given to him by persons who had taken him a prisoner."

"You have some grounds for this assertion?" Judge Moran asked.

"Many grounds," Mason said. "Look at the contents of the man's pockets. Whatever money he had in the form of currency had been taken. All of the pages of a notebook on which there was any writing had been removed and a new filler placed in the cover. The man had cigarettes in a silver case but there were no matches and no lighter. In other words nothing with which he could set a fire. He had no knife. I believe that Douglas Hepner was held a captive before his death."

"Now just a minute, just a minute," Hamilton Burger said angrily, getting to his feet. "Here's another grandstand play unsupported by evidence, a mere statement of counsel that is injected for the purpose of drawing a red herring across the trail of murder. These are things that can't be proven."

"They certainly can't be proven if we bury the evidence," Mason said.

"Of course," Judge Moran pointed out, "even if it should appear that the decedent had been given injections of morphine, that wouldn't establish the point you are trying to make."

"It would fit in with evidence which I hope to produce to establish that point," Mason said.

"An order of exhumation should only be made under most extraordinary circumstances," Judge Moran said. He turned to Dr. Oberon. "Doctor, you noticed these punctures of the skin?"

"Yes, sir."

"And what made you think they were hypodermic punctures?"

"The appearance of the arm and the punctures. I thought they might well have been made by a hypodermic which had been administered . . . well, rather shortly before death."

"Then why didn't you try to determine what drug had been administered?"

"I . . . I was instructed not to."

"By whom?"

"I rang up the district attorney and told him what I had found. He asked me what was the cause of death and I told him it was a .38 caliber bullet which had been fired into the back of the head. He said, 'All right, you've got your cause of death. What more do you want?' and hung up."

There was a moment of silence.

"I was merely trying to keep from confusing the issues," Hamilton Burger said, "because I know only too well how easy it is for a shrewd defense attorney to pick up some piece of purely extraneous evidence and torture it into . . ."

"Nevertheless," Judge Moran interrupted, "under the circumstances, the autopsy surgeon should have followed up that lead. Let me ask you a few more questions, Doctor. Were there any marks indicating that this man customarily used drugs? In other words, were there any old puncture marks or . . . ?"

"No, sir, there were not. I looked the body over very carefully. With the confirmed addict we usually find quite a few such puncture marks and frequently there is a species of tattooing. The hypodermic needle will be disinfected by means of flame from a match. A certain amount of soot or carbon will be deposited on the needle and injected into the skin, leaving very definite tattoo marks. There were just these two marks in the right arm and there had been minor extravasation."

Judge Moran stroked his chin thoughtfully.

"I think perhaps the jury should be excused during this argument," Hamilton Burger said.

"The defense is entitled to . . . the Court is going to take an adjournment and give this matter further consideration. I dislike to adjourn at this hour in the afternoon but I'm going to continue this matter until ten o'clock tomorrow morning. It is quite apparent that the case has progressed up to this point with unusual rapidity. For certain reasons which I need not comment on now, counsel for the defense is placed in a position where he must rely on every Constitutional right which is given his client."

"I don't think the Court needs to comment on that," Hamilton Burger said acidly.

"I don't either," Judge Moran said. "I'm simply pointing out certain elemental matters. The Court feels it might be well to take a recess until tomorrow morning at ten o'clock unless there is an objection on the part of counsel. Is there any objection?"

"There is no such objection," Mason said. "The defense makes a motion for such continuance."

"The prosecution objects," Hamilton Burger said. "It is quite obvious that up to a point the defense let the case develop rapidly until it had seen the entire hand of the prosecution. It is equally evident that thereupon the defense started a whole series of stalling tactics. This whole question of asking to have a body exhumed because of a couple of pin pricks is absurd. There's no question what caused death. It was caused by a bullet fired from the defendant's gun after the defendant had threatened to kill the decedent."

Judge Moran listened patiently, then said, "The defense is entitled to know every factor in the case. Apparently what might have been a material factor was not investigated at the time of autopsy because the prosecution wished to keep the issues from being confused.

"What might confuse the issues in the mind of the prosecution might well be a very significant matter to the defense. . . . You're making a motion for a recess, Mr. Mason?"

"Yes, Your Honor."

"The motion is granted," Judge Moran snapped.

There was a considerable measure of excitement manifest in the demeanor of the few spectators who were watching the trial as Judge Moran left the bench.

The jurors, filing from the courtroom, glanced at the defendant, and now there was more curiosity, a certain measure of sympathetic interest in their glances.

Hamilton Burger, cramming papers down into his brief case with an unnecessary vigor that indicated suppressed anger, spoke briefly to his assistants, and strode from the room.

Della Street came up to grasp Mason's arm.

"You've got them guessing, Chief," she said.

Mason nodded.

A policewoman touched Eleanor on the shoulder, escorted her from the courtroom. Paul Drake came forward.

"What happened?" Mason asked.

Drake shrugged his shoulders. "I couldn't get near the place but I managed to see Suzanne Granger when she came out. She went right to the elevators and left the building. She was white-faced, she was so mad. You can see what effect the interview had on Burger. He's looking for an opportunity to commit a murder himself. What do you suppose happened, Perry?"

"There's only one thing that could have happened," Mason said. "Somehow Suzanne Granger's story contradicts that of Richey. You say that Suzanne Granger went to the elevators?"

"That's right."

Mason grinned. "That means Burger told her to go home, not to stay around the courtroom. We'll serve her with a subpoena as a defense witness. He won't be expecting that. This adjournment took him by surprise."

"How did you find out about these puncture wounds?" Drake asked.

Mason grinned. "In checking over the pictures of the body at the autopsy, I noticed that there was an enlarged picture of the right forearm. It was a picture that had no business being in the collection according to the theory of the prosecution. There was no apparent reason for taking it.

"I couldn't imagine why on earth that picture had been taken. Then I realized that the autopsy surgeon must have directed the taking of this picture because he wanted to protect himself.

"At first I couldn't see what it was. There were, of course, these small spots, but they could have been blemishes on the photograph. Yet there undoubtedly had been something that caused the autopsy surgeon to direct that picture to be taken. So I took a chance. It was, of course, a last desperate chance. The minute I'm forced to put on my defense I'm licked. My only hope is to find some weakness in the prosecution's case."

"How much chance do you have of doing that?" Della Street asked.

Mason shook his head. "A darn slim chance," he admitted, "but it's the chance I'm taking."

■ 15 ■

MASON, WHO HAD FOR HOURS BEEN PACING BACK AND forth in his office, said to Della Street, "Della, there has to be an answer. There's something that doesn't fit. Somewhere in here there's a key clue that . . ."

Suddenly Mason broke off and snapped his fingers. "I've got it! It was right under my nose all the time. I should have had it sooner. I muffed it."

"Muffed what?" Della Street asked.

"The keys."

"What about them?"

"Remember," Mason said, "that when we entered the Titterington Apartments I tried different keys until I found one that opened the front door?"

She nodded.

"And," Mason went on excitedly, "we went up to the apartment that Hepner had maintained under the name of Newberg. I tried *that* key on the door. It slipped into the lock all right but it didn't work the latch. I thought then I was on the wrong scent, but I tried the other keys just as a matter of routine and one of them opened the door."

"I don't see what that proves," she said.

"On that type of apartment," Mason said, "the front door has a lock that can be worked by any key to any apartment in the house. Hang it, Della, that other key is the thing we've been looking for."

"The key clue, eh?" Della Street asked with a wan smile.

"Damned if it isn't," Mason said. "Stick around, Della. Ride herd on the office. Keep in touch with Paul Drake. If you don't hear from me by nine-thirty, go on home."

She laughed. "Try and make me. I'm going to wait here now until . . . Chief, can't I go with you?"

He shook his head. "I need you to hold down the office and for all I know you may have to bail me out of jail."

Mason grabbed his hat and hurried out of the door."

Mason picked up his car and drove to the Titterington Apartments.

He rang the bell marked "Manager."

The same woman came to the door who had accompanied Sergeant Holcomb when Mason, Della Street and Paul Drake had been discovered in the apartment rented by Frank Ormsby Newberg.

Mason said, "I'm not sure if you remember me but . . ."

"Certainly I remember you, Mr. Mason."

"I want some information."

"I'm sorry, Mr. Mason, but as far as that Newberg apartment is concerned I can't . . ."

"Not about the Newberg apartment," Mason said. "I want to compare a key that I have with duplicate keys of the apartments."

"Why?"

"I can't tell you. I'm working on a lead."

She shook her head.

Mason took a twenty-dollar bull from his pocket and said, "I'm not going to *take* any of your keys. I simply want to *check* the keys of the different apartments."

"Why?"

"I'm trying to find out something about the way these keys are made."

"Well," she said, "I guess . . . no one told me you couldn't do that, although they warned me against you. They said you were pretty tricky."

Mason laughed. "The police always adopt a dim view of anyone trying to make an independent investigation. The police theory isn't *always* right."

She debated the matter with herself for a moment, then said, "I'd have to watch you, Mr. Mason, to see what you're doing."

"Certainly," Mason said.

She opened the door of a key cupboard and at the same

time took the twenty-dollar bill which Mason extended toward her.

Mason took a key from his pocket, started comparing it with the other keys.

"Is this a key to an apartment here in the house?" she asked.

Mason said, "I'm trying to determine whether another key might open some apartment here."

"Well, it certainly wouldn't. These locks are the best."

Mason, hurrying through his comparison of the keys, suddenly found a key that was identical with the key he held in his hand.

He held the key only long enough to make sure they were the same, noted the number of 281, then replaced the apartment house key on its hook without giving any sign. He went on comparing his key with the others until at last he came to the end of the board.

Slowly he shook his head.

"I could have saved you twenty dollars and a trip down here, Mr. Mason. All you needed to have done was to have telephoned me and asked me if some other key would have fitted one of these apartments. We're very careful about them. We've had some trouble and . . ."

"Well, I just had to make sure," Mason said, ruefully.

"How are things coming with your case?" she asked.

"So-so."

The manager shook her head slowly from side to side. "I'm afraid that girl's guilty."

"Of course," Mason said, "the fact that Hepner had an apartment here under the name of Frank Ormsby Newberg introduces an element of mystery into the case. I'd like to find out something about it."

"So would I," she said.

"Did he have any friends here in the building?"

She shook her head.

"Do you have many vacancies?"

"Very, very few."

"Let's take a couple of them at random," Mason said. "For instance, here's apartment 380. How long has the tenant been in there?"

"Some five or six years."

"260?"

"About two years."

"281," Mason said.

"Well, that, of course, is exceptional."

"Why?"

"That girl came here because she had a relative who was very ill and she had to be here off and on. She moved here from Colorado some place. It was temporary. Her relative died a week ago and she's moving out for good."

"Oh, I believe I read of the case. She's a blonde?"

"No, a brunette. About twenty-seven. Rather quiet but with a very nice appearance, well-dressed, good figure. She impresses you."

Mason frowned. "I wonder if I've seen her. What's her name?"

"Sadie Payson."

"I don't believe I am familiar with the name," Mason said. "How about 201?"

"That's a man. He's been with us six or seven years."

"You evidently have a bunch of steady, reliable tenants."

"That's the kind of a place I try to run, Mr. Mason."

"How long have you been manager?"

"For ten years. I've made it a point to weed out my tenants carefully, to get those who are steady and dependable. It's a lot better to have rentals coming in regularly than to have trouble with collections and having people moving in and out."

"That, of course, is true. But I don't see how you can weed them out."

"Well, I flatter myself I'm a pretty good judge of character."

"What about this man that you knew as Newberg?"

"That's one of the reasons I was suspicious when I saw his picture in the paper. He didn't fit in somehow. He was like a phony diamond. It's nice-looking and it glitters and it sparkles, but you just have the feeling all the time that there's something wrong."

207

"And that's the way you felt about Newberg?"

"Yes—after he'd moved in and been here for a while. When I first met him I felt that he was just the type I wanted. He told me he was studying to be an engineer and that he'd be away on field trips quite a bit.

"Well, it wasn't long before I realized the man wasn't really *living* in the apartment. He was just using it for some reason or other. You can tell when an apartment's being lived in. There's a feel about the place.

"Of course, Mr. Newberg would come and stay a few days. He'd sleep there lots of times, but you couldn't feel right about him. He paid the rent right on the dot so there was no way I could question him or ask him to move."

"Women?" Mason asked.

"Definitely not. I watched him on that. Of course a man's apartment is his home and ordinarily I don't snoop, but in this case if he'd been at all promiscuous . . . well, good heavens, here I am rambling on, and I had orders not to talk to you or give you any information about Newberg."

"Nothing wrong with what you're telling me," Mason said. "I really should hire you to sit with me in court and help me pick jurors. I see that you can judge character quickly and accurately."

"Well, after you've seen enough of people you can spot the ones that aren't on the up-and-up—at least I know I can."

"Thanks a lot," Mason told her. "I'd like to visit with you and talk about people, but since the police told you not to talk to me I'll be on my way."

He went out, walked twice around the block, came back ten minutes later and pressed the button opposite the name of Sadie M. Payson.

There was no answer.

Mason opened the front door with his key and went up to the second floor. He walked down to 281, rang the doorbell, and when he received no answer, inserted the key in the lock, twisted it and found that the lock worked back smoothly.

The lawyer withdrew the key, stood in front of the door, hesitating.

Abruptly a woman's voice on the other side of the door said, "Who's there?"

Mason said, "I'm the new tenant."

"The new tenant! What in the world are you talking about? I'm not out yet."

"I'm the new tenant," Mason said. "I have the key. I'm sorry if I'm disturbing you but . . ."

The door was flung open. An indignant brunette, pulling up a zipper on a housecoat, regarded him with flashing eyes. "Well, I certainly like that! And I certainly admire your crust! I'm not leaving until midnight. I haven't moved out and I haven't surrendered my key and the rent's paid until the first."

"I'm sorry," Mason said, "but it's imperative that I get some measurements of the apartment."

She stood there in the doorway, bristling with indignation. Behind her, Mason saw two suitcases, open on a bed, being packed. There was a traveling bag on a chair. She was evidently wearing only the housecoat and slippers. She said, "Why, if you'd have come walking in here you'd have caught me . . . undressed."

"But you didn't answer the door."

"Of course I didn't answer the door. I didn't want to be disturbed. I've just had a bath and I'm getting my things packed and then I'm going to the airport. The

Mason pushed his way into the apartment.

"I'm sorry," Mason said. "I understood you were leaving and I have to have measurements for some of the things I'm buying."

"I'm leaving at midnight. I haven't checked out, and the rent's paid."

"Well," Mason said, with his best smile, "I guess there's no harm done."

"No harm done because I threw on a housecoat when I heard your key in the lock! Haven't I seen you somewhere before? Your face . . ."

"Yes?" Mason asked as she broke off abruptly.

"You're Mason," she said, "Perry Mason! I've seen your

209

face in the papers. That's why you looked familiar! You're the one who's defending that woman. You . . ."

She started to slam the door.

Mason pushed his way into the apartment.

The woman in the housecoat fell back toward the rear of the apartment.

Mason kicked the door shut.

"Get out," she said. "Get out or I'll . . ." Her voice trailed away into silence.

"Call the police?" Mason asked.

She whirled abruptly toward one of the suitcases, came up with a gun that glittered in her hand.

"I'll do something more effective than that, Mr. Mason."

"And *then* what will you tell the police?" Mason asked.

"I'll tell them I . . ."

She started groping for the zipper on the housecoat. "I'll tell them that you tried to attack me—and I'll make it stick."

Mason stepped forward. "Before you do anything like that," he said, "permit me to give you this document."

"What . . . what's that?"

"That," Mason said, "is a subpoena to appear in court tomorrow and testify on behalf of the defense in the case of the People of the State of California versus Eleanor Corbin alias Eleanor Hepner."

Her eyes showed dismay, then determination. Her hand found the zipper on the housecoat, jerked it half down. She ripped a jagged tear in the cloth. Mason, lunging forward, grabbed the hand that held the gun, pushed the arm back and up, twisted the gun from her grasp and put it in his pocket.

She flung herself at him and Mason threw her over onto the bed.

"Now," he said, "sit down and quit acting like a fool. I may be the best friend you have in the world."

"You," she exclaimed, "the best friend! I like *that!*"

"I may be the best friend you have in the world," Mason repeated. "Look at the spot you're in. You posed as Douglas Hepner's mother, living in Salt Lake. You

210

worked with him on a racket that started out as a free-lance detective business, getting twenty percent of smuggled gems, and developed into blackmail.

"Then Douglas Hepner is found dead with a bullet in the back of his head and you are on the point of taking a midnight plane out of the country."

"So what? What if I am? This is a free country. I can do as I damn please."

"Sure you can," Mason said, "and by doing it, put a rope right around that pretty little neck of yours. If I were as unscrupulous as you seem to think I am, I'd like nothing better than to let you get on the plane and then drag you into the case and accuse you of the murder. That would save Eleanor from a first-degree murder rap."

"He was killed with her gun," the woman said.

"Sure he was," Mason said, "and she'd given him her gun as protection. Somebody had been jabbing him with a hypodermic needle and he was under the influence of morphia when he died. He was probably so groggy he only had a faint idea of what he was doing. Under those circumstances it would have been easy for anyone to have taken the gun from his pocket and shot him in the back of the head."

"You say he was under the influence of morphine?"

"I think he was. He'd been jabbed with a hypodermic."

"That," she said, "explains it."

"Explains what?"

"I don't have to tell you," she said. "I'm just getting things straight in my own mind."

"No," Mason told her, "you do have to tell me. I've served a subpoena on you. You're either going to talk to me now in private or you're going to talk on the witness stand in public—with newspaper reporters making notes of everything you say."

"You can't bluff me."

"Somewhere," Mason said, "you have a family—a mother, a father, perhaps you've been married and separated and have a child. You don't want those people to get that picture of you. You . . ."

She blinked back tears. "Damn you," she said.

"I'm simply pointing things out to you," Mason said.

"You don't have to drag my family into it."

"You'd be the one who was dragging your family into it," the lawyer told her. "You and Doug Hepner were working a racket. I don't know how much of it was handled for the reward, how much of it was blackmail, but you had a system of signals. When Doug wanted someone blackmailed he'd make himself agreeable until he had them hooked for a week-end trip somewhere. Then he'd telephone you and give you the name and address. You'd show up and be Hepner's wife, sort of a complicated badger game. You'd threaten to name the woman as a correspondent and . . ."

"No, no," she said, "it was nothing like that. I didn't sink that low."

"All right," Mason told her, "what was it?"

She struck a match and lit a cigarette with trembling hands. "I got teamed up with Doug when I went to Europe as a secretary for one of the Governmental agencies. I served a trick over there and came back. I thought I was smart. I smuggled in a little jewelry—not too much, just what I could afford. It got past the Customs all right but it didn't get past Hepner."

"How did he know about it?" Mason asked.

"I suppose I talked too much. I talked to another girl who had been with me over there. She was my closest friend, but she fell head over heels in love with Hepner on the boat, and babbled everything she knew.

"Well, one thing led to another and I became Doug's partner."

"Also his mistress?" Mason asked.

"What do you think?"

"Go ahead," Mason said.

"Doug was clever, unbelievably clever. He had a magnetic personality and he could insinuate his way into anyone's good graces. We worked a great racket. He'd travel back and forth to Europe. He'd get enough information lined up to keep going for quite a while in between trips."

"On smuggling?" Mason asked.

"The smuggling was the small end of it," she said. "The blackmail was the big end. Doug would get a line on gems that had been smuggled. He'd turn in enough to the Customs for his twenty-percent take to give himself a standing and an apparent occupation. The rest of the time it was blackmail."

"Who did the blackmail?"

"I did."

"Go on."

"I had an apartment in Salt Lake. Over the telephone I'd pose as Doug's mother. When he had someone ready to be picked he'd get them out on a week-end trip. Obviously I had to know just as soon as they got started. Well, Doug would telephone me, but he did it in such a way that he always put the girl on a spot. He'd call me as his mother. He'd introduce the girl over the telephone and would say something out of a clear sky that indicated he was intending to marry the girl.

"You know how that would make a girl feel. She was starting out on a week-end trip and then it would appear that the guy's intentions were honorable and he was thinking of marrying her . . . well, that was my cue. While Doug and the girl were away I'd take the first plane and get into the girl's apartment. I'd really go through it and, believe me, I know how to search. If there was anything in the apartment I found it. If it was very valuable I appropriated it. The girl couldn't afford to make a complaint, but if it was run-of-the-mine stuff then I'd show up later on as a Customs agent. I'd state that I was very sorry but that we had traced the gems and that it was going to be necessary to swear out a warrant for arrest and things of that sort.

"Quite naturally the girl would turn to Doug for advice and he'd act as intermediary and finally suggest that I could be bought off. Well, you know what that meant. There wasn't any end to it."

"But what about Eleanor?" Mason asked. "Had she or her family been smuggling?"

"If they had, I didn't find anything when I searched their apartment."

"I don't get it. Doug seems to have been in love with Eleanor and was planning to marry her. And he has you search her apartment?"

"You don't get the sketch. Doug wasn't really in love with Eleanor and never had any intention of marrying her. But he was working on something big, something that was really terrific. He was on the trail of a regular professional smuggling ring. And he needed her help. He was just stringing her along."

"Did he know who was in it?"

"Certainly we knew who was in it."

"Who?"

"Suzanne Granger."

"Go on," Mason said. "Tell me the rest of it."

"Well, Doug needed somebody that he could use, someone who had a definite background. It was a deal that he couldn't use me on, or at least he *said* he couldn't."

"You doubted that?"

She said, "There had been many women in Doug Hepner's life. Eleanor was just another leaf on the tree, and when the leaves begin to fall you don't count each individual leaf. You simply rake them up in a pile and cart them away or burn them."

"You're bitter," Mason said.

"Of course I'm bitter."

"At Eleanor?"

"It wasn't her fault. Doug started playing her in the routine way, or at least that's what he made me think. He started out with her on a week end when her whole family was to be away, telephoned from Indio and . . ."

"And you went to search their place?"

"Yes. I had to watch my chance. I got in and searched the whole place. I drew a blank. I went back to Salt Lake. I didn't hear from Doug for a week. Then he got in touch with me. He said he had been working on a big deal.

"I don't think he'd really fallen for Eleanor. He was on something big and he was playing square on the financial end. He was going to give me my cut. At least I *think* he was."

"Go on," Mason said.

"Well, Doug said he could use Eleanor, that she could pose as a jealous neurotic. He thought that he could get her into the apartment next to Suzanne Granger."

"And then?"

"Then Doug made his usual play for Suzanne. He got her to go to Las Vegas with him over a week end. He telephoned me from Barstow. I was on a plane within an hour of the time he telephoned. I went through that girl's apartment and, believe me, I went through it. I thought, of course, she might be using her tubes of paint as a means of smuggling."

"What did you find?"

"Not a thing."

Mason said, "It came out in testimony today that Ethel Belan saw Eleanor with a whole bunch of gems—at least that's what she claimed."

She said, "I'm going to tell you something, Mr. Mason. No one else knows this. On the morning of the sixteenth Doug telephoned me. He was excited. He said, 'They almost got me last night, but I've got the thing licked. It was a different setup from what I thought it was and it was so clever it had me fooled for a while. You'd never have guessed their hiding place. But I've got the stones now and if I can ever get out of here without being killed we're going to be sitting pretty. This is a professional smuggling ring and your cut on this is going to run into big money.' "

"He was excited?"

"Yes."

"And he was evidently in the apartment house?"

"He must have been right in Suzanne Granger's apartment."

"And when was this?"

"About ten o'clock in the morning of the sixteenth."

"But you'd searched Suzanne Granger's apartment."

"I'd searched it Saturday and, believe me, I'd made a good job."

"How did you get in?"

She said, "I've developed a technique for that."

"And what about this apartment you're in now?"

"This is my hideout here. I posed as a woman who was nursing a sick relative who wasn't expected to live. I had a key to Doug's apartment and he had a key to mine. Of course I didn't dare use hotels."

"His apartment was searched," Mason said hastily.

"That's what bothers me—and it frightens me."

"You didn't search it?"

"Heavens no. If he'd had the gems he'd have come to my apartment with them the first thing. I waited here for him all day and that night. When I finally found out his apartment had been searched I dashed back to Salt Lake, packed up everything in the apartment and waited to see if he'd call me there.

"That's when your call came in. I thought you were one of the gang teamed up with Suzanne Granger, so I played it straight and told you just what Suzanne could have told you. Then I hung up, threw my suitcases into my car and got out of there."

"Didn't you think it was dangerous to come here?"

"At first. Then I realized no one knew of this place. The rent was paid for three months so I decided to stay on. There was always the chance I'd get some clue as to what Doug had done with those gems. If I could be on the spot and get them I'd be sitting pretty. Otherwise . . ." She broke off with a little shrug of her shoulders.

"Do you know who killed him?"

"Eleanor killed him. I think she found out when he got the gems . . . I don't *know*. All I *know* is that Doug had the gems before he was killed."

"And he was dealing with a professional smuggling ring?"

"Yes. One that operated on a big scale."

"And Eleanor wasn't in it?"

"Heavens no. Eleanor was helping him. She had set the stage for spying on Suzanne Granger."

"And you knew that Doug Hepner had coached her to take the part of a jealous mistress, a woman who had used that approach to get herself into Ethel Belan's apartment? You knew she had instructions to threaten to kill Doug Hepner to keep anyone else from having him?"

She hesitated. "If I say that will it help the girl?"

"It may result in her acquittal."

"And if I don't admit that it may mean she gets convicted?"

"Yes."

She paused, took a deep breath. "I don't know that she isn't guilty. I don't have to say a thing."

Mason said, "There'll be a terrific battle over whether I can get your testimony into the evidence. I think the judge will let it in. In any event, if you'll tell the truth, I'll try. The district attorney will claim it's hearsay, not part of the *res gestae* and too remote.

"However, before I can lay my plans I'll have to know where you stand and I'd have to know the facts."

"I'd have to take the witness stand?"

"Yes."

She shook her head. "I can't do it. You called the turn. I have a child—a daughter, eight years old. I don't want newspaper notoriety. I can't be cross-examined about my past."

Mason said, "You can't let Eleanor walk into the gas chamber for a crime she didn't commit."

She shook her head. "I'm not going to help you, Mr. Mason."

Mason's face was as granite.

"You're going to help me," he said. "You don't have any choice in the matter. That's why I served that subpoena on you."

She said bitterly, "You have lots of consideration for that Eleanor Corbin, who has a fortune back of her, but think of me. I'm leaving here with just what you see on the bed."

Mason said, "I'm sorry. The honest part of your business was one thing. The blackmail was something else. You're going to have to begin over."

"On what?" she asked bitterly. "On what's inside of this housecoat! That's the only asset I have in the world,

217

except a bus ticket to New Mexico, thirty dollars in cash, and . . ."

"I thought you were taking a midnight plane," Mason said.

Her laugh was bitter. "My days of plane travel are over. I'm going by bus, but I didn't think I had to tell the apartment manager that."

"All right," Mason said, "now listen. I'm not making any promises but if we can get this case solved it *might* be that we could recover the gems that Doug Hepner told you about. It might be that we could break up that smuggling ring."

"And then you'd grab . . ."

"No," Mason told her, "that's what I'm trying to tell you. That would be your cut."

She studied him with thoughtful eyes. "You're dealing with a tough bunch," she said.

Mason said, "My secretary, Della Street, is going to come and get you. You're going to a place where you'll be safe. Tomorrow morning you're going on the witness stand. If we recover those gems you get the reward. Then you promise me that you're going to turn your back on blackmail and rackets and are going to be the kind of a mother that your child can be proud of."

She regarded him steadily for a moment, then got up and put her hand in his. "Is that *all* you want?" she asked.

"That's all I want," Mason told her.

■ 16 ■

DELLA STREET WAS WAITING FOR MASON WHEN HE entered the courtroom. She handed him a chamois skin bag containing the gems that had been taken from Eleanor's cold cream.

"Everything okay?" Mason asked.

"Okay, Chief," she said. "Sadie's waiting down in the car. One of Paul Drake's men is with her. When you want her, step to the window and flip your handkerchief. Drake's man will be watching. He'll bring her up."

Judge Moran took the bench and the bailiff pounded the court to order.

Judge Moran said, "The Court has decided that under the present circumstances there is no reason for ordering the exhumation of the body of the decedent. However, the Court wishes to state that it is the duty of the coroner's physician not only to determine the cause of death but to discover any contributing causes. Apparently there is no independent reason to believe that the puncture marks in the arm of the decedent were made by a hypodermic. So far we have merely a conjecture on the part of the autopsy surgeon. The present ruling of the Court is that an exhumation will not be ordered. If there should be any new evidence indicating independently the presence of morphia, or that the decedent had been held a prisoner against his will, the Court will again consider the matter.

"Now as I understand it, counsel for the defense wished to ask additional questions on cross-examination of the witness Suzanne Granger."

"If the Court please," Hamilton Burger said, "we are prepared to resist such a request on the part of defendant's counsel. We have some authorities . . ."

"What sort of authorities?" Judge Moran asked.

"Authorities indicating that in a criminal action the defendant cannot cross-examine piecemeal, that he must conclude his cross-examination of a witness before the witness is excused from the stand."

"You don't need to cite authorities to that point," Judge Moran said. "The Court is quite familiar with them. However, Mr. District Attorney, in your search of the law did you also find a series of authorities holding that the trial judge is completely in charge of the order of proof and the examination of witnesses and is obligated to exercise his authority in the interests of justice?"

"Well, of course, Your Honor," Hamilton Burger conceded, "that is a general rule. However, in this case . . ."

"In this case," Judge Moran said firmly, "you put the witness Richey on the stand. You didn't ask him about overhearing the conversation which Suzanne Granger had with the defendant. That matter was brought out afterward. Thereupon you put on the witness Richey for the second time. The Court granted you permission to do that. The Court feels that defendant's request to interrogate Miss Granger in regard to the matters testified to by Richey is a reasonable request under the peculiar circumstances of this case—I repeat, Mr. District Attorney, *under the peculiar circumstances of this case*. The Court, therefore, orders Miss Granger to take the stand."

Suzanne Granger arose, started toward the witness stand and said, "I am very anxious, Your Honor, to take the witness stand. The district attorney refused to . . ."

"Never mind that," Judge Moran said. "You will take the witness stand. You have already been sworn. You are to be cross-examined by counsel for the defense. You will not volunteer any information. You will wait until questions are asked and then you will answer those questions, confining your answers to the subject matter called for by the question. In that way we will give the prosecution an opportunity to object to any improper questions."

Mason said, "You have heard Mr. Richey's testimony?"

"I did."

"You returned to your apartment on the fifteenth of August and found that it had been searched and that acts of vandalism had been committed?"

"Yes, sir."

"You complained to the management?"

"I spoke to Mr. Richey about it."

"And what happened?"

"He went to the apartment, surveyed the damage, ordered the janitor and the maids to clean up. He asked me if I wished to notify the police. I told him I did not."

"Why?"

"Because I was satisfied that it was the work of . . ."

"Now just a moment," Hamilton Burger said. "I object, Your Honor, that this is not proper cross-examination, that the question is incompetent, irrelevant and immaterial,

220

that the reason the witness did not want to call the police is entirely outside the issues of this case, and that if she had in her own mind an idea as to what had happened or why it had happened the prosecution is certainly not bound by some *thought* the witness may have. The witness can be examined as to *facts* and not as to *thoughts*."

"I want to show bias and prejudice against the defendant in the case," Mason said.

"Very well, reframe your question," Judge Moran said. "The objection to the present question is sustained."

"Did you," Mason asked, "state to Mr. Richey that the vandalism was the work of Eleanor Hepner, or Eleanor Corbin as the case may be, who was spying on you in the adjoining apartment?"

"Same objection," Hamilton Burger said.

"Overruled," Judge Moran said. "Answer the question."

"I did."

"Was there any evidence, any fact, any proof that caused you to believe she had done this?"

"No evidence, no fact, no proof. It was my intuition if you want to call it that. Now I also want to state that . . ."

"Don't volunteer any information," Judge Moran said. "Wait until you are questioned."

She tightened her lips.

"Now then," Mason said, "later on you returned to your apartment?"

"I did."

"And Mr. Hepner called on you that evening?"

"Yes."

"Prior to the time Mr. Hepner called did you take a shower?"

"I took a tub bath."

"Was it possible for anyone to have been concealed in your closet?"

"Definitely it was not. I looked in the closet. I unpacked a suitcase. I took some clothes out of the suitcase and hung them in the closet. There was no one there."

"Thank you." Mason said, "that is all."

Hamilton Burger conferred in whispers with his associates, then said, "That is all."

"Very well, you may leave the stand," Judge Moran said, his manner showing that he was very puzzled.

"The prosecution rests. That's the People's case," Hamilton Burger said.

Perry Mason got to his feet. "Now, Your Honor," he said, "at this time the defense wishes to make an opening statement to the jury as to what it expects to prove."

"Very well," Judge Moran said.

The courtroom, which was now filled with spectators, broke into whispers and was quieted by the bailiff.

Perry Mason quietly stepped forward to stand in front of the jury.

"Ladies and gentlemen of the jury," he said, "we expect to produce evidence to show that Douglas Hepner was engaged in a very unusual occupation, that he made his living by means of collecting rewards as a free-lance detective.

"We expect to show that Douglas Hepner had been a gambler, that he had learned that the United States pays informers twenty percent of the value of merchandise smuggled into this country if an informer produces evidence resulting in the recovery and confiscation of the merchandise so smuggled.

"That was Douglas Hepner's occupation.

"Douglas Hepner knew the defendant—well. They had discussed marriage many times. But Eleanor Corbin wanted him to quit that business and he had promised to buy an interest in an importing business after their marriage and cease his so-called free-lance detecting.

"However, Douglas Hepner, at the time of his death, was working on one last case on which he wanted the defendant to help him. We propose to show that Douglas Hepner was on the trail of a ring of smugglers who were professional smugglers, who were making a profession of bringing gems into this country illegally.

"We propose to show that in order to break up this ring, thereby getting a last reward which he would use as a stake to buy his way into this importing business, Douglas Hepner enlisted the aid of the defendant Eleanor; that he deliberately cast her in the part of a jealous, neurotic mistress who was to secure a room in apartment 360 because Douglas Hepner thought that Suzanne Granger was part of the smuggling ring.

"Suzanne Granger was making frequent trips to Europe. She was doing a considerable amount of painting and she carried back and forth many tubes of paint, tubes which would make an ideal place of concealment for gems if she had been so minded."

Suzanne Granger jumped up, started to say something and was immediately silenced by a bailiff whom Judge Moran had placed at her side.

"Just a moment, Mr. Mason," Judge Moran said. He turned to the courtroom. "Miss Granger," he said, "you have repeatedly created a disturbance. The Court has placed a bailiff beside you. The Court intends to see that you conduct yourself in an orderly manner and do not interrupt proceedings of this court. Any further attempt at an interruption will be treated by the Court as a contempt. Do you understand?"

"Am I not going to be given an opportunity to . . . ?"

"Not at this time, not in this manner and not at this place," Judge Moran said. "Remain seated and be quiet. Now, Mr. Mason, go on with your opening statement."

"We expect to show," Mason said, "that Douglas Hepner was mistaken about one thing, and that was the identity of the woman who acted as custodian of the smuggled gems and the location of the smuggled gems. We expect to show that the actual custody of the gems was in a place and was carried out in a manner far more ingenious and subtle.

"We expect to show that the defendant Eleanor carried out the instructions of Douglas Hepner; that she duly secured lodgings with Ethel Belan as has already been established by the evidence of witnesses.

"We expect to prove that at the last minute Douglas Hepner discovered the real secret of the smuggling ring; that Douglas Hepner had one other female accomplice, a woman who had been working with him for some period of time; that Douglas Hepner actually recovered a small fortune in gems and that he thereupon communicated with this woman and told her that his life was in danger.

"We expect to show that Douglas Hepner left the Belinda Apartments surreptitiously using the freight elevator, that he proceeded to a hideout apartment he maintained under a pseudonym; that he was followed by the conspirators who believed he had these gems in his possession. We expect to show that his enemies trapped Douglas Hepner in his apartment, doped him with a large injection of morphia, that he thereupon was held prisoner while a determined effort was made by the heads of the smuggling ring to recover the gems. That they not only searched him but ransacked his apartment; that he was held prisoner all day, and was given a second injection of morphine shortly before his death. That when they failed to recover the gems they killed Douglas Hepner under such circumstances that the crime would naturally be framed on the defendant Eleanor, hoping thereby to make it appear that any story she might tell would be a self-serving declaration subject to suspicion and regarded with skepticism by the district attorney."

Hamilton Burger, smiling scornfully, whispered to one of his assistants, then leaned back and shook with silent laughter.

"And," Perry Mason went on, "the proof of this is that Douglas Hepner *did* recover those gems and that the defense now has those gems in its possession and knows the identity of the smugglers."

Mason suddenly took a piece of chamois skin from his pocket, spread it on the counsel table, picked up the chamois bag Della Street had given him and poured a cascade of glittering gems onto the chamois skin.

Hamilton Burger jumped up. "What's this? What's this?" he asked, striding forward.

The jurors craned their necks.

"We expect," Mason went on, "to introduce these gems in evidence and . . ."

"Your Honor, Your Honor," Hamilton Burger shouted. "I object. Counsel can't produce his exhibits before the jury at this time. He can only tell the jury what he expects to prove."

"That's what I'm doing," Mason said. "I expect to prove to the jury that Douglas Hepner had recovered these gems."

"Those are the gems Ethel Belan described," Hamilton Burger said. "Those were in the possession of the defendant. The mere fact that the defense produces them now . . ."

Judge Moran interrupted sternly. "Counsel for the prosecution can argue the prosecutor's case to the jury at the proper time. It will not be argued now."

"I object to this evidence being produced in front of the jury."

Mason said, "I am merely showing the jury what I expect to prove, Your Honor, and I may state at this time that Douglas Hepner had made one very simple mistake. Knowing that Webley Richey, one of the clerks in the apartment house, was a member of the smuggling ring, he naturally assumed that Suzanne Granger, with her frequent trips to Europe, was part of the ring. The true, diabolically clever scheme didn't occur to him at first. When it did occur to him he found the gems. He found them in a hiding place so ingeniously constructed that it was extremely difficult to detect. However, in entering that hiding place he set off a burglar alarm and when he did that he knew he was trapped. There had already been one attempt on his life and he knew that if he were caught leaving the apartment house with the gems in his possession it would be sure death.

"So he locked the door of the apartment. He telephoned his assistant to report what he had found, and he then concealed the gems in the one place where he thought he had any faint chance of keeping them secreted. He had to do all this in a matter of seconds.

"Then he unlocked the apartment door and stepped into the hall, expecting to be seized and searched, expecting to have to battle for his life.

"To his surprise no one was there. He was not molested. Knowing he didn't have the gems on him gave him a surge of confidence. He raced for the freight elevator and pressed the button.

"It seemed ages before the lumbering freight elevator came up and stopped. Everything seemed to be clear. He sneaked out the rear entrance of the apartment house and sought sanctuary in his hideout apartment. I do not think Douglas Hepner even knew he was being trailed, or once in his apartment he would not have responded to that knock on the door. Obviously he expected someone else, for he opened the door—and then Douglas Hepner knew he had gambled and lost. Hands grabbed him, arms held him, a hypodermic needle jabbed him."

"Oh, Your Honor," Hamilton Burger interrupted. "All of this is plainly improper. Counsel only has the right to outline the evidence he expects to put on. He is building up a suspense story here that sounds like a movie scenario. He can't *prove* this. He's talking about the thoughts and emotions of a dead man. He's outlining hearsay. He's rationalizing . . ."

"I think the objection is well taken," Judge Moran interposed. "Defense counsel has unquestioned oratorical ability. He is now telling a story, not reciting what he proposes to prove."

"But I do propose to prove it, Your Honor," Perry Mason protested. "I expect to put on witnesses who will establish the facts and these other matters are fair inferences to be drawn from those facts."

"Just *how* do you expect to prove these things?" Judge Moran asked.

Perry Mason said, "I have waiting downstairs a surprise witness who will prove these things. I need only to step to this window and wave my handkerchief and this witness will be on her way up."

Hamilton Burger, livid with anger, said, "Your Honor, I must object to this statement. There is perhaps no law that counsel should not be dramatic, but counsel must at least be truthful."

Mason stepped to the courtroom window, waved a handkerchief, said, "If I may have a moment's indulgence,

Your Honor, I have given the signal which will bring my witness here."

Hamilton Burger said, "Your Honor, I also wish to object to any proof concerning any statement that Douglas Hepner may have made to any persons about his life being in danger or about having recovered any gems. Unless that was a dying declaration it would be hearsay, it would have no part in this case."

Mason turned to face the Court. "Your Honor, this *was* a dying declaration. That is why the morphia becomes important. Hepner specifically told this witness that he doubted if he could leave the apartment house alive. It was also a part of the *res gestae*."

Hamilton Burger, so angry he could hardly talk, said, "Your Honor, that is simply an attempt to put the cart been a horse or the cart wouldn't have been there. Here before the horse and then try to show that there must have we have drama deliberately concocted. Counsel asks to capture the interest of the jury by going to the window and waving a handkerchief. Why all this cloak-and-dagger business?"

"Because," Mason said, "in the event this witness had been seen in the building she might have been killed before she could testify. I propose to show that Webley Richey and Ethel Belan were partners in a smuggling ring of enormous proportions and . . ."

"Ethel Belan!" Burger exclaimed.

"Exactly," Mason said. "Why did you think one of her closets was three and a half feet shorter than any other closet in the building?"

"Here we go again," Burger shouted. "Counsel makes an opening statement that sounds like a dime novel, then he starts smearing the prosecution's witnesses. Let him cease this talk and put on his proof if he has any."

"That's what I'm trying to do," Mason said, "and I notice my surprise witness has just entered the courtroom. Miss Payson, please come forward and be sworn."

Sadie Payson marched up to the witness stand, held up her hand and was sworn.

After the first preliminary questions and answers, Mason said, "You knew Douglas Hepner in his lifetime?"

"Yes."

"What was your relationship to him?"

"I was associated with him in business."

"What sort of a business?"

"Recovering smuggled gems."

"Do you know when Douglas Hepner died?"

"On the sixteenth of August."

"At what hour?"

"I know when the autopsy surgeon says he died."

"Some time before that had you had a conversation with Douglas Hepner?"

"I had."

"Did he tell you that he expected to die?"

"Now just a moment," Hamilton Burger said, "I object to that question as leading and suggestive. It also calls for hearsay evidence."

Mason said, "It is part of the *res gestae,* Your Honor, and it is a dying declaration."

Judge Moran said, "It would seem to require that more foundation be laid before it can be described as either. At the present stage of the evidence I am inclined to sustain the objection. However, I would like to have you lay as complete a foundation as possible before the Court is called upon to rule finally on the matter."

Mason turned to face the witness. He picked up a sheet of paper which he had dropped over the pile of gems in the chamois skin on the counsel table.

As he picked up the paper, Sadie Payson's eyes caught the glitter of the gems.

"Oh, you *did* find them!" she exclaimed. "You *did* find them! Those are the ones Doug telephoned about! He told me he had them. He told me they . . ."

"Order, order!" shouted the bailiff.

"The witness will be silent," Judge Moran thundered.

But there could be no mistaking the spontaneous nature of the exclamation Sadie Payson had given. No amount of rehearsal could have accounted for that joyful exclamation.

Judge Moran said, "Court is going to take a ten-minute recess. The Court would like to see counsel for both sides in chambers. Mr. Mason, I would suggest that those gems should not be left lying there on the counsel table. If you wish to mark them for identification you may deliver them to the clerk for safekeeping.

"Court will take a ten-minute recess."

■ 17 ■

IN THE JUDGE'S CHAMBERS, HAMILTON BURGER, SHAKing with rage, pointed his finger at Perry Mason.

"That was a cheap trick to get the witness to exhibit emotion in front of the jury! It was a deliberate attempt to get testimony before the jury which Perry Mason knew the Court should exclude. That paper had been carefully put over the gems and was deliberately removed. This whole presentation turns a court of law into a carnival side show!"

"That whole thing was perfectly proper," Mason said. "Douglas Hepner recovered those gems the day before his death. He was drugged and held a prisoner. They tried to find out what he had done with the gems. Actually what he had done with them was very simple. He had recovered the gems and he was going to try to leave the apartment house. He had tripped a burglar alarm when he found the hiding place of the gems. He knew that the chances of his escape were slim. Eleanor's overnight case was lying there on the dressing table. It was open. He stepped over to that overnight case, unscrewed the tops of several cream jars, forced gems down inside of the jars, then hurried from the apartment house as though trying to make his escape."

"You're not grandstanding in front of a jury now," Hamilton Burger said. "I want to see some proof."

229

Mason glanced at his watch. "You will," he said, "within a few minutes. Fortunately the Customs officials are a lot more open-minded. They have secured a search warrant and are at the moment searching Ethel Belan's apartment. I am quite satisfied that they will find that her closet has been very skillfully subdivided so that the back part of it represents a place where smuggled goods can be deposited. If you'll notice this map, which was drawn to scale and which was introduced in evidence as a part of your case, you'll note that the closet in Ethel Belan's apartment is approximately three and a half feet shorter than the closet in the Granger apartment. Yet there is no structural reason why the closets shouldn't have been of the same length.

"And if you want to keep your face from being red in public, you'd better get Ethel Belan and Webley Richey into custody before this thing breaks wide open and before they've made good their escape. I deliberately made my opening statement in the way I did so they'd know the jig was up and try to escape. That would clinch the case against them and . . ."

Hamilton Burger bellowed, "I don't have to take advice from you. I don't have to . . ."

The telephone on Judge Moran's desk tinkled into noise.

"Just a moment, gentlemen," the somewhat bewildered jurist said, and picked up the telephone.

He said, "Hello," listened for a few moments, then said, "I'll call you back."

He hung up the telephone and turned to the district attorney. "It seems," he said, "that Mr. Mason left word with the Customs officials to telephone me as soon as the search warrant had been served. They found a concealed partition in the back of Ethel Belan's closet. There were no gems there but there is an estimated two hundred and fifty thousand dollars' worth of illegal narcotics.

"I think, Mr. District Attorney, that you might do well to reconsider the entire situation before going back into court."

Hamilton Burger's expression was that of a man whose entire world is collapsing around him.

Judge Moran turned to Perry Mason. "I feel you should be congratulated, Mr. Mason, on your apparent solution of this case, although I deplore the dramatic manner in which you presented the facts."

"I had to present them in that manner," Mason said, "otherwise Ethel Belan and Webley Richey wouldn't have tried to escape. As it was, when I produced those gems they felt certain I had them dead-to-rights.

"And don't congratulate me on being astute. I should have noticed the significance of one closet being three feet and a half shorter than the others, and should have appreciated the fact that there were only two apartments Webley Richey could have been in where he could have heard that conversation. He was trapped by having remonstrated with Suzanne Granger about it and counting on her not telling the district attorney about it.

"If he hadn't overheard that conversation while concealed in Suzanne Granger's apartment there was only one other place where he could have been concealed and overheard what was said and that was in Ethel Belan's apartment. But he couldn't have been concealed in there unless he had been in some sort of a specially constructed place of concealment because the defendant had entered the apartment shortly after he did and she didn't see him.

"Just because I have a client who is flighty, who became panic-stricken and resorted to falsehood, I almost failed to look at the evidence with a coldly analytical eye."

Judge Moran glanced at Perry Mason. There was grudging admiration in his eyes. "Some very clever reasoning, Counselor," he said, "but I still deplore your dramatic use of my courtroom."

The judge turned to Hamilton Burger. "I think, Mr. District Attorney, it's your move. The Court will give you another ten minutes to make it."

Hamilton Burger started to say something, changed his mind, heaved himself up out of the chair, turned, and without a word lunged from the judge's chambers. A moment later the door slammed.

Judge Moran looked at Perry Mason. A faint smile softened the jurist's face. "I deplore your procedure, Mason," he said, "but I'm damned if I don't admire the effectiveness of your technique."